MAKE ME HOT

Bayshore #5

Ember Leigh

ABOUT 'MAKE ME HOT'

One of two things happens when Maverick Daly walks into a room: you either want to be him, or be with him.

Maverick lives in the fast lane: gorgeous one-night stands, souped up cars, a penetrating gaze that will either paralyze you or light your panties on fire, depending on which category you fall in above.

But I'm off-limits to him. He could never see me as anything other than Scarlett: Plain Childhood Bestie. Even though I'd cut off a pinky toe for a chance to be desired by Bayshore's most available bachelor, it could never work with us. He's Mr. One-And-Done, and I'm Ms. Longing For Forever.

I'm usually able to keep his after-hour shenanigans out of mind, until a gourmet-casual food truck competition thrusts us into a tiny kitchen for five weeks. Maverick is launching his career, and I'm just trying to help out my good ol' platonic bestie. And while the flames are leaping off the grill, the heat is rising between us. Until it gets so hot that—pop goes the sexual repression.

The past two decades of being friendzoned? Out the window.

Now we're lovers with a side of what comes next? I've known him my entire life, but I'm meeting a whole new side of him. A side that is begging me to dive headfirst.

We're gunning to win the competition, but Maverick just might win my heart instead.

DEDICATION

This book is dedicated to my real-life food truck, which served as a wonderful source of fodder for this novel, and continues to surprise me every time I think I've fuckin' seen or done it all.

contents

CHAPTER ONE

SCARLETT

"Excuse me, is this seat taken?"

The soft question from my right makes me jump out of my internal thoughts. I've been nursing this chardonnay for far too long. It's warm. My hand hurts from gripping the stemmed wine glass. And honestly, I've just been fiddling with it as a way to keep my hands busy so I don't reach across the table and strangle one of my more annoying table mates here in the middle of the Bayshore Theatre's reception hall.

I twist to look at who's asking me. A middle-aged woman I don't know is grinning down at me, gesturing to the open chair to my right as if there's any question. She could be an aunt or a distant second cousin. Not *mine*, of course, since this isn't my wedding. This is the Daly wedding. Grayson Daly, to be exact. I squint at her, trying to place some Daly features in her face. She might have their nose. I peg her as an aunt.

"No, no, seat's not taken." I make a shooing motion to show her how fine it is that she steal the one open chair at my round table.

"Are you sure?"

"Absolutely." I move the chair toward her as a gesture of how okay it is. The seat represents the plus one I'd planned on coming with...until we broke up three months ago and I'd forgotten to alter my RSVP. "It's just the ghost of my ex-boyfriend, so I'd be happy for you to take him off my hands."

Mrs. Probably-Their-Aunt titters nervously and drags the chair to a neighboring round table. The reception is full of an astonishing number of Daly family members who I never heard about growing up. Not that I hold a PhD in Daly Genealogy or anything, but I should have at least received some sort of honorary-Daly award by now.

I've been hovering around the Dalys for damn near two decades. Tagging along on pool days. Going to the same school, elementary through high school. Hell, I've been Maverick's closest female-friend-he-doesn't-fuck since we were twelve years old.

"Ahhhhhh." It sounds like gas escaping a vacuum chamber, but actually it's the most annoying of my table mates. Veronica. The girl that Maverick came with. His "date," even though everybody and their brother—especially his own brothers—know that Maverick doesn't date. This girl absolutely will not stop making these long, drawn-out noises as she critically assesses some aspect of the reception. "I really disagreed with the peony selection. They could have put some thought into the color scheme." Now she's shaking her head, grimacing while she leans over her half-eaten plate of food to sigh about the flowers with the other woman at our table, Maverick's cousin Betsy.

There aren't many instances when I wish my ex could actually be near me these days, but I wouldn't have been upset if he rolled up now just so I could stop feeling like the odd woman out among this impromptu trio at our dinner table.

It doesn't help that Maverick got swallowed into the Daly crowd, and Betsy's date has been using the bathroom for approximately a half hour. I wouldn't be surprised if it was related to the weird collard-and-kale dish that we were served tonight. One look at that limp pile of greenery and I felt sorta queasy, too.

"It's like, who was behind this? Who puts peonies with carnations?" Betsy scoffs with incredulity, and I'm feigning intense interest in the people milling around post-dinner so I don't have to critique the flower selection along with them. As if I'm looking for someone and just can't seem to find him.

Definitely not looking for my ghost ex-boyfriend. After two lackluster years together, breaking up with Tom was the hardest thing I've ever had to do. I'm pretty sure he still thinks we're getting back together, too. At least, that's what Maverick reports. Because thanks to the tiny-town effect in Bayshore, Maverick and Tom are coworkers. Of course.

A belly laugh that I would recognize anywhere, even beyond the grave, drifts through the air. I snap my gaze around and find the source. *Maverick.* He's halfway across the reception hall, his head tossed back in laughter as he and his older brother Weston are looking dapper and fit for a fucking modeling contract in their black-on-black suits.

I don't know Hazel, Grayson's new wife, very well, but I know *of* her plenty. And this woman would only have a wedding decked out in mauve and black-on-black, with owl centerpieces surrounded by white peonies—and, apparently, carnations, though I never would have noticed if it weren't for my lovely tablemates. Hazel is the only one in Bayshore who could pull off this slightly morbid yet wildly elegant theme.

I'm certainly not complaining—the look is perfect for Maverick. I might be Maverick's platonic bestie since the time puberty rolled around, but I haven't been blind all these years. The man's hot enough to make lava seem palatable. Hot seeks out hot. Which is why Veronica, for all her irritating gaseous sighs and peony complaints, looks like a next-gen Kardashian with lips so plump they could only be destined for Hollywood.

But you know what hot doesn't seek out?

Me. Which is why I'm on the outskirts of this carnation-calamity conversation, the laid-back sidekick stuffed into a skintight dress, second-guessing all my eyeshadow decisions and wondering what, exactly, Maverick and Veronica would be getting into later, and whether or not he cares at all about her personality.

"Lettie." Maverick's raspy baritone floats through the air, settling inside me with pinpricks. I smile up at him as he comes around the table. His longish tresses, so dark brown they're almost black, are slicked back in a trendy yet formal look. His jawline could cut glass, and his normal stubble has been replaced with a freshly sheared face. Not that I notice or care about these things ever. He jerks his chin at the space beside my seat. "You get rid of Tom's chair?"

Helpless laughter cascades out of me as he settles in beside Veronica. Finally, the table feels right again with him here. Now if only Betsy's boyfriend would come back, so I could resume blending into the male shadows like I'm used to.

"Your aunt needed the chair," I tell him. He's scooting in his chair, returning to his half-finished plate. Veronica's is half-finished out of concerns for her figure, but Maverick's is half-finished because he got interrupted by a call for an impromptu family pic. And let me tell you, seeing all those Daly sons side-by-side takes a certain type of willpower. Especially when Maverick insisted on scaling Grayson's shoulders in a precarious tower with their brothers leaping in the air beside them for a photo op.

"He'll be pissed when he shows up and finds out you let Sally have his chair. And she's my *cousin*, by the way."

He still hasn't formally acknowledged Veronica since he sat back down, and she still hasn't blinked in his direction. Not like they're required to. Hell, I don't know what the rules of flings are these days. I never knew to begin with. You could probably search the entire United States for a more loyal, commitment-focused twenty-something than me and not find her. Which just makes mine and Maverick's friendship all the more hilarious.

He's Mr. One-and-Done. And I'm Ms. Hunting-for-Forever.

Yet somehow, we pinky swore a BFF pact back in sixth grade and never looked back. He and I bonded over playing basketball, which blossomed into an easy sort of camaraderie centered around jokes and simply being present for each other that hasn't changed since. I'm pretty sure he sees me as a feminine-looking dude...one he can both share a beer with and talk about life's conundrums with, without the typical dude ridicule.

"Do I at least get some credit for knowing that she was on the Daly side?" I return to my plate, even though nothing here interests me. I'm quite content with the entire steak I consumed, less content with the warm chardonnay. I'm extremely physically active, so I need my protein. As in, *all* the protein.

He grimaces and shakes his head. "Max, three points. But only because my brother got married today."

"Wow." I let out a low whistle. This is the type of shit that Maverick and I are known for. Bullshitting, pure and simple. We could spend an hour splitting hairs about this imaginary score card we're about to invent, believe me. "Woulda thought that you'd be more generous with the points dispersal, considering that I was only one family tree limb off, but whatever."

"Hey. Those limbs are separate for a reason."

I stifle my laughter. His date is now looking at us like we're speaking Arabic.

"What happened with a tree outside?" she asks, her brows drawn together.

"Nothing." Maverick wets his bottom lip, finally swinging his gaze toward Veronica. He's got a plastic sort of smile on, the type I see him use all the time with his flings and hookups and one-night stands. The type of smile I'd call him out on. But Veronica doesn't know him well enough to realize she's being played.

Or maybe that's what she's there for in the first place. To be with the player.

"I gotta go to the bathroom." Veronica offers an even more plasticized smile and stands. Betsy follows her lead, sending Maverick a look that I don't understand, and the two saunter off through the bustling reception hall.

"Those two became fast friends," I say, now that it's just us here. Betsy's date either is having a bowel emergency forever or just snuck out on her. Based on her preoccupation with the carnations, I'm thinking they're heading for a breakup.

Maverick stabs at what little remains on his plate. "Yeah?"

I watch him move around the potatoes for a moment. "You're not that enthused about the food." *Or the girl.*

"Looked way better sitting in the pans than it tastes, but hey." Maverick drops his fork and leans back into his chair. "I'll give Gray shit about it for the next five years, so I don't mind."

"You could have done a way better job," I tell him, crossing my arms over my chest. My cleavage has been on display tonight, which was my plan as a recently-single woman, but also uncomfortable. I wear dresses twice a year, if that.

He smirks, and for a tantalizing moment his gaze drops to my cleavage. "Sometimes I forget you have boobs."

My body shakes with silent laughter. This is how not interested in me sexually he is—he doesn't even remember I'm female. We put the *pal* in *platonic,* if you misspelled it intentionally.

"Consider this your annual reminder." I point to my chest. "I've got knockers."

"Yeah, but you can't really knock anyone out with them," he chides.

"Don't sit there and criticize the potential of my *breasts,*" I say. "Just because they aren't as big as your date's doesn't mean they aren't secretly trained as MMA fighters."

He snorts, turning his fork over, but some of the humor has drained out of him. Maybe it was too weird to compare me to his date. He's probably going to go barf in the toilet just imagining me naked, which is what I've assumed his response would be since we were teens.

It's not what my response would be to seeing *him* naked. No, my response would be way different. I'm not going to lie and say I haven't imagined it already, but that scenario will only ever live in my imagination. Besides, it would be too weird to finally know exactly how long or thick his *unmentionable* is—also things I've imagined once or twice *only,* I swear. Friends shouldn't see friend's naughty bits, much less imagine them.

"But seriously," I barrel on, determined to steer the conversation back to safe territory where my boobs aren't the center of conversation. "You could have made a better meal than this."

"Probably."

"Grayson should have hired you."

He huffs, shaking his head as if it's an absurd idea. "I'm not *that* good."

"Well, you're good enough to feed large groups of people, that's for sure." I jerk my chin out in the general direction of the bathroom doors. "Look. Here comes Edward E. Coli."

Our long-lost table mate is heading our way, looking haggard after his extended journey into the bathroom stall. Maverick twists, the start of a smile playing at his lips. "Who?"

"Your girlfriend's new best friend's boyfriend," I say with a *duh* tone.

"She's not my girlfriend. You know this."

"Fine. Gal pal. Whatever."

A moment later, Betsy's boyfriend sits back down at the table with a sigh. His tie is loosened slightly, and I can't tell if he just got back from a secret make-out session with *another woman* or if his body really was rejecting the dinner. This is how unexciting my life is. I spend most of my time theorizing about the exciting aspects of other people's lives, because my daily existence is spent doing one of three activities: working, exercising, or babysitting my niece and nephew.

I'm really rocking at being twenty-six. I'd have a quarter-life crisis if I could get the time off from my serving job. Instead, I'll just tack on a few extra push-ups and work out my stunted life aspirations at the Cleveland gym where I practice aerial silks. It's my one solace in life. Well, that and bullshitting with Maverick.

"Man," the guy says with a sigh as he crosses his arms. "I'm ready for beer."

Maverick lifts his half-drunk glass of brew in salute to Edward E. Coli. No, that's not his name. *Patrick.* That's it.

"Always time for another beer," Patrick-not-Edward says.

"Especially when the beer is going the be the majority of your dinner," I say, nodding toward his plate. "You didn't eat much."

"Tasted like bleached cutting board," Patrick says with a grimace. "They shoulda brought one of those food trucks out."

"Bayshore has food trucks?" Maverick says dully, like he's only half-listening. But I know it's his defense mechanism. He's pretending he's not interested, because he doesn't want to talk about it, even though he knows he should. I know this man too well.

"Bayshore has one food truck hidden away," I say pointedly, pulling a face at him. I try to kick him under the table for good measure, but I only reach the middle leg of the table, jostling the whole thing. Maverick narrows his eyes at me.

"No it doesn't," he says. "It's not a food truck yet."

"You do food trucks?" Patrick says, a brow lifting.

"No," Maverick says.

"Yes," I say at the same time. "He's been building one for the past couple of years as slow as a snail."

"It's just a little side project I've got going on," Maverick tells Patrick, his tone dripping with *it's seriously nothing*.

"What kind of food you gonna sell?" Patrick asks. I could kiss him. I make needling Maverick about his unexplored culinary talent an official hobby, so I'm happy to pass the baton to Patrick.

"I don't have a menu set or anything," Maverick says, smoothing his palm over the slicked side of his hair. "But I make a lot of burritos, rice dishes. I've got a plate I want to make called the Hot Mess..."

"Dude, did you hear about that food truck competition happening soon?" Patrick jerks his chin toward Maverick. "You should enter! At least for the fun of it."

Maverick smirks just as Veronica and Patrick's girlfriend come back. Something hard slides over his face, and he shrugs noncommittally. "Eh, we'll see."

"What's going on, guys?" Veronica asks as she sits down next to Maverick, sending a conspiratorial smile toward Patrick's girlfriend. "Anything fun happen while we were gone?"

"Just about to get another round of drinks," Maverick says before Patrick or I can say anything about the food truck.

"Ooooh, get me another *blanc*," Veronica purrs in the way in an actress would in a bad porno. She wraps her arm around his, leaning in to plant a sloppy kiss on his lips. Maverick seems surprised at first, but he melts into it. I admit I spend a little bit too much time side-eyeing their kiss, because A) it's a train wreck I can't look away from and B) I spend too much time wondering what it would feel like to kiss Maverick.

It's not like I *want* to kiss Maverick, even though I'm pretty sure if he asked me at this point, I'd say yes. As long as we could establish that it was for science, because I wouldn't do *anything* that would disrupt our decade-long friendship. It's a long-simmering curiosity that I wasn't aware of until recently. I know everything about this man—I should know how his lips taste too, right?

Again, for *science*.

Despite how well I know Maverick, there must be plenty I don't know about him. The way Maverick looks when Veronica breaks the kiss is a look I've never gotten from him, not even after fifteen years of knowing him. The type of look a girl like me could never coax from him, either.

A familiar, aching heaviness stretches across my chest, something I know well but don't often pry into. It's easier to look away, to offer a smile, to watch him cycle through women from afar and tell myself I don't care.

But when Maverick's gaze drags back to find mine, there's something electric there that pins me to my spot, reviving the recent question that has circled dangerously inside my skull like a shark after fresh blood:

What would it be like to be the girl on his arm?

CHAPTER TWO

MAVERICK

"Just thought I'd get this party started before we get too drunk." Veronica's whisper comes out in a hot burst at my ear. It's the kind of sexy murmur that dudes pay by the minute to listen to. But it doesn't give me goosebumps. Not by half.

Instead, much like that sloppy kiss she laid on me, it reminds me why I should never have fucking invited her.

"Let me head up there before they cut the cake," I say, sneaking one last glance at Scarlett before I push to standing. I'm trying to tell her with my eyes to follow me. So we can start concocting a plan to ditch Veronica, critically analyze the dessert menu, and then eventually head back to my place where we can get properly trashed.

But she's not meeting my gaze. Instead, she's tugging on the extra-long curl of hair framing her face, wrapping it around and around her index finger as she watches Patrick or maybe a conversation across the room. I excuse myself from the table, weaving through the happy crowds toward the bar at the far end of the reception hall.

This day has been great. Hazel and Gray's wedding counts as the best one I've ever been to, sub-standard dinner menu included, but I'm not sure how long it'll retain that title, since Dom and London are getting hitched later this summer, followed by Connor and Kinsley this fall. Weston and Nova are either already secretly married or are planning to do so in a cave along the Italian coast or something equally as wild.

Most guys would see their four older brothers getting hitched and think, *fuck, I better find someone fast.* Not me. I'm the loose caboose of the Daly clan. Not only fiancée-less, but completely single.

Just how I like it. And that's how I'll stay, simply out of spite for my father. He and my mom are looking to me now to round out the *Happily Married Daly Brothers* squad, and they can look as long as they like. It's not gonna happen.

Besides, I know the truth, even though my four older brothers willingly submitted to the ball and chain. I'm not fit for the eternal monogamy shit. And yeah, I tried once or twice before. It never ends well. And you know what they say about the scientific process: try a couple times, give up, and get drunk instead.

I smile to myself as I wait at the bar—Scarlett would have enjoyed that joke. A hand on my shoulder startles me out of my thoughts. Weston is beside me, jostling me.

"We're on the same drinking schedule, brother."

"If you mean a one-way street to being toasted, then yes," I say, smoothing the side of my hair again. I'm loving this chance to get nice clothes on and slick back my hair. I'm usually greasy and covered in oil after each shift at work, and I forgot what it was like to go to something fancy. The last time I got dressed up, it was the night Dom premiered his Bayshore cardiology clinic, which was a year and a half ago. Time flies when you're fixing hot rods and fucking full-time.

"Don't get too drunk you can't roast Gray," Weston warns. "I flew all the way from Aruba for this, you know. I refuse to accept anything less than him getting roasted by every single one of us."

"I know, you *flew from Aruba.*" I roll my eyes, but it's out of love, I swear. He and Nova are on their yearly USA rounds, splitting their time between Ohio and New York. Their rental car is yet again something that is permanently out of my budget and based on the amount of work I've heard they're getting in Aruba, I can only assume they're rolling in cash.

Which marks four of the five Daly brothers in the *Successful* category.

But I'm not jealous or bitter. I swear. Hand on the Bible and everything. I'm having a good old time being a mechanic and fucking my way through the tri-county region. Isn't this what every man dreams of? Cars and women. I'm living the life. If I repeat it to myself enough, it'll become true.

"Why don't you come down to visit us?" Weston asks, shoving his shoulder into mine. "You know you can stay with me and Nova."

"I have no one to go with," I reply.

"Didn't you bring your girlfriend tonight?" Weston pins me with a *duh* look. "Bring her."

I look over my shoulder at the table, my gaze landing on Scarlett. No, wait. She's not my girlfriend. She's *Tom's* girlfriend, even though they're on a hiatus that is destined to end any second now. Weston is talking about Veronica, who is less *girlfriend* and more *girl I've fucked on a handful of occasions.*

"We're not, like…"

"Ahh, yeah. I get it. You could come by yourself, you know."

I grimace. "I don't do shit like that, sorry."

Weston nudges me just as the bartender sidles up to us, gesturing for me to order, because of course he is the most respectful of the five of us.

"I'll take an IPA. Actually, make that two." I'm thinking it will be nice to hand one off to Scarlett when I get back. She's been nursing something I can tell she barely likes, based on how slowly she's drinking it. That girl can toss back beers, so I know she's probably secretly crying out for one. I can see through her fancy charade. That girl never wears a dress.

How do I know? Because I would have fucking noticed. And oh my god, Scarlett has a body she wasn't advertising to the world. I can't tell whether I should be intrigued or repulsed by this secret knowledge, so I'll just pretend I don't care.

We've never crossed that line. I don't intend to now. Besides, Scarlett is spoken for, and if I somehow did try something with her, in a parallel universe? I can already hear her laughing me out of the room.

"Anything else?" the bartender asks.

"Whatever he wants," I say, jerking a thumb toward Weston. "Oh, and uh, sauvignon blanc." I almost forgot about Veronica's order. And the girl altogether.

The bartender nods and moves toward Weston to take his order. Weston sends me an amused look.

"Thanks for buying my drinks at the open bar, bruh."

"Hey, anytime." I send him a snarky grin, looking out at the happy buzz of friends and family around us. Weston gives his order to the bartender, and then turns back toward me.

"Things are going well at the shop?" He doesn't mean it in the same way as if my dad would ask, which he never does. Weston genuinely wants to know that I'm happy. Not prying to find out if

I've started saving for a vacation home or broken my first million in my retirement account.

This is why Weston is the best and I am, well, the dropout. Not only that, the dropout who became a mechanic. I'll never be able to live it down in my father's eyes, which is why we haven't spoken in a full year and a half and we've been within six feet of each other only for family pictures today.

"Going great," I tell him, receiving the two IPAs happily. I start sipping on my own as I stuff a ten-dollar bill in the tip jar. "Lots of work. Money's good. Living the dream."

Weston nods at me, but he doesn't look convinced. I swear I repeat that phrase—*living the dream*—to myself at least five times a day. As if sheer volume will somehow make up for how little my life embodies the phrase. I raise my bottle of beer to Weston in a silent *see you later*, but he stops me.

"You forgot your wine," Weston says.

"Fuck." I form a triangle with my fingers and scoop up the glass of white wine. "I'll catch you later, brother. I gotta go get these women drunk."

Weston slaps my shoulder, and I weave back to the table through the throngs of people. I set the triad of drinks at my spot, and then move Scarlett's beer in front of her.

"I figured you'd want one," I tell her.

Veronica starts cooing at my side, reaching for her wine. "Thaaanks, Mavie."

I sink into my seat, slinging my arm over the back of Veronica's chair. Scarlett is grinning down at the bottle of beer like it's sent from the heavens.

When Scarlett looks at me, she's got a mischievous twinkle in her eye. One that pairs nicely with the swell of her breasts in that skintight dress and the plump rouge of her lips. "Thaaanks, Mavie," Scarlett says before she brings the bottle to her lips.

She says it with just enough twang that Veronica doesn't realize she's being made fun of. I fight to stifle the laugh that bubbles up inside me. I shouldn't laugh. I *won't* laugh. Even though Scarlett and I both know what she's doing.

Scarlett's throat bobs as she takes a healthy sip of the beer. In that moment, I make my decision: I *am* going to ditch Veronica. It won't be hard to conspire with Scarlett about what we could do post-reception. She's been coming over at least once a week to my apartment since her break-up with Tom. Usually we find each other on drunken nights out at the High-5's in downtown Bayshore and end up making our way back to my place for late-night quesadillas, which Scarlett claims are the best in all the land. I'm not here to argue with her, so it seems like today would be a good time to remind her that I have all the quesadilla fixings back at my place after this sub-par dinner.

My palms are itching, I'm so excited to enact this plan. I knew inviting Veronica to my brother's wedding wasn't the smartest idea. I just knew that I couldn't invite Scarlett, and showing up alone to a wedding isn't my style either. I would have taken her in a heartbeat, but her ex Tom is a bullheaded motherfucker, and he would have gotten the wrong idea. He knows how tight Scarlett and I are, but I'm not trying to start that much drama over a wedding.

"So you work at that sports car shop on the east side?" Patrick asks me, picking up the *what do we all do with our lives* thread from earlier in the evening.

"Yeah. Going on two years."

"You must have a sweet hot rod in your own garage, then," Patrick says with a knowing smile.

"You think?"

"All mechanics do," he says, and there's something about the way he says *mechanic* that rubs me the wrong way. Maybe it's the same thing my dad hated when I told him I wanted to be one. I don't fucking know. I try to tamp down my irritation, because this dude is here with my cousin. But he's half right. I do have a pet project in my garage, but it's not a hot rod. It's the food truck I don't want to get into.

"No hot rods to speak of," I tell him, preparing myself for the backlash from Scarlett. She's going to call me out. I can already feel it.

"Not even an old coupe that hasn't run since the sixties?" he presses.

"Not even that," I confirm, glancing at Scarlett. But she's not even listening to us. Some guy—definitely not from the Daly side—has stopped at our table and started chatting with her. He's got wide receiver shoulders and the type of face that screams beefcake.

But he and Scarlett are somehow wrapped up in conversation and laughing as if they've known each other their whole lives.

"I'm thinking of getting a Miata," Patrick murmurs, more to himself than anyone else. My cousin and Veronica are buried in conversation. Scarlett was right. They *did* become fast friends.

"Ooh," Veronica squeaks suddenly, her hand shooting up to wave at someone across the hall. "There's my friend. Hang on, guys, I gotta go say hi." Veronica stands and tugs her short skirt down an inch before she totters off on her heels. I watch her as she weaves through the crowd. She's hot, there's no doubt about that. But something feels off.

I think it has something to do with the question that won't leave me alone in the quiet moments anymore: *Is this all there is?*

I found the stable job that I like well enough. I got my own place. I'm fucking the hottest girls.

What's next?

"Mav," my cousin starts, leaning across Veronica's vacated seat so she can grab my wrist. "I am in *love* with Veronica."

"You two should date," I say.

Patrick snorts, then recovers himself. "I'd be into that."

Betsy shoots Patrick a withering look, then swings back to look at me. "Are you two serious?"

"Define serious," I say, unable to keep the shit-eating grin off my face.

She sends me the same withering look she sent her boyfriend. "You know what I mean. You're always with a new girl. But you brought this one to Gray's wedding! Doesn't that mean you two are like, I dunno, dating at least?"

It means I'd rather suffer than show up without someone on my arm to something like this. I look back at Scarlett again, eager for her to catch wind of this conversation. I'm just waiting for her to pipe up. But the beef cake has dragged a chair to our table—Tom's chair is returning, basically—and they're buried in conversation still.

Something weird and hot pummels the lower part of my stomach, but it's brief, and I have better things to think about. Guess that rules out quesadillas tonight, which is actually more of a letdown than I can process right now.

"Why do you look so upset? Does just saying the word 'dating' make you mad?" My cousin snorts, squeezing my wrist one last time. I try to laugh it off and bring myself to the conversation happening here, but it's hard not to watch what's unfolding with Scarlett and her new friend. I feel like Tom would be pissed about this, not that I'm going to tell him. But I can practically feel the breeze whooshing past me as Scarlett's attention centers fully on her new friend.

"I don't see the point in tying myself to one person," I tell Betsy. My words are rehearsed. I've told my mom this at least a dozen times in the past six months.

"Not even someday?" Betsy asks with a lifted brow.

I shrug. Truth is, I wanted the happily-ever-after a long time ago, but nobody wanted it with me. You only need to meet heartbreak once to know she's a bitch that's better off avoided. Besides, I've cycled through enough girls to give up on the fantasy. My brothers might have found it, but I've got plenty of research that says it's not in the cards for me.

So why not just have fun and forget about it?

Betsy falls into conversation with Patrick again. Sharp laughter from the other side of the table drags my attention back to Scarlett. Beefcake is telling her a story, and she's *really* laughing, not the fake kind she offers to customers at E. Lago, the lakefront restaurant she works at, when they ask her why her hair doesn't match her name. The dimples are out, and she's clutching her stomach.

"Stahp," she's wheezing. "I'm gonna pee my pants.

"You aren't even wearing pants," Beefcake reminds her, which makes her snort further.

I roll my eyes. Such a stupid line. I'm reaching for my phone to send her a furtive text reminding her that quesadillas are on the menu later when Beefcake leans a little closer.

"Promise me a dance later, okay?" His tone is one I know all about. It's the tone I use when I'm trying to fucking *seduce* someone. I rub the back of my neck, pushing my chair out a little so I can angle away from what's happening in my direct line of vision. She shouldn't have worn that dress. It looks way too good on her. Like, to the point where it crossed even *my* mind what it might be like to peel that thing off her and see what lies beneath.

Scarlett has always been just another one of the guys for me. She's distantly female in the way we all know tomatoes are technically fruit, even though it's not something you really talk about with anyone. Well, Scarlett would never enter into my *fucking* category. It just doesn't fit, in the same way a tomato does *not* go in a fruit salad.

I take a hard pull at my beer, and then I stand. It's time to go harass a brother or something. Because I can't stand another second at this table watching Scarlett giggle like a schoolgirl.

The heat streaks through me again as I brush past the *new, happy couple,* trying with all my might not to notice them. Because if I look at Scarlett a second longer, with that smile lingering on her ruby lips and the dangerous swell of her breasts in that tight-ass dress, I'm liable to chop up a tomato and call it a strawberry.

CHAPTER THREE

MAVERICK

It's midnight, and I'm at home in my happy place: the kitchen.

I've got a killer buzz going, since I've been nursing beers since approximately six p.m. Other people might call this blatantly drunk, but I'm a twenty-six-year-old bachelor who works in a garage with coworkers who double as alcohol sponges. My tolerance is what I like to call *robust*. But I'm not dumb enough to go to bed this drunk. Which means the quesadilla plan is back on.

I'm chopping scallions while mushrooms sizzle in the sauté pan. I wipe my hands on a dish towel slung over my bare shoulder. I cook shirtless usually, which makes me not the smartest chef in the kitchen, even though I'm the *only* chef in the kitchen right now.

And yeah, Scarlett was right. I could have done a better job with Gray's wedding dinner, but I'm not ready to put myself out there like that. Cooking is something I do because I love it. I don't need to put it on blast and end up hating it, which is probably what would happen if I had to feed all 150 mouths that showed up at the Bayshore Theatre for the reception.

My phone buzzes. It's a series of pictures from my Mom. She's up late, riding the high of her first married son, no doubt. One of the pictures she sends is a shot of me with the mic in my hand, addressing Gray and Hazel at the main table during my speech. It's hard not to smile, even though my cheeks hurt from how much I laughed and smiled tonight. The rest of the wedding was a blast, and of all our brothers, my speech was the funniest *and* the shortest, which are absolutely related.

Dom dragged on forever talking about soul mates and Grammy Ethel while staring so hard at London I thought she was either going to get pregnant *again* on the spot, or maybe just go into labor right there. Dom has gotten a new type of intense now that he's in love, and I swear to God, if he talks one more time about finding true love with our inheritances, I'm going to put him into a coma myself.

I ditched the reception once the "Macarena" started. I ditched Veronica, too. Both are hard no's for me. Even the gal pals, as Scarlett calls them, aren't really scratching my itch these days, which has me a little worried. I learned early on that long-term shit wasn't for me. I got burned when I was eighteen by the girl I thought I was going to spend the rest of my life with. I was the stupid sap googling ideas about how to propose to her, while she was googling thirsty guys in our area and sending out nudes behind my back. It's easy to say we were too young to know better—because we were. And now I know better. My heart can't handle that shit, so I'm not touching long-term with a ten-foot condom.

My stomach grumbles in anticipation of this awesome fucking quesadilla. I sidestep to the fridge, pull out a package of bacon I forgot about, and get a different skillet ready to go. This late-night snack just reached tenth-level awesome. Once the bacon is popping on the stove, I wipe my hands again and pull out my phone from the back pocket of my dress pants.

And just like that, I'm sending Scarlett a picture of the situation on my stove.

Her response is lightning fast. I swear to God, sometimes I think that she and I are actually telepathic and the cell phones are just a decoy. We never used to talk so much via text and calling, but in the past few years, our friendship has blossomed from low-grade lifelong friends to high-grade BFFs. She sends me a picture in response: her middle finger against what I can tell is her blanket as a background. She's probably wrapped up on her couch. That's *her* happy place, at least what she does to wind down at the end of a day.

MAV: Girl, you coulda had these.

SCARLETT: Musta missed the invite. Did you send regular mail or Fed-Ex?

MAV: Guess you didn't hear it when you were sucking face with that football player.

Heat flushes my chest, and I set the phone down, turning back to my stove. She never sucked face with that dude, but she might as well have. I saw him cop a feel on the dance floor, sliding his hand down the curve of her hip to squeeze that compact cantaloupe I noticed once or twice tonight. I might have been hovering like the Older Brother Police, even though I'm not her brother and I'm only older by two months.

Still, though. She needs someone to watch out for her. Scarlett is fresh meat, and dickheads can smell that. I would know. I'm one of the dickheads.

SCARLETT: There was no Hoovering, thankyouverymuch. His breath smelled like cod and stale beer.

MAV: Good combo. I think I'll put it on the menu for our next dinner night.

SCARLETT: You're such an asshole, you know that, right?
MAV: Shut up and come get your quesadilla.

My heart is racing now, and I don't exactly know why. I flip the bacon, turn the mushrooms, and get my tortilla ready. There's barely enough here to make two, but I'd share if needed.

SCARLETT: Sorry, not trying to be the third wheel with your gal pal.

I smirk, sensing my window. I swipe through screens so that a moment later, the phone is ringing. I put it on speakerphone and set it on the countertop. She picks up on the second ring.

"Don't even start with the bribery," she says in lieu of a greeting. "I'm on my couch and perfectly comfortable."

"But I made you a quesadilla," I say, fighting to keep the smile out of my voice.

"Listen, you make the best food in Bayshore, but even that juicy ass strip of bacon isn't enough to coax me into listening to that girl laugh in the wee hours of the morning." She pauses. "Wait, am I on speakerphone? Maverick!"

"You are on speakerphone," I confirm, snapping off the burner for the mushrooms.

"Oh, God," she wails dramatically. "Why do you do shit like this? Did she hear me?"

"No, Scarlett, she didn't." My heart is pounding. I turn the bacon again. "She's not even here."

An immense silence fills the air for a moment, and then Scarlett says, "Oh."

"Like I said, I made you a quesadilla."

"Mav, I'm druuunk."

I sigh, snapping off the burner for the bacon so that I can drain the grease. In times like these, it would be so much easier if we lived together. That seems like a weird thing to bring up. But we'd be roommates. I wouldn't feel weird asking any dude to do the same.

"So am I. And this is gonna help."

"Can't you just send it to my apartment with one of those bicycle delivery guys?"

"Yeah, because I have one of those guys living with me."

"Well, you should, with how much food you make and tempt me with when I can't come over. It's high time you convinced a bicycle delivery guy to move in."

"Maybe *you* should move in," I say, the weird yank in my chest returning. My heart is pounding between my ears. There. I said it. "That way, you'd be stumbling out of your bedroom right now instead of across fucking Bayshore."

"Oh yeah, I'll just move in. Great idea." The sarcasm is bleeding through the phone. "I'm sure your gal pals would love showing up for their night of fun and finding a female roommate in your apartment."

"We're living in the twenty-first century, Scarlett. Men and women can live together as friends. They were doing it in the nineties, even. Didn't you watch *Friends*?"

"That was a little before our time," Scarlett says.

"Yeah, well, brush up on your history and watch Netflix sometime." I move my cast-iron skillet to the stove with a *clunk*.

"Is that the cast-iron?" Scarlett asks.

"It's the cast-iron."

"Are you putting the sauce on it?"

She's referring to a homemade aioli that I use on basically everything. "I'm putting the sauce on it."

She groans again. "God, you are *such* an asshole!"

I look at the clock. It's almost twelve thirty. Plenty of time to go pick her up and continue having fun tonight. "What if I came and picked you up?"

"Can you drive right now?"

I blink, assessing the internal state of my organs. "No. But once I eat this quesadilla…I probably could."

"You can't eat the quesadilla without me. That defeats the whole purpose of eating quesadillas together."

"How about I send a taxi?"

She launches a sigh. "Maverick Ian Daly. No. I'm not going to be shuttled around like one of your quesadilla whores."

"So what you're saying is you don't want me to turn this into a FaceTime video so you can watch me plate this food?"

"Exactly."

I press the button to initiate the video call. A moment later, she's frowning on my phone screen. I prop up the phone and wave, giving her my biggest, cheesiest smile.

"So good to see you!" I say in my fakest professional voice.

A smile is tugging at the corners of her lips, which are still brilliantly ruby red. Her raven hair falls around her shoulders in soft waves, the fancy updo dismantled, which is a gut punch I wasn't expecting on this call. "Not likewise."

"All right. I'm trying to be a good friend by letting you witness this sacred act of creation. But if you'd rather not support me…"

"No, no. It's fine. Just call me in the middle of the night to force me to watch you eat something I can't have. Very thoughtful."

I'm laughing as I drizzle oil onto the cast iron skillet and get the tortilla into place.

Finally, she says, "Are you planning on cooking on those washboard abs or do I get to actually see what you're doing?"

"Oh, right." I half forgot that the phone was pointing at my stomach. Though it never hurts to remind her what I'm working with. Sometimes I think she has no appreciation for how hard I work on my body. She never lets on if she does, though, and in times like these—tipsy, feeling loose and free—I like to push the envelope and see if she'll bite. Just to see if there's really a window there. "Didn't you know? I *am* the quesadilla."

She snorts. "Not at all what I ordered."

But of course, Scarlett never takes the bait. It's because we're just friends. That's all we'll ever be. It's all we *can* be. Besides, who wants to be the guy who gets ridiculed for chopping up a tomato and putting it in a fruit salad?

That guy would be me if I ever dared try. And Scarlett would laugh me out of the kitchen.

I struggle to get the phone set up on a nearby shelf so that the stove is on display. When I get just the right spot, Scarlett says, "I don't think I've ever gotten this intimate with your hairline before."

"How's it look?"

"About what you'd expect for a guy in his late twenties."

"Mid-twenties," I correct her.

"Fine. I'm sure it won't affect your standing with the gal pals. They like older men, right?"

I place myself in direct line of the camera so she can see how hard I'm glaring at her before I turn back to the stove.

"You know, this is kind of like those reality TV shows," she says a moment later as I'm warming the tortilla shell. Then she groans. "God, Mav! That's right! You need to do the reality show!"

"What now?" I reach for the cheese blend I prepared earlier and sprinkle some onto the shell.

"The freaking competition thingy that Edward E. Coli was talking about!" She tuts. "No, his name was Patrick. Fuck. Whatever. You know who I'm talking about. Your cousin's boyfriend."

"Why do you call him Edward E. Coli?"

"Because I told myself he got food poisoning from the weird dinner and that's why he spent so long in the bathroom and I had a whole story going in my head. Whatever. Just—it doesn't matter. Maverick, *do the competition!*"

I sigh, shaking my head.

"Don't shake your head like that."

"I'm nowhere *near* prepared to enter a competition."

"Um, actually you are." Her phone rustles, and her side of the video call goes dark.

"What are you doing?"

"Looking this thing up. I can't believe I forgot. You're doing it."

"I'm not," I remind her. "I have a full-time job."

"Mmhmm."

I fold the ingredients into the tortilla shell and start toasting the sides. It's looking good. No, it's looking *great*. My stomach rumbles again with impatience. Scarlett's really missing out.

"Wow," she says a moment later, just as I'm turning the stovetop off. "I found it. And this thing is *cool*."

"I bet."

"Your lack of enthusiasm is noted," she says, and then her face returns to the video. Her lips form an O, and the first thought that streaks through my mind is not the sort of thing I usually think about Scarlett: *fuckable*. I've got a thing for big red lips wrapped around my cock, but it's too weird to think about. So I shove it back down into the recesses of my body never to be thought about again. Easy enough.

"I almost missed the plating," she whispers.

"Yeah you did. See? The competition isn't worth it. It almost made you miss the plating." I bring out the famed lime-green plate that we always use for quesadillas and slide it on without much fanfare. This is "the plating." It's nothing, really. But to us, it's a big deal. Because we're fucking weird.

"That was a good one," she murmurs.

"Pretty intense." I turn off the last burner and get out my big slicing knife. The backwall of my kitchen has a magnetic strip on it and it's filled with ten different knives. I could only be an amateur chef or a serial killer with this collection.

"So, seriously, Mav. You should apply for this competition. It's a Midwestern food truck competition. If you get picked, you'll participate in five different challenges throughout the Midwest. They all get taped and compiled into a fun little reality TV show. You could be famous!"

"I don't really want to be famous."

"Well, you could be the winner and jumpstart a new career."

"Scarlett, I already *have* a career." I run a hand through my hair. The gel is no longer effective, so thick strands fall onto my forehead as I finish cutting the quesadilla into four pointed wedges.

"Yeah, but your calling is cooking."

I scoff. She's right, but there are too many obstacles on that path. It's better not to walk down it. Just let things unfold as they will throughout the next few decades. If I have no expectations, there can be no failure. Besides, I couldn't stack up to my older brothers. Not one of them. So why bother?

Because you know there's something bigger out there.

"My calling is paying rent and having a good time," I say, but the words sound hollow. She's right. We've had enough late-night conversations about how bored I am at the garage for her to call me out like this. Part of me still thinks that I just need to tough out the routine for a few more years before it becomes more natural and maybe even pleasant. The other part of me knows I need to stick with it to prove to Dad that I knew what I was doing when I dropped out of college.

Even though I'm not sure I've ever known what I was doing.

Least of all now.

"That is the most bullshit answer I've ever heard," Scarlett says with an incredulous laugh. She mimes choking me.

"Well aren't you Ms. Drunk and Feisty."

"I'm Ms. Comfortable on the Couch and Sick of Your Shit."

"My name had a better ring to it," I tell her, pointing at the camera with a quesadilla slice.

"Listen. I can't make you take this once-in-a-lifetime opportunity that could possibly earn you fifty thousand dollars—"

"How much?"

"Fifty thousand dollars to the winner. They want new food truck businesses only. You already have the truck done. Why wouldn't you try it?"

Frustration finally bubbles over. "Scarlett, I don't *have*"—I make exaggerated air quotes here—"anything for this. Yeah, I own the physical body of a food truck, but I don't have equipment. I don't have a cash register. I don't even have a fucking menu. Least of all a...a *business plan* or something."

I'm saying all of these things because I've been thinking about it, deep in the recesses of my mind. There's a tiny note taker who lives in the darkest cave of my brain, and he processes and logs all of the things I consciously ignore. His name is probably Stan. And what he came up with was all the imagined advice and responses from my brothers: Weston would say *fuck yeah, go for it!* Dom would lecture me on having a business plan and a nest egg. Connor would implore me to crowdsource and let him build my app. Grayson would be gung ho but cautious, with plenty of stories about he and Hazel owning their own businesses.

And I'm over here wondering why I have an imaginary note taker in my brain named Stan.

It's all just a little too much. And this is *before* I've ever spoken the idea out loud. Imagine actually going for it.

"You can *get* all of those things. You can make them or buy them or create them. The competition doesn't even begin filming until early July or something. So that's plenty of time to get your shit together."

"And once I get my shit together, I'll be up against a bunch of guys who know what the fuck they're doing."

"It says new food trucks—" she begins.

"Right. So Mr. Owned A Restaurant For Five Years can waltz in with his brand new food truck to demolish me. Listen, there's too much. I can't do it all on my own." I realize I've had nothing but excuses. But they're valid. And she's being drunk and idealistic.

Or maybe I'm being drunk and negative.

"Then find the help?"

I chew my quesadilla, so intent on shooting down this idea that I can barely focus on how damn good it is. I wrack my brain for a foolproof exit, and as I chew and glare at the phone screen, it comes to me. "Fine. I'll do it if you help me."

She snorts. "What?"

"You want me to do it so bad? Then help me out."

"You're fucking kidding me."

"Nope." She'll never agree to it. She works full time and then some at E. Lago in the summer, and she'd never take the time off work. And all the rest of her free time is eaten up with watching her niece and nephew. Every second of her summer is spoken for. She doesn't have time to launch this huge new business with me. "You be my right-hand woman, and I'll do it."

She covers her face with her hands. "How did I somehow know you'd say that?"

I go for my second slice of quesadilla. "Well. There's the deal. Accept or not."

She's quiet for a loooong time. We go through a fierce yet important battle of staring at each other, smirking cockily, sighing heavily. Finally, she groans and throws her head back.

"FINE, Maverick," she says, looking both disgruntled yet impossibly cute. She purses her lips in a way I've never seen before. Or maybe I've just never noticed without that shade of red on her pretty pucker. And then she adds, "You win. I'll fucking do it."

CHAPTER FOUR

I wake up the next morning warily. It's not normally how I wake up, but from the second my alarm goes off at seven, I feel like there's something I'm forgetting. Something big around the corner.

I yawn and roll onto my side in my queen bed. The big window of my bedroom is covered with dark red drapes, but I can see the bright sunlight spilling in around the edges. I went to bed extra-late last night, thanks to my marathon conversation with Maverick, which means that I am going into my practice morning with a sleep deficit and mildly hungover.

Another yawn escapes me, and I roll onto my back, thoughts drifting to our conversation. For some reason, Mav likes to cook shirtless. I can't tell if he's a cooking oil masochist or just wants to remind the world what they can't have. His washboard abs leave no room for debate. It doesn't matter what the debate even is—his abs win.

And it's getting really annoying.

Wisps of my dreams from last night return to me. Maverick was definitely there. How could he not be? I squeeze my thighs together, a little sigh escaping me. There's something really sexy about watching him cook, and I say that as his friend. I can acknowledge when my friend is attractive. It doesn't mean anything. And it especially doesn't mean that I'm wanting to experiment with Maverick, even though I technically do want that.

My hand drifts to my panty line, my eyes fluttering closed again. Last night was just too much. Between his black-on-black formal wear, the slicked back hair, and his beefy shoulders straining his shirt, it simply *wasn't fair* for him to follow all of that repressed attraction with actually showing me the sculpted body that teased me all night.

Because now what?

My middle finger slides into my panties and nicks the swollen nub of my clit. I make a slow swirl around it, biting my bottom lip. God, I'm so fucking horny. I pinch myself once, relishing the jolt of pleasure that streaks through my limbs. My imagination fills with Maverick's face. His forearms. The sexy rasp of his voice when we talk in the morning or when I catch him off guard with a joke. God, what would he taste like? His kisses. Soft, punishing, or somewhere in between?

The circles around my clit quicken, my belly growing taut as I imagine Maverick pinning me up against a wall. And then I yank my hand out of my panties and sit up.

"This is too awkward!" I tell no one. I roll out of bed, finding my wide green eyes in the mirror beside my bed. "I'm just horny," I reaffirm to my reflection. My pussy is *throbbing*. I can practically see my bedsheets pulsing with my arousal.

But it's true. I'm just horny. I haven't had sex in a long time. Like, a *really* long time, because Tom and I had stopped having sex for months before we broke up. So that means that all my pent-up sexual energy is being directed at a person who makes no sense for me. I couldn't even fathom a one-night stand with Maverick for *so many reasons,* but most of all because he's my best friend.

So masturbating to his image is totally out of the question.

I hurry to the bathroom and splash water on my face. Hopefully this will knock some sense back into me. After a quick wake-up routine, I pull on my training clothes—skintight shorts, sports bra, and a sweat-wicking tank—and grab my go bag, which is already sitting ready at the door.

I always leave it out for myself for the mornings I get my schedule to align with a Cleveland practice session. Because these mornings are few and far between. It's an hour drive each way, and a two-hour minimum class or session once I'm inside the gym. Sometimes, I barely make it back to Bayshore in time for work.

I've learned to cherish and treasure these precious sessions. Between helping out Flor, my own work schedule, and the sheer distance, I'm lucky if I make it twice a month. Once I hit Route 2 heading east, I crank the music—Katy Perry, *thankyouverymuch*—and let myself daydream about all the things I normally squash.

Because that's what going to Fly By in Cleveland allows me to do: dream a little. My practical side—and probably anyone who knew about this crazy hobby—tells me it's pointless to even practice such an obscure art form. But I try to tell that voice to shut up. It doesn't usually listen.

It's different with Mav—that's what I'm thinking about as I pull up to the gym in Cleveland. I encouraged Mav to go after his hobby because he can make a living out of it. Because he's that good. But what could I do with silks?

Whenever I consider it, I can just hear my older sister Florence sneering about the ridiculous waste of time it would be when there are more important things to focus on, like *paying the bills*. And she's not wrong—if this were *her* life. But it's mine. I can't take another round of judgment about this thing that is so close to my heart. So I keep it tucked away, barricaded, so that nobody can touch it except for me.

As soon as I set foot in the brightly lit foyer of the aerial silks gym, some of my tension dissolves. Everyone here knows me, and some of my instructors call me their rising star. I don't like to let that go to my head though. They probably tell everyone that.

The class I'm attending starts with some stretches. It's me and six other women, and we're all chatty and laughing as we go through the familiar routines. Yoga mats are brought out, followed by kettlebells and resistance bands. Then we go into more advanced work: head stands, popping back, yoga sequences that make us all groan.

Once our warm-up routine is done, we've already been at it for an hour. The good stuff is almost here. We take a small bathroom and hydration break, and I head for my stuff stashed in the cubbies along the far wall. As I approach, my phone is vibrating against my water bottle, making a strange metallic *bzzzz* noise.

It's my sister Florence. I stare at the vibrating phone for a moment, considering not picking up. I'm in the middle of my workout, after all. This is *my* time. But if I don't pick up, she'll just call again. And again. The guilt starts to pool inside me. I remember the last time I didn't pick up the phone when she called, and it was when her daughter Louisiana was being rushed to the emergency room.

"Hey, Flor." I press the phone between my ear and shoulder as I unscrew the cap of my water bottle. "What's up?"

"Listen, I've had this *crazy* morning." I can practically see her sitting on the stool at her kitchen island, pressing the tip of her middle finger to the spot between her eyebrows like she does when she's stressed. "Can you come watch Fifi and Louie for a little bit?"

Fifi is my nephew, Felix, and Louie is my niece, Louisiana. It seems backwards, but for these cute little hellions, it makes sense.

"Uhhh." I begin my usual cycle through a short mental list of excuses. *I'm about to walk into a paid aerial silks lesson* would bring up too many questions, but *I'm busy* is too vague. "I'm not exactly in Bayshore right now…"

"I have to go pick up Greg from jail," Flor says, a defeated sigh escaping her. Greg is her boyfriend. Her baby daddy. Her emotionally immature life companion who once told me that reading newspapers was a task reserved for women. "It's not as bad as it sounds. But it'll take a couple hours."

I take another sip of my water, staring at the wall clock in the gym. I woke up at seven a.m., drove an hour, and paid forty dollars specifically for the part of the class that has yet to begin. "Is there any way you could ask Mom…?"

"She's on her way to work."

I roll my lips inward. Mom gets to use the work excuse because she's a nurse. But since I'm a lowly server peddling alcoholic beverages and subsisting on tips, I have to answer the call whenever my sister needs me. In a nutshell, the world needs my mom's services, but mine? Not so much. Something the illustrious Greg also told me once.

Behind me, the girls are already transitioning into the silks portion of the practice. Long, ribbony strips of fabric dangle from the ceiling in pairs. Teal, Black, silver, purple. I look over my shoulder at my classmate Robin as she tugs at the silks and then pulls herself up, dangling above the floor simply by the strength of her arms.

"I have to be to work at three," I tell her. It doesn't matter. It never does.

"We should be done by then," she insists. But I already know that somehow, I'll still be late. Because Flor and her life *always* make me late for work.

When I'm quiet, she adds, "You'll have plenty of time. Besides, if I'm going to be late, you can just take them to Mom and Dad's. Dad's getting off at two."

Taking them is no small feat. It involves bribery and meltdowns and bargaining and a strict promise of ice cream upon arrival, which is almost never honored and always comes back to bite me in the ass the next time I see my beloved niece and nephew. My eyes flutter shut.

Because here I am again. Back in this familiar place.

"Yeah," I finally say, a large whoosh of air exiting my body. I work my jaw back and forth, staring at Jenna as she executes a slow somersault through the strips of fabric. She hooks her left foot around the silks as she descends, creating a knot up her calf. "I'll head back into town. Probably won't be there for an hour, though."

"Oh, thanks, sis!" She only calls me *sis* when I give her the answer she wants to hear. "They can't wait to see you."

I don't doubt what she says, but at ages four and six, Fifi and Louie can't wait to see the mailman each day either. "All right. I'll start heading out."

We hang up and I stare at the cap of my water bottle until my vision goes blurry. I'm in this position more often than I'd like—bailing out my sister so she can get on with her super important life. Never asked what I might be giving up or sacrificing so that I can help her *yet again*. Each time I get disgruntled by another request to watch the kids or run an errand or go buy dinner for them somewhere, I am immediately put in my place by either my parents or the universe or both.

My parents love to remind me how hard it is to navigate life with two kids. They had two; now Flor has two. I have none, so according to them, my time is spent doing cartwheels and twiddling my thumbs. Actually, half of that is sort of true. But instead of twiddling my thumbs, I hook them around aerial silks.

It's the only thing that keeps me grounded, ironically—twirling around in the air. I don't get out to Fly By half as much as I want to, but when I do—and can actually complete my session as God intended—I'm riding high for a full week afterward.

But if my family found out I ditched Flor in her time of need to go play around with silks or focus more on my forward bends, they'd ridicule me for an entire year. So I keep it to myself. Not a single soul in my family knows about this, and that's how it'll stay.

Besides, it might sound stupid, but I feel like I owe her. Back when I was a senior in high school and first discovering silks, I bailed on her when she needed me so that I could go to one of the first aerial silks sessions of my life, and guess what? Louisiana almost died from an allergic reaction, Greg's car wasn't working, and the only family member available at the time—me—was out twiddling her thumbs and doing cartwheels.

My body feels heavy for a cocktail of reasons. Not only did I only get in a third of my usual workout, I'm both disappointed and feeling guilty. Because that's the other side of this super weird commemorative coin: I dread being asked for help in managing Flo's life, but I also hate myself for dreading it because *she's family* and *I should do whatever I can to help her.*

It's lose-lose for me and me only.

I pack up my stuff in the black backpack that serves as my purse. I'll change at her house once it's time to leave, and I'm already figuring out excuses I can give my boss when I roll in anywhere from ten to forty minutes late today. I jog over to the instructor, Robin, who always jokes that her parents picked the best name for her since she loves to act like a bird in the sky.

"Hey, I have a little family emergency, so I have to head out," I tell her. My gaze is drawn to my classmates in various stages of scampering up the silks. Jenna is already fully engaged in the middle of her silks, one thigh wrapped as she executes a back bend, her arms extended toward the ground. She is a beautiful swan wrapped in fabric. *Fuck.* I wanted to be the swan today.

"Oh, is everything okay?"

"Yeah, should be fine." I muster a small smile. "I don't know when I'll be able to come back. Hopefully soon."

Robin touches my wrist softly. "Wait. I wanted to talk to you about something." There's an undercurrent of excitement in her gaze that makes my heart start racing. "A famous performance troupe has opened up an understudy position. They're West Coast based, which I know is a little far. But I wanted to submit your sequence for consideration, if you'll let me."

I blink about a hundred times at her, unable to compute. "Sorry, what now?"

Her grin widens. "You're our rising star, Scarlett. I wasn't kidding about that. I think you have a shot at being selected by them. The experience you'd gain would be...incredible. Unfathomable. I think you'd *love* it."

I'm sputtering. "I—I have a job and stuff—"

"I know. It's a little unrealistic, but"—she shrugs, her eyes brimming with fantasy—"what if we just gave it a shot? The worst that can happen is you say no and they go with their second pick."

I squeeze the straps of my backpack. Everything in me wants to say no, to push my sister and her life to the front and center of my own life like I'm used to doing. But the pulsing core of me, buried under layers of practicality and pessimism and negativity is screaming *FUCKING DO IT.*

I just encouraged Maverick to do the same thing last night. Why not me? My chances of being picked are infinitely smaller than his, but still—what if I did it just to show myself that my passion deserves a secret spotlight?

"Okay," I blurt. "Yeah, I...if you think so. Are you sure? I mean, my sequence—"

"Is fabulous," she interjects. "I plan on using the videos we took last month. You looked amazing. I'll do all the submission stuff for you, okay? I just needed you to give me the green light."

My heart is racing now, and I'm nodding like a bobble head. "Yeah. Awesome. Wow. I just—okay."

She squeezes my arms. "Eeek! This is so exciting. I'll send you information about the troupe so you can look into them in the meantime." She winks, drifting away toward her silk at the front of the gym. "Drive safe, Scarlett."

Once I get to my car, I dive into a protein bar. My phone starts ringing just as I take the first bite.

"Heeeey," Maverick is saying as I bring the phone up to my ear. He has a habit of greeting me first, even when he's the one calling.

"What's up?" I press the phone to my shoulder as I turn the key. It sputters and then doesn't turn over. "Fuck." I try again.

"Is that your engine?"

"Yeah." I sigh, trying it again. It sputters to life a moment later.

"Girl, let me look at it."

"Could you? No rush on it, though." Tom used to handle all of that stuff, but I'm not about to bring my car into his workplace anytime soon. "It started acting up about a week ago...maybe longer."

"Scarlett, you gotta tell me these things. I could have looked at it and fixed it by now."

"Well, I didn't want to bother you." I ease out of my maple tree–shaded parking spot and into the bright late-May sun. "You do that shit eight hours a day. I know you don't go home each day thinking *Man, I'd love to work on just one more car.*"

"It's different if it's one of my friends," Mav says. "Where are you now? Want me to come look at it?"

"No, it's your off day. You don't need to bother."

"Scarlett."

"I'm heading to Flor's right now." My blinker ticks dully as I hit a stoplight right before the freeway.

"You watching the kids?"

"Yeah. Then working until close." I pull onto freeway, and soon Lake Erie is sparkling in the distance. I've always loved living close to the lake and in Bayshore. I sort of thought I'd have tried out a new place by now. I've always wanted to bop around the USA, backpacking or road tripping or maybe even just uprooting all together. But once Fifi and Louie came around…that fell right off the table quicker than a cat…pushing something off a table.

"Can't wait for today's newest Greg-ism," Mav cracks.

"Yeah, me neither. I'm about ready to publish my first book of his quotes." My sister's boyfriend could have his own line of merchandise dedicated to the ridiculous things he says. One of the more notable recent quotes: *Why do you want to move out of your apartment, Scarlett? Apartments are for unmarried, single people. You can't look for a house. Houses are for complete families.*

Must have missed that rule in the Life Handbook, Greg. I'm not sure what it says about Flor that she continues to be with him.

"You want to stop over after you get off?"

"No. I want you to enjoy your day off and not worry about my stupid car."

"Okay. You'll stop over once you get off, then."

I grin, shaking my head though he can't see it.

"Besides, we have some things to talk about," he adds.

My stomach pitches to the floor. I'm suddenly wracking my brain for recent memories. Did I act inappropriately at the wedding? Did we do something we shouldn't have? Maybe I somehow accidentally activated a video call while I *almost* masturbated to his memory, and now he knows I'm distantly attracted to him. "We do?"

"The food truck competition. Duh." I can hear his cocky smirk, and just picturing it sends a shiver up my spine.

"Oh my god, that's right." I grip the steering wheel tighter, both relief and anxiety prowling my body. Thank *God* that's what his chat is about, and not some potentially awkward and friendship-ruining thing like *You admitted you're in love with me, and I think we shouldn't see each other for the next year.* "I completely forgot."

"So you weren't serious?"

"No, no, it's not that." It's just that I was temporarily blinded by my own adrenaline-inducing advancement toward a secret hobby I don't want anyone to know about. But really, if I'm being honest with myself, I know I don't have the time to help Maverick with as much as he's going to need in order to get this thing going. But I also can't let him rest on his laurels like he's been doing for the past, oh, five years when it comes to his insane gift in the kitchen. I owe it to him to figure out a way to help.

"I was serious," I tell him. "I *am* serious. We just need to hammer out a schedule or something."

"Exactly. So I'll see you tonight."

He hangs up before I can protest. Not that I was going to protest very hard. My counterargument is weak at best, and it only hides a deeper truth that I'm hesitant to acknowledge: seeing Maverick is always the highlight of my day.

And I welcome every chance I get to see that man.

Only problem is, I keep wanting more of him. And Maverick is only willing to give so much.

He'll never hand over what I'm most eager for: a future.

CHAPTER FIVE

SCARLETT

It's eight p.m. and dusk is settling on Bayshore. I'm off work, and the entire evening stretches ahead of me. Tomorrow is Monday, one of my off days, and as of right now, Flor hasn't asked me to babysit or buy her groceries yet. I'd head to Fly By, but they don't have classes on Mondays, so I'm feeling a particular type of free as I sip on the ice-cold IPA that Maverick shoved in my hand the second I parked at his apartment complex.

In addition to free, I'm feeling a particular type of confused.

Maverick's simple black tee is the stuff that pornos are made of as he rests his hands on the frame of my car and inspects my engine. He wipes his forearm across his forehead as he continues the silent conversation with my car. I'm sitting on the sidewalk watching him like a crazed fan or the most pathetic apprentice.

"Everything look okay?" I ask him.

He grunts in response, per mechanic protocol I guess, and fiddles with things that I don't know the names for. I set my beer down and lean back on the sidewalk. I'm still in full E. Lago regalia, which includes black pedal pushers and a soft blue short-sleeve polo.

"I think I'm gonna go change," I say.

He jerks his head into a nod but doesn't look at me. It's kind of hot being ignored by Maverick while he's performing this hyper-masculine task. Because yes, I'm hopelessly attracted to grunting, sweaty *dudes*.

Not saying that I'm wildly attracted to Maverick, of course. Just distantly. It's more of a concept; kind of like how scientists theorize about dark matter, I've also theorized about being hopelessly attracted to my best friend.

I'm mulling this as I go up to his apartment. I've had a key for about a year now. Tom found out about it and thought it was super weird, and we half-fought about it, until I reminded him that I needed the key to water Maverick's plants when he went on vacation a year ago and never gave it back. Throughout the two years that Tom and I were together, my friendship with Maverick was never an issue. It's just so apparent how platonic Maverick and I are that I don't think the idea of *something happening* between us ever crossed Tom's mind.

And it shouldn't have. Because I'm a loyal ass girlfriend, and besides, I come in roughly last on Maverick's list of girls he'd like to fuck.

The pleasant scent of Maverick's apartment settles over me as I enter his home. I take a deep breath—it's leather and musk and something earthy, a combination of his body wash and raw, manly pheromones. I drop my bag on his couch and slip my shoes off, followed by my shirt. I've got my belt unbuckled and my pants half off when it occurs to me to get my regular clothes out. Except I can't find them. My pants slide to my ankles and I'm elbows deep in my backpack when the front door opens.

Maverick steps inside, his eyebrows shooting to the sky. "Uhh, sorry?"

"No, no, it's fine." I fumble to find my clothes and finally retrieve my black tank top. Maverick's seen me in a bathing suit before, so it's not like this is *scandalous* or anything. Still, though, I swear I can feel his gaze sizzling on me as he walks to his bedroom.

"Didn't realize you wore thongs," Maverick says, his voice muffled from inside his bedroom. My eyes widen. Shit. I *did* wear a thong today. That's slightly more revealing than my bathing suit. Still, I shouldn't feel embarrassed, even though I totally do.

"Yeah, well, it's almost laundry day. I'm running out of options." I force a laugh. I'm not sure why this feels like a personal failure, but it does.

His boots clunk against the floor as he comes back into the living room. I still don't have pants on, and my heart is pounding so hard I can barely make my hands work. Why am I acting like this? He stops walking, the sudden silence between us swallowing me whole. My cheeks are burning as his attention sizzles across me again.

"I forgot this wrench. I'm going back down," he says, and clomps toward the front door.

"Okay, cool, see you down there," I say, my voice unnecessarily bright and hollow. Once the door clicks shut behind him, I bury my face in my hands. What is going on with me lately? I'd blame this on Maverick's sexy outfit at Grayson's wedding, but that's not the entire truth. Honestly, I've been thinking about Maverick like this for a few months. Longer than Tom and I have been broken up. Fleeting thoughts. Flickers of firefly light at the back of my mind.

But one thing's for certain: I can't follow this train of thought further. I take a deep breath and bring myself back to the present, where the truths are solid and unyielding: Maverick is my best friend, and he is attractive, and that is all. I would never risk our lifelong friendship simply because I got a little case of the lusty-whimsies and started thinking Maverick was somehow on my radar.

I tug my shorts on and slip on my black Chuck Taylor low-top shoes. When I'm back outside, Maverick is buried under the hood of the car tinkering with something. I hum to myself and return to my abandoned beer, downing the rest of it in one go.

"Okay, so, you fixed everything already and it's perfect, right?" I ask after I've replayed the awkwardness in his apartment fifty times in my head.

He's grimacing, squinting at something on the side of the engine in the waning light of the day. Strands of his dark hair cross his forehead, and then he props his hands on the sides of my car, veins bulging in his forearms.

"I think I know what's wrong," he says, rubbing his shoulder across his mouth. "But I can't finish it today. I'm running out of light."

The all-business edge in his voice is an odd thrill. "But it's not fatal, right?"

Finally he twists to look at me, a dimple flashing in his cheek. The smile he sends me is the kind that could send Ariana Grande into a tizzy. "Not fatal. Actually, not even expensive."

"Oh, you're charging me?"

"Thousand an hour." He stands up and reaches for the hood, exposing a tantalizing creamy sliver of his abs. The hood comes down, and he picks up his scattered tools, jerking his chin toward the apartment building behind me. "Okay, let's go figure out the rest of our shit now."

I hop to my feet, and we walk back up to his second-floor apartment. Once we're inside the cozy confines of his bachelor pad, I head for my favorite spot, which is the overstuffed armchair facing an overstuffed loveseat. I feel like whatever weird slip we had in here earlier is forgotten now. Things feel normal again. Maverick glimpsing my thong didn't change anything. *Phew*. I snuggle into my spot, goosepimples flaring on my thighs.

"You cold, Lettie?" Mav's gentle rasp makes every inch of me perk up. He's heading to the refrigerator, and I couldn't even tell that he'd noticed me.

"Why do you ask?"

"You're burrowing like a newborn kitten."

"Yeah, I'm a little cold."

"Hang on." He abandons whatever he's doing at the fridge and heads to the bedroom. He comes back a moment later with a long-sleeve black tee. He grins as he drops it into my lap.

"Thank you for adhering to my wardrobe requirements," I say with a cheesy smile.

"I know better than to give you something pink."

"Do you *have* something pink?"

"No. But when I say 'pink' I mean 'anything that isn't black.'"

"Good boy," I tell him before tugging the shirt over my head. Maverick makes fun of me for not owning anything more vibrant than gray, but I just don't see the point of diving into a color palette when black clothing provides everything my soul requires. I nestle into the comfiness, which is made better by the fact that it smells like Maverick. "Okay. What's next on the agenda?"

"You helping my ass." He comes over to the loveseat, setting two IPAs on the coffee table between us.

"So you really want to do the competition?"

He shrugs. "I looked into it a little more this morning. I feel like we could pull it off."

There's that word again: *we*. I never intended to hand over every ounce of my free time when I encouraged him to participate, but helping my best friend is worth it. "I *know* you could pull it off."

"Not me alone," he clarifies. "I need you with me."

I purse my lips. "You really don't."

"That was the deal. If you do it with me, I go for it. If not..."

I wave away the words that remain unspoken in the air. "I know, I know. I remember."

"Except you forgot once already."

"It was a temporary forgetting. Now I permanently remember."

Maverick's smile is ear-to-ear. "Okay. So what's our name?"

I blink about a hundred times. My brain is an expansive tapestry of nothingness, despite how much I struggle to think of a witty food truck name. "Uhhh."

"Lettie and Mav," he says.

"Least creative of all time," I say. "Besides, that means we'd have to work together forever."

"It's just for the competition."

"No, this the real deal," I remind him, pointing at him with the neck of my beer. "The competition is just jumpstarting it. You're starting your food truck business here; the reality TV show is just what will get it going faster."

He doesn't look convinced. "This is just for the reality TV show. Trust me, I can't quit my job for something like this."

"You never know. It might end up panning out."

He just shakes his head and grabs a notebook, clicking the top of a pen. "We'll come back to the name. I've got a menu drawn up already."

"That was fast."

"It's been hanging out in my head for a year or two." He starts scribbling, which is just further proof that he needs to follow this path. "This is the first time I've ever written it out though."

While he writes, I realize that we really need the guidance of the actual application. "Hey, where's your laptop?"

"Bedroom," he says, frowning at the notebook.

I brush past the couch and head to his bedroom, flipping the light on. His bedcovers are rumpled, the dark gray sheets looking extra soft for some reason. What would it like to be wrapped up with him here? I pause in the middle of the room, forgetting what I even came in here for. Despite his being my closest male friend, we've never shared a bed, not even on an accidental drunken night. I usually come to his house and not the other way around, and if I crash here, I always opt for the couch.

How many other women have seen this bed or tainted these sheets? The thought is sobering, acting as a jumpstart to my legs again. I snatch his laptop off a small desk tucked beside his dresser. Veronica was probably the most recent one to grace his apartment. I don't even want to imagine the things they probably did in this room. Between those sheets. Her hair splayed out against the dark gray of his pillowcase.

I'm not going to think about it anymore. I'm not sure why it's even occurring to me in the first place. Back in the living room, I open up his computer on my lap and am greeted with the password screen.

"Is your password still 'ilovehugetitties'?" It sounds like I'm joking, but I'm not.

He smirks. "Yeah."

Yet another reason he and I are better off as friends. He'd never be satisfied with my wimpy B-cups.

I open up a web browser and search for the competition application. He scratches a few more things into his notebook and then glances up at me. "Don't get into my porn, okay?"

"Trust me, I don't want to see what gets your pulse racing." I find the official website for the competition and click through the info screens until I find the official entry page.

"Nothing freaky," Maverick replies. "Just the run-of-the-mill erotic shit enjoyed by your average red-blooded American man."

"And I know how disgusting most men are, so I'd rather not see evidence that you're just like the rest of them."

He snorts. "I had no idea you held such a high opinion of me."

"Only on occasion."

He grins as he scribbles toward the bottom of the notebook. Silence settles between us as we get lost in our own tasks. I've got the full list of entry requirements, which I email to both of us. I'll print it out later. Finally, Maverick breaks the silence.

"So Tom was pretty disgusting too?"

The question makes something icy coat my stomach. "Tom was disgustingly normal."

Maverick's shoulders shake with quiet laughter. "Now that's a sick burn. I thought he was an okay guy."

I'd tell Maverick all about the five separate occasions that Tom went down on me and did a half-assed job or the boring sex that became our complacent norm. Or how he'd always drop hints that we needed to start making babies before I got too old. The way he'd caution me against getting too skinny or fit or else I'd fully look like a pre-teen boy.

And then, the final straw, the ridicule he dished out when he discovered my monthly membership payments to the aerial silks gym. The way he'd called me out for being irresponsible and idealistic and dumb with money. That we could have been halfway to the down payment on our future house if I hadn't spent all that money.

But we don't talk about things like that.

And honestly, Tom's words might as well be Flor's or my mom's, or anyone else important in my life. It's why I refuse to share silks—or the fact that my instructor submitted my application for the understudy position—with anyone. I want us to win the competition and use my cut of the money strictly for furthering my silks career, like a giant, pulsating *FUCK YOU* to everyone who tries to control my life, my dreams, my passions.

In this fantasy world where we win the competition *and* I get selected as a silks understudy for a prestigious West Coast troupe, I'll figure out the perfect use of the earnings so that it's only used creatively.

"He is an okay guy." I sniff, scrolling through the requirements list. "Just not okay for me."

Maverick is quiet again as he finishes his menu. Then he rips it out of the notebook and passes it my way. "What do you think?"

NAME TO BE DETERMINED
Something witty and tasty
Definitely not 'Lettie and Mav'
AHI TUNA WRAP: pan-seared ahi tuna steak with sesame seeds, garlic, ginger, cayenne, rolled into a whole wheat tortilla with avocado, and wasabi slaw.
SPICY CHORIZO SCRAMBLE: crumbled Spanish chorizo, scrambled eggs, goat cheese, sriracha, served with corn tortillas.
BISON BLAST OFF: house-made bison patties, topped with caramelized onions and white cheddar.
THE COW TIPPER: there's so many patties on this hamburger, a cow will tip over!

I'm smiling by the time I read through his trial menu. "This is amazing! But you forgot to add the ravioli."

He glares at me. There's nothing Maverick hates more in the culinary world than ravioli. Some sort of childhood aversion that followed him into adulthood for no good reason, so of course I have to tease him about it. He rubs the back of his neck.

"I'll probably change it all."

"No, I think this is really on point with the competition. It's the Midwestern truck challenge! How could we not play on cow tipping?"

"Even though we've never been once."

"We might have to before the show starts, just to beef up our street cred."

Maverick leans back on the loveseat and nods. "Beef up? More like beef over." He snorts at his bad joke. "We'll call it a morale-building activity."

"Right. Go, Team! Tip cows! And all that." I tut as I scan the official contest regulations. "Oh, Mav. It says here that all hotels will be paid for by the show, but that it extends to only the official participants. Any other visitors will be denied entry and prohibited from utilizing the show-sponsored accommodations."

His brow furrows. "So?"

"That means you can't have your regularly scheduled *booty calls*, if you get picked to compete."

He looks unfazed. "You mean if *we* get picked."

"Right. So that would be"–I scroll back up to the top of the page—"five weeks of celibacy. Think you can handle that?"

His eyes narrow. "I thought you said you had a high opinion of me."

"I do. Just not, like, when it comes to getting laid."

He lifts a brow. "I'm not a fucking maniac, you know. I'll survive."

"Okay. Just wanted to make sure you're clear on the rules." It's fun to tease him in general, but it's even better when he gets genuinely annoyed, like right now. "Veronica can't come, no matter how hard you try to sneak her in."

He rolls his eyes. "Veronica won't be coming, don't worry."

"Oh, no? She was so fun to listen to when she laughed. What's wrong with her?"

He pauses a moment, something heavy and electric in his ice-blue eyes. "Disgustingly normal."

At that, we both crack up laughing.

It's time like these I swear to God we're meant for each other. Like I can read all the depths of his heart and soul from just the little glances we share. It feels so evident, so real, so obvious.

But I think I'm the only one who feels it.

And even if he did? I'd be too scared to ruin what we have.

Lettie and Mav need to stay best friends, and that's it.

CHAPTER SIX

MAVERICK

"Fuck."

My voice echoes though the empty interior of the step van—which is just the formal name for my big ass food truck—as I take my final measurement. I've been here since eight this morning, part of my new routine that I started last Sunday when I got serious about applying for the show.

There's nothing particularly wrong. It's just that I say *fuck* about every fifteen minutes when I'm in here doing measurements. I've been stressing about the floor plan on the daily for three days now, and today, I'm pulling the trigger.

I'm buying the equipment.

My footsteps clunk heavily over the metal floor as I head to the back door. I painstakingly rehabbed this old step van from rusting obscurity after inheriting it from Grammy Ethel three years ago. Nobody's really sure where Grammy got it from, or why she kept it around long enough to hand off to me. Dom has implied no fewer than fifteen times since hooking up with London that this step van has plans for my love life, which is insane for a couple reasons. First of all, I don't have a love life. Second of all, if this food truck is involved in me finding love, which Dom is convinced of, he's going to be disappointed when it turns out I fall in love with a new hamburger recipe and not a woman.

It's been sitting in the big storage unit my parents have been renting for God knows how long on the west end of town. My truck is parked next to twenty-five years' worth of lake-themed Christmas decorations and all the unused baby cribs that my brothers and I cycled through. I knew the second I saw it that I wanted it to be a food truck, even though I never thought it would be happening *this* soon.

And things aren't just happening soon. They're happening fast. A little *too* fast. It's making my head spin, and it would have flown right off my shoulders by now if it weren't for Scarlett.

A sick knot forms in my stomach as I fish my phone out of my pocket. I've got to be at work in approximately thirty minutes. It's right around the corner, so I should be fine. Except I need at least an hour to talk myself into pulling the trigger on this equipment purchase.

Seven thousand dollars.

That's how much I'll be sinking into outfitting this mobile kitchen. I about passed out when Scarlett shared the price quote with me last night, grimace and all. I told her I needed to sleep on it. Except I think I need to spend a lifetime on it just to be sure.

I swipe to call her. She picks up on the third ring, sounding slightly breathless.

"Hello?"

"You up?"

"Of course I'm up." She expels a loud burst of air. "Why wouldn't I be up? You're talking to me."

"I dunno. It's early. You could be sleep talking. You want me to call back later? Maybe on my lunch break?"

"Oh, I get it. You're stalling." She grunts softly and then sighs. I have no idea what she's doing on the other end. Running? Vigorous toweling off post-shower? Maybe something sexy…but no. I'm not allowed to think stuff like that about her. "You ready to buy the equipment now?"

"I don't know. I've cross-checked the quote list three hundred times. It all looks good. I just think we should wait until we get accepted to pull the trigger." I'm tugging at the front of my hair, making a slow lap around the inside of the truck, my work boots scuffing along the metal floor. "This is a huge investment, Lettie. It's going to eat up every last dime of my savings."

"I know it is. But you know what else? You'll keep saving money after this purchase. Hell, if things go wrong, you can resell it all."

"Not at full price though," I tell her.

"But at a high enough price to re-pad your savings. If you wait until you get accepted, it'll be too late. Remember—"

"I know, I know. They announce the final contestant line up one week before filming begins."

"Exactly. You think you can get everything installed in one week, when you'll also have to get your ass to the first filming location? Forget about it. You have the time now. This is an investment in your future, Mav. If it doesn't work out for the show, it'll still work out down the road."

I sigh heavily, because she's right, and we both know it. *Like usual.* "Fine. Let's say you're right."

"I *am* right."

"Yes, and it's annoying." By now, I can't keep the grin from covering my face. I look around me at the empty step van, trying to imagine it filled to the brim with equipment, counters, and sinks. I can barely fathom it. Yet every inch of me is dying to see it become a reality. "You got time today to put the order through?"

"I don't go in until four. I'm all yours."

The simple comment makes something hot streak through me. She *is* all mine. In more ways than I realized. There's something reassuring there. But now's not the time to think about it.

"Let's do it, then. I left my credit card on the kitchen island. Make it happen. I can come pick up the equipment this weekend."

"Okay." I can hear her beaming through the phone. "I'm on it."

"You think this is crazy?"

"Oh, I think this is more than crazy," Scarlett says. "This is crazy fucking great."

I'm left with a lingering smile once we hang up. I hop out of the back of the van and shut the door. I come around the side, past an enormous Christmas wreath that has tiny speed boats on it in lieu of ornaments, and I spot my mom heading my way, smiling like she knows a secret.

"Hey, Mom! What are you doing here?" I wrap her into a hug. I'm the shortest Daly brother by two inches, but my mom's still half a head shorter than I am.

"Just came to start looking for some old stuff that London and Dom might be using for their wedding." Their wedding is next on the docket, in August—which, if by some bizarre twist of fate I actually get picked for this show and make it through the challenges, I'll miss. But there's no way that will happen.

She smiles up at me warmly, the wisps of gray at her dark temples always serving as a stark reminder to me: *time is marching forward no matter how much you feel like you'll be 26 forever.*

"And what are *you* doing here?"

"I've been working on the truck." I shrug, looking back at it, which reminds me that I need to email that graphic designer again about starting work on a logo and wrap. The to-do list is never ending.

"You're buying something for it? Are you finally going to turn it into a food truck?"

I rub the back of my neck, laughing weakly. "Well, maybe. I mean, yes. I don't know."

She cocks her head in the way that says *come on now.* "Well, you're not doing it alone. Who's helping you?"

"Scarlett. That's who I was talking to. She's been a huge help."

My mom's smile grows even wider. The kind she uses when she looks at Gray and Hazel or Dom and London, or any of my other brothers and their partners. "I'm not surprised in the least. You've always been two peas in a pod. Why didn't you take her to the wedding?"

"Mom, I—" I'm not even sure how to respond to this. I know what she's getting at: Scarlett and I should be an item. But we shouldn't. And we never will be. "She was already going. Plus, she and I are just friends. We're not...I couldn't..."

Mom doesn't look convinced. "When are you going to stop telling yourself that?"

I roll my eyes. "Whatever. Lettie doesn't think of me like that, I promise you. Besides, she and her ex have this thing. She needs someone like him, you know?"

"I think she needs someone like my baby Maverick," Mom says, cupping my cheeks in her hands. She squeezes them together enough so that my lips smoosh.

"Okay, Mom, that's enough," I say, laughing. "I'm going to go try to forget you suggested me and Scarlett should be together. That's like telling me I should be with my sister, you know?"

Her smile grows mischievous. "You don't have one of those."

"Whatever. That's not the point."

"Then what is the point?" she presses.

"I'm not ready to settle down," I tell her. And it's true. At least, it was. "I gotta go." I'm flustered by the secretive way she's watching me. Like she knows something I don't. Parents get fucking weird after you turn twenty-five.

"Come over for dinner soon and tell me about this truck," she calls after me as I head for the main door of the storage unit.

"Not fucking happening if Dad's there," I shout over my shoulder. "Love you, Mom!"

The door clangs shut behind me, and I feel guilty for a moment. I haven't seen Mom half as much as I used to. But ever since my falling out with Dad after I dropped out of college, I haven't been very inspired to head to their house, much less to share this risky idea that could leave me flat on my face.

That's just fodder for him to go off about how much smarter it would have been to get my degree in engineering like I'd wanted to my senior year of high school. That way I could have room for advancement. I wouldn't be stuck turning to food service like any teenager at McDonald's. If he heard that I planned to drain my savings to get this equipment, he'd fucking leave the room. If he said anything at all, he'd tell me to call Grayson so he could talk some financial sense into me.

I can imagine all his retorts and then some. Because his stance on me has always been clear: Maverick—the youngest, the stupidest, the most hopeless.

So in a nutshell: fuck him and fuck sharing this with him.

We're both content to basically never speak to each other again. So I guess that's how it's going to be.

Sunshine lifts the corners of my lips as I head back to my car in the gravel parking lot. Lilacs are blooming from a huge bush nearby, and the smell is intoxicating. I'm so ready for another Bayshore summer. Except if we get picked for the show, I'll miss the entire summer.

Call Scarlett and tell her to cancel the order. It'll be easier to stay here and work on the truck more slowly. Besides, maybe Dad is right.

I head into work at a mental crossroad. Every inch of me wants to text Scarlett and tell her to wait on the purchase, but I'm damn near late to clock-in. I rush into the shop, forgetting my phone in the car. There's ten of us on the floor each day. Tom jerks his head into a nod from the next bay over as I head to my station, his mop of blond hair looking shaggier than normal. He's gained some weight and gotten scruffier since Scarlett broke up with him. The rest of my coworkers are lingering around the shop, all of us waiting for the shitty coffee our boss provides to kick in.

We're a quiet bunch at the start of the morning, but by noon, we're in full heckle-and-harass mode. My stomach is grumbling, and I'm itching to check my phone for updates. Work has been busy enough to forget about the pending anxiety, but now that I'm about to be on break for a half hour, it's trickling through my veins. Reminding me that this might be the worst mistake of my life. Before I can get my hands washed and some of this oil cleaned off my forearms, my boss is shouting for me.

"Daly! You got a visitor!"

I twist to look toward the door leading out of the garage. I spot Scarlett through the glass window. *Fuck.*

Everything inside me goes tight. It's not a good sign that she's here. And it looks even worse for Tom. I glance his way, finding his thick brows furrowing together, his gaze stuck on Scarlett through the window.

There's a low whistle from my coworker Adam in the next bay over as I scrub some of the oil off my arms with a paper towel. "Seems like she used to come around here for someone else back in the day," Adam says as I walk by.

"Shut the fuck up," I tell him.

"Your girl is here," another coworker, Trent, says to Tom, which prompts a glare. "But not for you."

"Daaaamn," Matthew says from across the shop.

Tom's glare swings my way. I already know I need to do some damage control, but first, I need to get Scarlett the fuck out of here.

I burst through the door into the cool front room of the shop. This is where customers pay or look at any of the fifteen different types of tires that cost an arm and a leg but do the same damn thing. Scarlett's in her normal attire—black jean shorts with a loose black tank. Except today, she's got a silver sports bra on underneath and slip-on Vans instead of the usual boots. They're tiny details, but I notice.

I'd find a way to give her shit about it, even though it's meaningless, but she looks spooked as I head her way. Her gaze flits over my shoulder to look toward the shop. We're always on display in there, like a zoo full of mechanics. I jerk my head toward the show room around the corner, where benches face the big windows looking out at the street.

"What are you doing here?" I ask in a low voice. I'm sure the receptionist, Renee, is listening, because she lives for knowing about our shit. She calls us "the bay boys" like we're there for her fucking amusement. And when Scarlett and Tom first broke up, she was the first to ask Tom out for a consolation drink.

"Emergency," Scarlett says, a wild look in her eyes.

"Make it quick," I say, wiping the collar of my shirt over my upper lip. "They're giving me shit in there."

She deflates, nibbling on her bottom lip. "I didn't want to stop in. But you weren't answering your phone—"

"I left it in the car. Is something wrong?"

"Something came up on the purchase order about the voltage," she says in a rush. "She asked me all these questions, and I had no idea, so—"

"Voltage for what?"

"The prep table?" She grimaces. "She said that they had a 240 volt, or a 220 volt—"

"We need 220," I tell her. "And that goes for anything else electric."

She clutches at the side of her face. "I was gonna tell her 240! I would have ruined everything."

"Was that it?"

She nods quickly, giving me a thumbs up. "Crisis averted."

"I'm gonna get my phone, so I'll check in later."

"Okay. I'm off to spend all your money."

I bite my tongue against a witty retort. I could spend the rest of my shift out here talking to her, but the pull of my coworker's judgment—and Tom's blazing suspicions—have me heading back toward the shop. But just before I pull open the door, I can't help myself. "Spend it all in one place."

"Not the usual advice, but okay." She grins and waves, pushing out of the waiting room and back toward the parking lot. I avoid looking at Renee as I head back into the shop, where low "Ooooh"s start immediately.

"Didn't realize you went for sloppy seconds," Adam teases as I head back to my bay.

"Will you shut the fuck up? She's practically my sister," I tell him, storming to grab my car keys.

"Eh, more like your brother," Adam goes on. He's the biggest douchebag of them all, the one guy I actually can't stand. I grit my teeth. We've gotten into it before, but it's not worth it over this. He loves to push until someone breaks and then claim it was all just good fun. I'm not falling for it again.

Tom appears in my bay a moment later, leaning against the work bench as he inspects something on the ground.

"So what the fuck was that about?" he asks in a low voice. I can hear the implicit threat there. The guys are getting to him, and I'm suddenly tired of how asinine this is.

"Dude, nothing. I asked her to do me a favor since I had to work today."

He sniffs, nodding. "You been seeing her a lot?"

"Not any more than usual. You know how I am. I've got a busy date book." I crack a grin, trying to make him understand just how stupid the idea of *Scarlett and Maverick* sounds.

He heaves a sigh. "Got any spare dates you can throw my way?" When he looks over at me, I can see the sadness in his gaze, the shit he doesn't show when he's buried under a car, trading barbs with the guys like everything is as fine as ever.

"I'll see what I can hook up," I tell him.

"I think I just need to fuck half of Bayshore. And then fuck up whoever it is that Scarlett is seeing."

"She's seeing someone?" A weird coldness slides across my chest. If she's seeing somebody, I sure missed the memo.

"Has to be. She moved on a little too quick." He leans in closer, his voice growing softer, more urgent. "We were together for *two years.* You'd think that fucking meant something. But not if she's got a rebound."

"I haven't met him if she's got someone," I tell him.

He frowns. "You'd tell me, though, right?"

"Of course." My heart is pounding, and I'm not exactly sure why. But Tom is squinting at me like he suspects something. Like maybe he can tell that I occasionally see Scarlett's perfect, apple-round ass cheeks in that tiny scrap of a thong when I close my eyes at night.

"I want her back, Daly. I thought we were getting married. And then...just out of nowhere..." He shakes his head and looks away, firming his hands on his hips. "She always dressed too much like a boy, you know?"

There aren't many alternatives to saying *I totally fucking disagree*, so I keep my mouth shut. Because now is *not* the time to mention how feminine that thong really is.

"She was bad with money, too. So bad. I think I need someone with tits. Huge tits. And those long, red cat claws, y'know? Someone who actually, like, wears makeup and shit. You know? I'm sick of these fucking tomboys."

Suddenly I feel like his therapist. I've said nothing, and it only prompts him to say more. I start washing my hands as intently as possible.

"I could have a new girlfriend by next week," he goes on. "I bet she wouldn't like it if I showed up at E. Lago with a new girlfriend, y'know?"

I'm scrubbing my knuckles raw. "She wouldn't like that," I confirm. Because it's the only thing that is mildly truthful.

"I think we'll get back together," he goes on, looking around the garage. "I know she wants to. I think we just need some time apart first. I need to go fuck, like, twenty girls, and then I'll be ready to go back to her. I want to get married soon, but I need to get some shit out of my system."

The cold feeling in my chest returns. I pull the lever for paper towels noisily, making a big show of it. Something about the thought of him going back to Scarlett twenty girls later is the least fucking amusing thing I've heard of all year. But I'm one to talk. "Yeah."

"Yeah," he wraps up, nodding, looking at me like he's really said something of substance. "Good talk."

I leave the bay and head for my car so I can snag my phone and sit in peace for a few minutes on my break.

Because between seeing Scarlett unannounced and dealing with all this talk about her and me like we're an item has me twisted in knots. It feels wrong, somehow, but not in the way that I expected.

It feels wrong like asking for steak and potatoes when all I want is a fruit salad.

CHAPTER SEVEN

SCARLETT

The following Wednesday is the application deadline, and we are ready to submit. The plan is to go straight to Maverick's house once I get off work.

That's been the plan *most* nights, in fact. There's barely been a day since Grayson's wedding, two and a half weeks ago, that we haven't video chatted or spent the evening planning together. By now, it feels like we've been living this way for years.

I'm humming along with One Direction—yes, another secret fave—on my way to Maverick's apartment. It's almost nine, and it's still daylight at this hour, a stark contrast to the *dark-by-five* winter routine here in northern Ohio. Every inch of me is hopping with excitement. We've been working our tails off to get this far, and while everything's not completely ready, we're as far as we could get by scrambling in two weeks.

I pull into an empty parking spot at Maverick's apartment complex and hurry up the stairs, tripping in my haste. My knee hits the top step, and I grunt as I collapse. A cackle echoes through the stairwell.

"Oh, fuck, did you see that?" I ask.

Maverick is standing in his doorway, propping the door open with his arm. "See what, ya klutz?"

I pop to my feet easily, thanks to my near constant headstand practice, snickering as I hurry inside his apartment. Sometimes, I feel like we're the non-weed version of Cheech and Chong. Maybe the IPA-and-artisan hamburger version, *Lettie & Mav*. Inside, his apartment is cool, the big windows letting in dreamy drafts of air. He's got full water views from his living room, which is what makes his place better than mine.

Well, the water view, and the fact that Maverick lives here.

The bay is tranquil at this hour, the orangey-red rays of sunset beginning to stretch across the horizon. Clouds are illuminated in weird, pregnant puffs across the sky, better fit for an episode of *The Simpsons* than real life. I drop my backpack beside my go-to armchair and toe off my shoes while Maverick opens up his laptop on the coffee table.

I'm just about to ask if he's ready to submit when the tantalizing aroma of *something delicious* hits me. Something is sizzling in a pan on the stove.

"What are you cooking?"

"My newest signature dish." He sends me a cryptic smile as he heads back into the kitchen. His black tee is pulled tight across his shoulders, and for some reason, it takes my breath away. No, maybe that's the smell of garlic taking my breath away. I really love garlic, after all. But when he reaches for the salt and his muscles ripple under the shirt, I have my answer.

It's definitely Maverick.

I swallow hard and look away. It feels somehow illegal to be drooling over Maverick when so many have drooled before me. My drool doesn't even register in the collection pan.

"Something for the competition?" I ask, trying to sound offhand and casual, when really I'm wondering when he got so *beefy*.

"Maybe. But mostly just to celebrate."

"Well we haven't submitted yet, buddy. Give me a few minutes, though." I position the laptop in front of me and pull open the familiar docs, making sure we have everything in line.

The rough draft of the logo: *check*.

Floor plan of the truck with list of equipment: *check*.

Example of a menu: *check*.

Introduction video: …

"Maverick?" I ask, noticing how strained my voice sounds. "Did you see that we need an introduction video?"

He's at my side a second later. "A what?"

I mumble as I reread the submission instructions, which are in size five font for some inexplicable reason. Probably so that well-meaning contestants like ourselves have everything ready except for *one crucial aspect* on the deadline day. "Introductory video. Straightforward video to introduce yourself to the judges, can be used in future promotional materials, should not exceed one minute." I turn to Maverick, my eyes wide. "Um, we need to make this. Immediately."

"Okay. Okay. I'm ready." He sinks onto the armrest of the chair.

"You're holding the spatula in your hand." I fumble to get my phone out of my backpack. "The food is actively cooking."

"Aren't those selling points?" He leaps up to tend whatever he's cooking, and returns a moment later. "I'm gonna tell the judges I'll be pissed at them if this video makes our dinner burn."

"OK, we'll be quick." I swipe through to my camera app, switching to video, and line us up so that Maverick appears behind me, perched on the armrest. "You ready?"

"I guess."

"Not enthusiastic enough," I tell him.

"Fucking born ready," he says, his deadpan making me laugh. I compose myself for when the video starts recording. The way both of our faces light up in the reverse-facing camera is pure gold.

"Hey, guys!" My voice comes out a full octave higher than normal. Maverick bursts out laughing.

"Who the fuck was that?" he asks.

I sigh tersely, ending the video. "Come on. We have, like, seconds to finish this."

"All right. Damn." He composes himself, and I press the record button again. He waves, I follow suit.

"Hey, America," he begins.

This time, I snort. "Seriously?" I stop recording. "We're not on *Good Morning, America*, here."

He groans and heads back to the stove. "It's not wrong to greet your country."

"Fine, fine, you're right."

He comes back a moment later, spatula now clutched in his hand as if he might use it to stab me. He grips my shoulder. "Press record."

I'm stifling giggles already, so I can tell the third attempt is basically failed as well. I line us up on the screen and press the big red button.

"We don't know what we're doing," I blurt, which makes him snort.

"But we know who we are," he adds, and then jerks his thumb toward me. "This is my best friend Lettie."

"And this is my best friend Maverick."

"We're like Cheech and Chong," he says, and I gasp, twisting to look at him.

"Did you know I was just thinking that earlier?" I ask.

He smiles at the camera. "See that? We're such good friends we're psychic."

"But not stoners," I add, sending a serious look to my camera. "You don't have to worry about us bringing in illicit substances." I wince, turning back to Maverick. "Should we restart?"

"No, let's show them who we really are," he says, his grin stretching ear-to-ear. "This is an introduction, after all."

We continue rambling unhelpfully and finish our video at fifty-eight seconds. It's ridiculous. Possibly funny only to us. But it'll have to do. Maverick darts back to the kitchen to finish his mystery dinner, and he starts plating food while I do the final run-through of the submission package. This time, we have everything in order. And after I finally press *SUBMIT,* I gasp.

"I did it," I croak.

Maverick lets out a whoop, dropping off our plates of food at the small dining room table. "Couldn't have been better timed. Let's fucking eat and get drunk!"

I join him at the table, and we use both hands to high five over the food. That's when I notice the fantastic plate of meat in front of me.

"Oh my god. What is this?"

He uncorks a bottle of wine with a loud *thhhup.* "Steak bites cooked in garlic butter. Side of redskin mash."

I groan, my head dropping to my hands. "It's already my favorite dish ever."

"And you haven't even tried it." He tuts, pouring two generous glasses of cabernet sauvignon.

"Damn, you're fancy tonight." We drink beer as a rule.

"It's time to celebrate." He sinks into the seat across from me and lifts his wine glass. "Cheers, bitch."

I laugh and we clink glasses. The steak is die to for: luscious, juicy, cooked medium well but not dry. Maverick's redskin mashed potatoes are the type that I could eat thirty-five pounds of and still want just a few extra scoops. The dinner whirls by, aided by wine and laughter and endless ribbing, and then we migrate to his balcony, where we continue drinking and talking and imagining what a reality TV show might actually be like.

"You know," Maverick says, once we've polished off the bottle of wine and have switched to beer, as God intended, "I wonder if the show is gonna make it out like we're together."

My heart rate picks up in the same way it does whenever I catch a glimpse of Mav's bulging biceps (which is annoyingly often tonight) or think back to the soft cocoon of his bed...and how badly I want a taste of it in there. A strange gulf opens up in my chest, swallowing my common sense.

I ask, "What do you mean?" Even though I know exactly what he means.

He shrugs, looking out at the dark bay. We've been lake-staring for over an hour at this point. "I ran into my mom at the storage facility the other day. She was going on about the idea of us doing this together and kept acting like I was hiding something from her about us."

Everything inside my body, all the way to my spleen, is clenched and anxious. "About us?"

He lets out a laugh, which perfectly conveys just how ridiculous the idea is. When he turns to me, he has the perfect casual smile on his face, beer bottle paused halfway to his lips. "Yeah. Like we've been dating in secret or something."

At this point, my organs actually freeze and begin to crumble. I really have no idea what's going on inside my body, but it's not good. "Oh. Oh, jeez."

"Yeah. I told her that was the most insane thing I'd ever heard. Like dating my sister." He laughs again and takes a pull of his beer. That gulf swallows my heart next, cracking a rib in the process.

"That's absurd," I echo, trying to sound as lighthearted as he does. It *is* absurd. I'm not lying. So why do I feel like this is a charade? "I could never date you. Not in a million years."

"Oh yeah?" He looks over at me, something dark and curious glinting in his gaze.

"You've slept with all of Bayshore," I tell him with a smirk. "I don't go for guys with that much mileage." When he doesn't react immediately, I add, "Or, you know, guys who are basically my brother."

"Right." Maverick takes another pull at his beer. "You're looking for that stable guy."

I laugh, but it feels hollow. "Looking, but haven't found him."

"Yes, you did."

I feign looking around, underneath my chair. "Where did I misplace him, then?"

Maverick sends me a sidelong look that says *come on*. "Right where you left him."

I shake my head, grabbing for my beer again. "Don't act like Tom is crying over me."

"He is. Well, more like...sighing."

"Is he telling you to get us back together or something?" My heart rate picks up again, but not because of Maverick's biceps, for once. I hate the idea that Tom is acting like a broken-hearted sad boi almost as much as I hate the idea that Maverick could never, not even once, see me as something more than his sister. There's a startling clarity in my tipsy state: *I want Maverick to want me.*

But he never will. Least of all when he's pushing for Tom and I to get back together.

So I'm going to push that thought back down into the weird hole it came from. Where it can shrivel and die. Because even though I'd love for him to see me as a desirable woman, I want us to preserve our friendship *more.*

Maverick doesn't answer me right away, so I push to standing, waving my drained beer bottle. "You want another?" I actually don't, but I need something—anything—to distract me right now.

Mavericks nods, and I head into the kitchen to grab another round of beers and officially begin forgetting what we just talked about. By the time midnight rolls around, I can barely stand, much less keep my eyes open.

Maverick tries to help me, but I wave him off. I can shuffle to the loveseat on my own, thankyouverymuch. I'm pretty sure I tell him this. But then my eyes drift shut, and I just don't care anymore.

When I wake up, sunlight is shooting right at me. Like a laser beam from the heavens. I squint, trying to orient myself. It's definitely daylight. No mistaking *that.* I grunt, rolling onto my back. Weird waves of sickness crash through my skull. I sigh, my dry tongue stuck to the roof of my mouth. There are a lot of bad signs accumulating right here. Still, though, I have hope for the day.

I throw myself onto my other side, away from the vengeful ray of sunlight. And once I roll over, my slit eyes widen immediately.

Because I'm not in the living room, like I thought.

I'm not on the loveseat, like I always am.

I'm in freaking Maverick's bed.

And Mr. Shirtless And Glorious himself is sleeping quietly beside me. One beautiful bicep bulging, his arm slung across his chest. His hair is mussed and draped across his forehead. And dammit, he's somehow more beautiful when he's asleep.

My mouth parts, and I stare at him for what feels like a solid half hour. By the time I come to my senses, I realize I must leave. *Now.* The clock on his nightstand reads nine a.m., and I need to hurry if I want to get any sort of work out in before I go to work today.

Once I start slithering out of his bed, I realize how comfy the sheets actually are. Soft. Gray. *Inviting.* Every movement releases a waft of Maverick's smell. And by the time my feet touch the ground, I realize that I'm not even wearing my clothes. I'm wearing *his* clothes. Which makes everything both better and way more terrible.

"Mmmrrrhhmm." Maverick shifts and drapes his beautiful bicep over his eyes. I'm once again rooted to my spot.

But I say nothing. Because what can I say? *Thanks for platonically dressing me, Oh Non-Biological Brother?*

I press a hand over my eyes as another gut-wrenching wave of discomfort sidles through me. The same discomfort that crops up whenever I try to frame Maverick in the whole *hey, he's just my sibling* light. The clarity of a new day does nothing to stem this discomfort either, not in the way alcohol or late nights or intense workout sessions assist.

In fact, the blinding sunlight and the scent of him—musk and leather—wrapped around me and the fact that I am not only near but also *draped* in his belongings send something so critical and raw through me that I almost want to puke.

I am in love with Maverick.

And he is the last man on Earth I could ever consider starting something with.

I roll out of his bed like I am a melted puddle of anguish. Very different from solidified anguish, of course. No, I'm mobile and pure. Like anguish should be. Once I'm army-crawling toward my work clothes, which are neatly gathered in a chair in the corner, Maverick grunts.

I pause, one hand on my work jeans.

"Lettie."

His voice is like sandpaper, except if it were sensual-grade and applied directly to one's clitoris. My thighs squeeze involuntarily, and I twist to look at him.

He's got one eye pinched shut, the sheets gathered around his waist like he's some sort of mythical creature born from perfect gray bedsheets. I'm sure there is an entire colony of hot men living beneath those covers, because everything about his bed seems suspect and otherworldly.

"Hey. Hi. Didn't want to wake you." I continue stealthily grabbing my clothes.

"Why are you sneaking off like a one-night stand?" The grit of his just-woke-up voice is enough to undo me. My eyes flutter shut, and I realize that I *cannot* be here any longer. I desperately need to retreat somewhere that I can address the sensations zipping underneath my skin.

"I, uh, I'm, you know. Just heading home." I'm sitting on the carpet in front of the chair, focusing intently on redressing myself without looking at him again. It's better if I don't look the bedsheet centaur directly in the face.

"Come back to bed." His voice is groggier now, which is both irresistible and a red flag.

Pros: I could sneak into his arms right now and see what happened and be protected under the *it was early morning and you told me to do it* clause.

Cons: He's probably actually asleep and unaware of what he's saying. Also, he probably thinks I'm someone else. Oh, and also, I'm technically not interested in delving into Maverick as a one-night stand.

So the decision makes itself.

"I need to get home," I say, my voice dripping with regret.

He grumbles unintelligibly, and I seize my window to get back into my own clothes. I peel off his ultra-comfy sports shorts and oversized Bayshore basketball tee. He was one of the best point guards in Bayshore High history, made even better by the fact that he did not care how many points he scored, whether or not he lettered, or basically anything at all. All Mav cared about in high school was getting laid.

And the shirt reminds me that really, not that much has changed.

I'm still in my basic black sports bra and the panties I came in, and I tug on my work clothes so fast that I'm not even sure I take a breath. I bolt into the living room where I gather my things at light speed. There is evidence everywhere of the great night we had: the dirty dishes, the empty wine bottle, the scattered notebook papers that Maverick filled with sketches of food service ideas.

I run away from all of it, hop into my car, and drive back to my apartment. I feel like someone scooped out my brain with an ice cream scoop and yet somehow left enough gray matter for me to drive a car—*thanks, hangover.* Back at my apartment, I stare at my rolled-up yoga mat for only a fraction of a second before I realize what task truly has priority right now.

I drop my things and race to the bathroom, turning on the water for a warm shower. I get naked, and immediately my hand drifts between my legs. I don't even make it under the water before my fingers are slipping between juicy folds, finding dampness that hasn't been waiting for mere minutes but maybe years when it comes to this man.

You're in love with Maverick.

I can't think about it. I don't know what to do with this information. I mean, I've always known that I *love* Maverick, deep in my bones, but in the same way that you know you need a car to get around in this city, or how I'd do anything to help my sister, even when I don't want to.

But being *in* love with him?

My fingers slip and slide over the tight bud of my clit. All I can see in my mind's eye is Mav. The scruff of his jaw and the way it matches the scruff on his chest. Those arms that look like they could pick me up a little too easily, toss me around, keep me pressed against him. Those washboard abs tapering off into a wonderland that I haven't even considered, know nothing about, but am dying to fucking explore.

A memory of Maverick with his chef's knife in his big, rough hand flashes through my mind, and my pussy pulses against my fingertips. I let out a choked cry. Oops—there it is. Big O achieved in less than a minute.

How long has that orgasm been waiting to get out? I was so hard up that the mere thought of Maverick in the kitchen sent me over the edge. In an alternate dimension, I'd tell Maverick about how I achieved orgasm simply imagining him chopping carrots. But no way in hell am I ever telling him in *this* dimension.

I step into the shower, letting the warm water envelop me, wash away the weird feelings. One thing is certain. Whatever I feel for Maverick needs to be washed down the drain today.

The idea of *Lettie & Mav* in a romantic sense is going to remain a fantasy. And nothing more.

CHAPTER EIGHT

MAVERICK

There's a two week wait for the results of the submissions, and I cycle between complete arrogance and crippling uncertainty like clockwork every single day of those two weeks.

On the one hand, I'm completely fucking certain that we'll make the cut, because Scarlett and I did an amazing job.

But on the other hand, who knows what our competition looks like? We could be the laughingstock of the submission pile. Immediately scrapped. And truthfully, my thoughts veer this way far more often than I like to admit.

Because why would they pick something from *my* brain, from *my* fingertips? If Weston had done it, of course he'd be entered into the list of contestants. Shit, if it were Dom, he'd be the damn judge on the show. Both Connor and Gray would elbow their way into the top three somehow, I already fucking know.

But me? I'm destined to be the one who almost made it but didn't. I've always been that guy. Shooting for the stars but landing in the neighbor's backyard.

I couldn't hack college. I couldn't prove to even a single girl that I was worth taking a chance on, back when I believed in the fantasy of romance. This is the bitter pill that I've swallowed too many times but thought I'd swallowed for the last time once I'd settled into my career at the garage.

And maybe Scarlett didn't realize it, but she's handing me the pill and a glass of water.

So what does anyone do when faced with crippling insecurity?

Drink. And normally fuck, but I'm too anxious these days. Or maybe it's not anxiety. Maybe it's something else I don't want to think about or even pretend is real. Something that has a lot to do with Scarlett, but damn if I'll give those thoughts any airtime.

She makes it easy to avoid thinking about *that which I should not fucking indulge* because she's basically MIA from the day we submitted the application to now, two weeks later. Scarlett picks up lots of call-off shifts, and she's constantly helping out her sister and that shitty excuse for a boyfriend that woman has, so there are stretches of time when our schedules don't line up and I just don't see her.

Normally, it's okay. But lately? It's got me gnashing my teeth.

It's early evening Wednesday when I'm finally off work and heading home to wash the grease off and forget about how many dick jokes we made that day. There's an informal bad dick joke contest ongoing between all of us, and today's winner was Luke with this gem: *Where do bad dicks go? To the penistentiary.*

And my dick needs to head into a penistentiary with how often I've thought about walking in on Scarlett and her thong a few weeks ago. I never thought that pitiful excuse for underwear (seriously, it's just a string, people) would crop up in my thoughts so fucking much when I let my mind wander. Has she *always* had ass cheeks like fucking juicy apples? Knowing her, they'd be organic apples. She's got an organic Honeycrisp ass, and I can't even tell her.

My penistentiary sentence is extended by a year after my thoughts wander yet again to the thought of bending that Honeycrisp ass over the side of my bed and giving it a slap just hard enough to make the apple shine. Fuck. I've got to stop thinking this way about Scarlett. Or else my penistentiary sentence will include solitary cock-fine-ment.

That was a bad joke. Scarlett still would have laughed.

Inside my apartment, I shuck my clothes and hop into the shower. Yeah, I jack off. So what? I force myself to think about a faceless bombshell, but she's got Scarlett's ass, so there's that.

Once I'm dried off, dressed, and still horny for something I refuse to give into, I pick up my phone and check my email. I've been looking every day after work, just in case they send some update email. Nothing has come so far. Some days, I wonder if they even got our submission, but Scarlett has sent me enough reassuring texts with screenshot evidence of our submission that I have to believe it went through.

The emails load. I scroll lazily, half-resigned, half-hopeful.

And there it is.

RE: The Great Midwestern Food Truck Challenge (GMFTC)

My stomach pitches to my feet, and I chuck the phone onto the sofa. I can't look. Not without Scarlett. I can't bear the brunt of the bad news alone. She needs to be here. So I'll wait. I look at the stove clock. It's six-motherfucking-thirty. No way I can wait two more hours until Scarlett gets off, and then what if she can't come over?

I have to know now.

My stomach swallows itself hole and then turns inside out as I scoop my phone up again. Throwing it somehow made the email open, and the words are waiting for me.

Congratulations! Your mobile food business, FORK OFF, has been selected to compete in the Great Midwestern Food Truck Challenge!

My eyes progressively grow wider as I read on—*you and your crew will receive all-expenses-paid accommodations at each of the five challenge locations; you will be responsible for arriving at each desti-nation city in your own vehicle; each challenge will eliminate a com-peting crew until one winner remains at the final stop in Minneapolis, MN*—until my eyeballs hurt and I have to stop to process.

I read the email a second time. A third. And then a fourth.

And then I shout. "We fucking made it!"

My legs are moving before I can even make the conscious decision. I bolt out the door, feet thundering down the steps. I'm excited enough I could run the entire way to E. Lago, but the car will be faster. I'm not sure I take a breath the entire drive to the restaurant. Once I park, I practically fall out of my car. I can no longer walk. I can't even think. The sheer excitement of qualifying is probably enough for me. I don't even need to compete now. This high alone is fine.

A few people mill around the entrance of E. Lago as I barrel up to the double glass doors. I yank open one side, shouldering past a distracted young couple paused in the doorway looking at a phone. The scent of steak wafts in the air as I enter the happy clamor of the restaurant. I'm craning my neck to find Scarlett bopping around somewhere when the perky hostess greets me.

"Hey there! Welcome to E. Lago. How many today?"

"Where's Scarlett?"

Her face scrunches slightly in confusion. "I think she's in the kitchen..."

My heart is racing. I clutch the back of my neck. "Can I sit at the bar?"

"Sure. Go right ahead."

I'm starting to feel like a crazy person. I need ten celebratory drinks immediately. And to tell Scarlett, of course. I slide onto an empty bar stool, staying vigilant for my best friend. The bartender is busy with some others further down the row of stools, so I'm left to bounce my knee and compulsively run my hand through my hair on my own. I must look like I'm desperate for a fix of something.

I guess that fix is Scarlett.

She breezes through the swinging doors from the kitchen a moment later. I lunge out of my seat, as if to save her from falling off a cliff. Except this is a very casual lake-front restaurant, not a life-or-death bid to save Scarlett from plummeting into a ravine. She gasps when I grab her. When her gaze snaps to me, I can read everything in her face. The surprise. The warmth. The amusement.

"Mav! What are you—"

"Scarlett." Suddenly, I can't remember what I'm supposed to say. I'm staring into her eyes after two weeks of very low Scarlett doses in my life, and her grin feels like sitting down after walking for days. Has she always been this pretty? Her cheeks are pink, and she's watching me with a little smirk that begs me to kiss it off.

Kiss. Scarlett.

"Are you—" she begins.

"We fucking made it." The words tumble out of me. The logjam begins to unwind. Her eyes go wide, plump lips parting, and that fucking idea pops in my head again: *you should kiss her.*

Except no. Not her. Not now. Not *ever.*

Right?

"Are you fucking serious?"

"Yes. We're in the competition."

She squeaks, hands shooting to cover her mouth. "Are you fuck-ing *serious*?"

"Yes! We did it!" I whoop and gather her into my arms for a hug, without thinking, without even deciding to. She melts against me, and my insides release a collective sigh.

Damn. It feels a little better than I thought to have her here. I squeeze tighter, lifting her off the ground for good measure.

"So you're seriously serious?" she asks once I convince myself to let go of her.

"I wouldn't fucking joke about this." The bartender approaches me finally, and I turn to her. "This is an amazing day. Can you make me two mojitos?" The bartender winks at me and grabs for the tumbler.

"I can't drink on the job," Scarlett hisses.

"I'll save it for you," I tell her with an evil grin. "Until you get off and we can start celebrating properly."

Another server comes through the double doors behind her and Scarlett glances back into the kitchen. "Okay. I need to get back to work. What was I even doing?"

"Reveling in our success."

She snorts. "Right. Before that, I mean."

"No idea. But you know where to find me when you're ready to take a secret sip of celebration."

She laughs, her green eyes goddamn twinkling as she breezes to-ward the main dining room to tend to her tables. The bartender is a pretty blonde who looks like she's probably in her last year of college or so. Just my type. Usually.

"You got good news?" she asks.

"The best news." Also the most terrifying, because now that the excitement is wearing off, the truth is settling in. *What comes next?* What does the competition look like? How do I tell my boss that I suddenly need the next one to five weeks off work? What the fuck am I going to cook for these food truck judges? And most importantly, *what the fuck do we think we're doing?*

"And what news is that?"

I open my mouth, ready to spill the beans, but I remember that we have to be tactful about this. Scarlett needs to talk to her supervisor. This is *our* adventure. Together. I can't go blowing my load on the first set of ears that comes my way.

"Let's just say a great adventure is about to happen." When the bartender hands me the first drink of two, I raise it in salute. "To new adventures."

She sends me a coquettish smile, winking as I take my first sip. She finishes making my second mojito, her gaze lingering a little too long on me. Pink stains those round cheeks as she glances up at me for a third, then a fourth time. I know this situation for what it is. In the playboy world, it's called *The Window.* She is giving me the chance to pursue her—to climb through the window—to take this into full-blown flirtation territory. The subtle shift in dynamic is barely perceptible, and only finely trained pussy hounds like myself can smell the hormonal shift.

But oh, it's shifted. She opened the window. And I just have to climb through it.

I take another sip of my mojito. The weird thing is, I don't want to climb through the window. Like, at all.

I just want Scarlett to get off work so we can act like freaks celebrating our victory. It's not weird to want to spend time with a friend. So why do I feel like it's somehow wrong?

After the bartender moves on to new arrivals at the other end, a hand clamps on my shoulder. I know that it's Scarlett before I see her because of the waft of jasmine and amber that envelops me. I'm smiling before she says a word.

"Don't you start hitting on her," Scarlett says, sending me a playful smirk.

"What are you talking about?"

She lifts a brow. "I saw the way she was looking at you."

"I was just sitting here minding my own business."

"Yeah, sure. You're always just minding your own business. Until somehow that business follows you back to your bedroom and leaves their business panties in your bathroom."

I narrow my eyes. "Wait, did you find—"

"Listen, I don't want to get caught in the middle of something messy at my job, so let's just say the new girl is off limits. Okay? Can you handle that?"

I roll my eyes as outrageously as I can manage. She doesn't need to know that I kind of like it when she thinks she's reeling me in like this. She doesn't need to know that I'd already nixed the idea of pursuing the bartender for reasons I refuse to dive into. "You act like I can't control myself."

"Well," she begins, but instead of finishing her sentence, she gestures at me, implying what she didn't say: *just look at you*.

And maybe this is just another sign that we're insanely close. Sometimes, we don't speak but still manage to communicate.

"Don't you have tables to wait on?" I ask.

She laughs and pushes through the swinging doors into the kitchen, the curve of her tight calf muscle snagging my attention before she disappears entirely. All the servers wear the same powder blue, short-sleeve polo shirts and khaki shorts or pants, but she's the only one who somehow gives it an edge. Maybe it's because I know how saucy she is underneath the plain clothes.

And as of recently, I also know the ass she's hiding beneath the plain clothes.

Seriously, Mav. Enough. This is where being a pussy hound gets me in trouble. Scarlett cannot be hounded. If I'm hunting for those sweet kittens, then Scarlett must remain what she's always been: the guinea pig in the corner. Fluffy, fun, good for some laughs. An unexpected comfort when sad. Occasionally terrorizing the neighborhood when released accidentally.

Scarlett the guinea pig.

The doors burst open again, and Scarlett breezes past, a big tray balanced on her palm and shoulder. She doesn't look at me, which is fine, because I'm looking hard at her. At the taut curve of her bicep, betraying a strength you wouldn't guess from her slight frame. At her nearly pitch-black tresses swept up into that messy bun that, if I'm totally honest, is my favorite look on her. At the tiny wisps of dark hair framing her high cheekbones, which don't need any makeup-enhancement to make you fucking notice them.

I'm torn between her cheekbones and her lips as my favorite part of her face.

"Whatcha thinking about?"

The bartender is back, sending me a coy smile. I suck in a deep breath, feeling somehow caught.

"Uh...nothing much." Just trying to decide which feature of my best friend's face is my favorite, because I'm a pussy hound who's not supposed to go after guinea pigs. "Great mojito."

"Got any plans later?"

Wow. I dragged my heels on seizing that window of opportunity, so the bartender is making it even easier now. Somewhere inside, I'm tempted to follow the train of thought. Because I'm used to it. Because I know how to travel that path. Because why not, she's hot.

But this is our adventure together.

"Scarlett and I are going out when she gets off work," I tell her.

"Oh?" Her face crumples slightly. "Are you two together?"

"No, no. It's just...we're celebrating. The good news."

She nods slowly. "Well...if you change your mind..." She sends me a hopeful look before heading off to tend another customer. I down the last of my first mojito because on the inside, I'm reeling. What the fuck was that? Did I just turn down a perfectly fine invitation to sex? Scarlett asked me to, sure. But her request was unnecessary. Because there's no way in hell I want to start something with her coworker, not even for a night.

Something is wrong. I suspected it earlier, and this just proves it. Maybe it's because I'm in my late twenties. It's that testosterone drop I heard about once and it scared me ever since. My libido is gone. Done. Completely dead. *Goodbye, casual sex. It was fun knowing you.* I'll have to content myself with shower-time jack-off sessions thinking about Honeycrisp ass cheeks and that's it. I might as well be eighty years old.

I dip into the second mojito. After a little bit, Scarlett drops off a plate in front of me with a cocky smile.

"That's an oops," she explains before breezing away again, but I doubt that it's truly a mistake. It's my exact favorite plate from E. Lago—a beef brisket wrap with charred corn and the stupid good fire sauce they make in house. It's like Taco Bell, a southern bar-beque pit, and some gourmet street taco had a lovechild and poured orange sauce all over it.

I smash it in record time. I'm not even shy about it. Scarlett's eyes go wide the next time she heads to the kitchen and sees my empty plate.

"Damn. You need a second one?"

"Wouldn't say no to it."

"Where do you put all this food?"

I shrug. "Where it belongs."

She snorts and whisks away my empty plate. Now I'm just counting the seconds until we can escape together and start figuring out the details. I leave her mojito mostly untouched, though I do start nursing it after a while. I did buy it for her—she should at least get one sip.

By the time Scarlett gets cut, there's enough left for her to take a solid gulp. Which I encourage her to do when she finally approaches the bar, untying her apron.

"Celebrate with me." I push the glass her way, just as the bartender returns with my bill. I slide two twenties her way.

"I can't believe you actually saved it for me."

"Why wouldn't I? It's what friends do."

Friend. Guinea pig. Scarlett.

She tosses back what little remains in the glass and slams it onto the bar top. "Tasted like iced down saliva. Thanks. Now let's go."

I get my change and leave a 50% tip. Now the evening can truly begin. I push through the main doors and out into the warm, fresh dusk. The lake air is invigorating. Every cell of my body is vibrating with a type of bliss I'm not familiar with. I feel like I have it all. Which is strange. Usually, I feel like there's something missing in life. But not right now.

"Let's go sit at the lake and think about how fucking awesome we are," I suggest.

Her nose crinkles as she laughs. "See, my plan is usually the opposite. I end up thinking about all my failures."

"Same here, except with the good news we got today, we deserve to feel like successful assholes for a second."

"Just for one second though," she says with a tut. We follow a winding path that leads down a small hill toward the lakefront. Once upon a time—two and a half years ago, to be exact—my oldest brother Dom made the newspaper for getting into a fight right here.

Scarlett was working that day, too, and watched the whole thing from the window.

I sling my arm over Scarlett's shoulders as we come up on the boardwalk. "Where should we sit?"

"Over here." She grabs my hand dangling over her left shoulder and clutches it while she leads the way. She steers us toward a small jetty that lines one of the small marinas dotting the downtown Bayshore area. Our footsteps clomp down the wooden walkway, and we wave or nod to the fishermen posted up on benches, waiting for a bite on the line.

At the end of the walkway, she disentangles from me and sits down on the edge of the jetty, her legs dangling off the side. She looks up at me, shielding her face from the rays of the setting sun. She's bathed in orange and crimson.

"All we need is a bottle of champagne." I ease down next to her.

"And a picnic blanket and some truffles," she adds. "Though that might feel too much like a date."

"Friends can eat truffles and drink champagne," I tell her.

"Yeah, but what it leads to isn't that friendly."

"I've never had champagne and truffles together, so I wouldn't know the dark trail of destruction it leads to like you apparently do."

"Bad outcomes all around," she says, swinging her legs off the side of the jetty. "You'll lose your job. Something might randomly explode. There will definitely be fighting."

I nod, surveying the water chopping against the steel posts plunging into the water below us. "So you're saying I shouldn't make a truffle-infused dish for the competition."

"Not if you want to win." She looks over at me, a playful smile dancing across her lips. The sun hits her just right. Dark wisps of hair, lifted by the lake breeze, cross her forehead, and we get caught there, trapped like an insect in time's delicate web. Dangling, waiting, watching. I don't know if seconds or hours pass, drinking her in like this.

"What?" she finally asks. And that's when I realize it's been too long. This got too weird.

I don't know what I'm doing, and I don't know how to make it stop.

"I was just thinking about the menu. Sorry." I jerk my gaze back down to the water. White froth circulates on the surface. "We have a lot of shit to get done before this competition starts."

"You're damn right we do," she murmurs, squinting out at the water. There's something heavy in her voice, something I can't quite pin down. All I know is that it doesn't matter, because I'm at her side and she's at mine. "You scared?"

My stomach plummets. Scared doesn't even begin to cover it. "I feel like I could puke hourly for the next week."

She snorts, shoving at my arm. "Well you better not puke in the food. Because we need to really win this thing, now that I'm about to tell my boss I need the next *five weeks* off."

I sigh, doubt creeping in. I shouldn't have asked her. But now we're in it. Now we *need* to see it through. "If she gives you any shit, just blame it on me."

"Yes, my best friend roped me into a reality TV show—*sorry, Cheryl.*" She laughs, kicking her legs. "It's okay. I need to get out of there. I need the break. I don't know that I ever want to come back."

Her admission jars a cold fear into me. "But you will come back, right?"

She doesn't answer me. Instead, she just looks at me and grins, her answer spelled out in all the devilish details of her smile.

CHAPTER NINE

SCARLETT

It takes me a few days to piece my world together, now that we have the good news tucked into our back pockets. There's officially six days left until we have to report to Cleveland for the start of the competition, which is *not* the scariest idea I've ever entertained in my life. So don't worry, I'm not having anxiety spirals every half hour or anything.

Lies. I'm so fucking nervous I could crumple onto the floor and never get up again.

Luckily, I have plenty of real-life distractions to assist with not thinking about certain things, like the all-consuming anxiety or the fear that burrows like a tick that we'll fail out of the competition right there on our own turf.

Right now, I'm standing in my sister's shoddy two-bedroom house on the outskirts of Bayshore, right where it turns into the back part of a quarry. Occasionally, it smells like farts for hours at a time.

Real great part of town over here. I've been collecting my courage in tiny segments since we got the good news, preparing myself to inform my sister that surprise, I'm fucking leaving!

She won't be distraught about me leaving for any other reason than her losing the free childcare I provide, so I've been carefully constructing my armor. I already got in a practice run with my boss, who was oddly supportive of the opportunity. She couldn't promise me full-time hours when I return, especially if we end up making it the full five weeks, but she promised I wouldn't be cut entirely from the schedule. And that's good enough for me.

Fifi and Louie are hard at work on coloring in their respective coloring books as I pace the living room, waiting for Florence to come out of her bedroom. She and Greg have been discussing something heatedly in there since I showed up. I'm not sure if it's about me, or the kids, or something related to his recent stint in jail, and honestly, I don't care. I just need to get us all on the same page, schedule-wise.

"Doing a good job, buddies," I tell the kids. This is par for the course when I babysit. Get them focused on something creative. Bring out the best in them. Remind them how cool and good they are. I am the antidote to their mother, who thinks that all creative endeavors should be limited to childhood and Disney movies.

"Aren't you gonna make one?" Louie asks without looking up at me.

"I have to go to work, sweetie." I check my phone. I came over here early so that I could give the kids some extra hang time and so that I could give Florence her usual half hour of tardiness. It doesn't matter what she's doing—she's going to be a half hour late. Even if it's just showing up to her own living room.

"I thought you were staying with us again," Fifi whines.

"You know that when I'm wearing this outfit"—I gesture to my *oh-so-attractive* blue polo and khakis—"that it means I'm going into work."

"But you can just change your clothes and stay," Louie says with a shrug, the ever-practical older sister.

"I'll let you call my boss then."

Louie's eyes light up, and her hand shoots out. "Okay! I want to talk to your boss!"

"No, I want to talk to her boss," Fifi says, his chestnut brown hair falling into his eyes as he scrambles to put himself in front of Louie and stick his hand out further. "I'm going to do it first."

"It was my idea!" Louie shouts.

"I was the one who said she had to stay!" Fifi shoots back.

"Actually, it was *my* idea for you to call my boss," I say, totally unfazed by the random outburst of fighting. This is only the first of likely ninety fights that have yet to occur today. They're just getting started. "And neither of you can call him, because she's..."

"She's what?" Louie presses, which means I have to follow through with an excuse.

"She's in the bathroom right now," I finish. The bedroom door down the hall creaks open, and my sister comes out, her eyes on the floor as she heads my way.

The kids are hopping around now, chanting "She's in the bathroom!"

Flor frowns.

"Good morning to you too," I say once she starts rifling through papers on the coffee table without much of a glance my way.

"I said hi in the hallway," she mutters.

"Didn't hear you." I can already feel the seismic shift of her mood settling over me like a boulder. She's not happy today. But this conversation must be had. "Hey, you got a second? I need to head out soon."

Her brows knit together like I just belted out a song lyric in Japanese. "Heading out? I thought you were watching the kids today."

My stomach plummets to my feet. "What? No. I'm literally on my way to work."

Her mouth thins into a frightening line, and her hands go straight to her forehead. "Fuck."

"Mommy, watch your mouth," Louie says.

"I don't know what I'm gonna do," she says, heading into the kitchen. The despair is trailing behind her in thick waves. I'm practically choking on them. The knot in my gut cinches tighter.

"Can't Greg—"

"It's his second court date," she says, pressing her lower back against the countertop as she faces me. She looks exhausted. I try to stay out of the drama of their daily lives, but she makes it hard to fully disengage. "He has to be there. You can't just not show up for your own court date."

"Right, but—"

She cuts me off with a long, annoyed sigh. "What did you want to talk about? I don't know what I'm fucking supposed to do."

Not exactly the lead-in I was hoping for. She might be more receptive to the bad—I mean, technically good—news from me if the babysitting issue is resolved first, so that should be addressed first. "Well, listen. We'll figure it out. What time is court? Let's call Mom and—"

"She can't help today. That's why you were supposed to."

I glance back at the living room, where Fifi and Louie are tearing pages from the coloring book and making paper airplanes like we always do together. "Flor, I gotta work today. I can't—"

"We can't switch this date. We already switched it once."

I sigh, eager to stick to my originally scheduled plan of breaking the news to Florence. Now, I have to organize last-minute childcare on top of it, but I can't back down from telling her. It needs to happen today. Because I've only got six days left before I leave.

"I'll figure something out. Promise. Now, I have to tell you something."

She sniffs, crossing her arms over her chest. "You pregnant?"

I laugh. It's the most outrageous suggestion she could have come up with. "No. Absolutely not."

"You and Tom were together for a long time."

"Yeah, and we've been broken up for months now."

She shrugs, offering a wry grin. For a moment, she looks like her old self. Bright blue eyes shining with that big sister warmth, which I see so rarely anymore. If I focus hard enough, she can still become the Florence who used to sit cross-legged with me on my bedroom floor while she painstakingly tested out eyeshadow combinations on my eyelids. Even then, I was doing it for her. Because she wanted to. Because I've always wanted to make her life better if I could.

"Breakups don't mean a thing when it comes to making babies." She jerks her chin toward the living room. "Look at Felix. He came when Greg and I were broken up."

Part of me wishes the breakup had stuck then. But alas. It never does. And I wouldn't have gotten my BFF Felix out of it. So we'll call it even.

"Fair enough, but no, the kids are not getting a cousin anytime soon. I'm actually about to go on a trip."

Curiosity flashes across her face, but it dissolves quickly. "What kind of trip?"

Excitement bubbles up inside me, and I can't squash the silly grin. "Maverick and I applied to be on a reality TV show. It's a food truck competition. I'm going to help him out."

She nods slowly, her face neutral. "Okay."

"It starts filming in about a week." I pick at one of my nails absentmindedly. Here comes the hard part. "If we do well, it'll take a few weeks to film...and we'll get to travel all over the Midwest."

She's still nodding, but now her gaze looks vacant. She's looking past me, over my shoulder, out into the living room. The silence between us is punctuated by the occasional chirp or squeal from the kids as they play.

"I'm really excited," I finally add, as a way to remind her to respond.

Her gaze snaps to me. Her eyes widen slightly. "Wow. That's awesome. Must be nice to be able to think about...I don't know...anything other than feeding your kids."

I gnaw at my upper lip, trying to fight the swell of frustration. I scratch my forehead. I never know how to respond to these moments. "It's...important to Maverick. This is his passion—"

"You know those shows are rigged, right?" She finally pushes away from her perch against the countertop and heads to the fridge. The white light spilling out from the inside illuminates her frown in stereo. "They'll find some way to kick you off. I guarantee it."

I stare at one of the dull tiles of the kitchen floor. "Well, it's not really about winning. I just want to help my friend."

"Is it worth it?" She pulls out a two-liter of soda, setting it on the countertop with a heavy *thud*. "I mean, if you don't even want to be doing it."

"I *do* want to do it."

"How long will you be gone?" Her voice is more lifeless than the *hissss* of the carbonation escaping the twist cap.

"A few weeks, probably. At most."

Her jaw sets, and she sighs. "Fuck." She pours herself a cup of soda and takes a long swig. The silence between us is so vast, yet noisier than ever. I know what that silence contains. It's her disappointment. Her worry about what she'll do with the kids, so she can continue going to work and supporting her family.

"Well, that's why I wanted to let you know now," I offer hopefully, "so we can start figuring something out. I mean, I'll be back—"

"And in the meantime?" She lets a heavy, threatening pause slide by. "If I lose my job," she says as she replaces the two liter back in the fridge, "it's your fault."

This is why I'd been constructing my armor the past few days. These zingers don't just slice, they take root. Now I get to worry about Florence losing her job over the childcare hassle. Hello, premature guilt! What a timely arrival, just as I'd allowed myself to feel excited.

And I never know how to respond, because maybe my heart is so big that it drowns me. I feel beholden to the children. My sister can't get her shit together, so I must do everything possible to make sure they make it out okay. Even when that includes taking on extra duties in Florence's life.

"Flor, you have other options besides me," I tell her, unable to keep the frustration at bay. The kids start taking turns screaming in the living room, which is a nice punctuation to the rising tension. "I mean, I'll research some daycare options—"

"That requires me having money, Scarlett. Which I don't have. Least of all now, with all the legal fees we have to pay."

But that's not my fault! Greg should stay out of trouble because he's a grown-ass man! I clamp my mouth shut, looking back at the kids. Felix is pretending to be a dinosaur—I think.

The bedroom door creaks open and then footsteps thud down the hallway. Greg's head pokes out a moment later. "Can you guys keep it down?"

"Sorry, Daddy," Louie says in a sing-song voice. Greg goes back into the bedroom without so much as a hello.

"I have to go get ready," Florence says, setting her empty glass next to the sink, which is still full with the plates from last night's dinner and probably the night before that. "Since you're fucking leaving me up shit creek, can you at least stay today?"

I don't know what to say other than, "Yeah. I'll call into work and let them know I'm not coming."

Florence sighs, which I guess is her version of a thank you, and heads back to her bedroom. I'm left with the alternating squawkers, who are jumping on the couch now, despite knowing full well they absolutely should not be doing that.

"You guys. Get down." I use my stern voice, which only makes them giggle maniacally and stop bouncing to the max height. Now, they're just bouncing slightly, which in children's brains, is the same as doing what the adult said.

But it's hard to concentrate on getting them to listen. Even harder when my chest feels like a rubber band ready to snap and I'm practicing what I'll say to my boss when I finally work up the courage to call off work one day after I informed her I'd be bailing on E. Lago for up to five weeks. I need to do it ASAP, too, because I'm supposed to be showing up there in less than an hour.

And more than that, I'm still stuck on the infuriating lack of encouragement. Not even a whiff of excitement. Couldn't even get a "Hey, that sounds cool."

It stings, and it's not even *my* passion. It's just a reminder that I shouldn't—and never will—share my own passion with anyone. Maverick might be the only exception, but only because I think he'd understand somehow—especially now. But even then, it's better just to never mention it, because the last thing I want to do is get my hopes up about the silks troupe understudy position.

But the stupidest part? Is that I still want Florence to be involved even mildly in my successes and joys. I should have learned by now—my happiness cannot be shared. I must preserve it and barricade it.

While Florence and Greg are getting ready in the bedroom, I step outside onto the front porch to call my boss. Stepping away from the energetic black hole Florence sucked me into helps; so does the fresh air. Because as I'm dialing E. Lago, I get a sneaky little idea.

Flor might not be excited for me, but you know what?

I'm going to make sure her kids get excited for Aunt Scarlett. If for no other reason than to show them that life might have more interesting options than *go to jail* or *work yourself to death*.

Today's art projects are officially focused on food truck menu art.

Take that, Florence the Grump.

CHAPTER TEN

MAVERICK

It's nine a.m. on Monday, and not just any Monday, but *the* Monday.

Today, we're going to Cleveland, and this whole insane adventure lurches into the next act.

I've been making laps around the food truck, checking the tires, triple-checking the lug nuts, making sure the engine is still in place. I've never felt so manic, so wild, so absolutely brimming with energy. Is this what people feel like when they chase their dreams? Unhinged. Ready to shriek with laughter at the slightest murmur of a joke. Perpetual nervous gut. Wondering where I put the damn keys even though they've been in my pocket since seven.

"Mav?"

Scarlett's husky lilt wraps around me like a loving squeeze on the wrist. Some of the nervousness fades away.

"Over here." I prop my palms on the side door of the truck, checking the seal. "Just making sure we're good to go."

Her footsteps scuff softly over the cement floor of the storage unit. She stops at the far end of the truck, watching me. The look on her face says it all.

Can you fucking believe it?

"Dude." I laugh weakly. "I can't believe—"

"I know," she finishes. "Do you—?"

"No," I interrupt, and the two of us burst into laughter. It was hardly a complete conversation, but we said all we needed to. "I guess that's our pep talk, right?"

"Fuck yeah. Go, team. Let's do this!"

I draw deep breath and nod. "Here we go." I pull open the passenger side door, which is how you get into the cockpit of my gleaming, refurbished kitchen-on-wheels. The exterior of the truck was wrapped four days ago, with the brand-spanking-new logo and design that one of my friends whipped up for me, cartoonish forks and all. The sides are emblazoned with "FORK OFF" in a modern font, and I can't believe how legit it makes this whole venture feel...or how big of an imposter I feel.

Now's not the time for those thoughts. I turn the key, and the truck rumbles to life. Scarlett steps aside and waves me out. I ease out onto the gravel of the storage unit lot, and once I'm clear, Scarlett hops into her own car and pulls it into the spot my truck had occupied. That's where her car will stay during the show, and the food truck is going to tow my car.

It's just a regular old reality show caravan.

I make quick work of hitching my car to the back, and when everything is set, we clamber into the truck. We buckle our seat belts, watching each other with big grins.

"Are you ready?" I ask.

She screams as a response.

"Holy shit, we're doing it!" I hit the gas and the truck lurches into motion. Scarlett is catcalling and pumping her arms in the air. The truck fills with warm, beautiful sunshine as we emerge beyond the shade of the trees. This is what memoirs are made of right here. A twinkling lake in the distance. Your best friend at your side. Unknown adventures waiting on the open road. A huge thud rocking the truck.

We share horrified looks.

"Maverick..." she begins.

I shake my head and park the truck. I climb past Scarlett and out the side door, and a dismal sight greets me at the back.

My car sits about twenty feet behind the truck. The hitch came undone. Scarlett's at my side a moment later.

"We don't really need the car, do we?" she whispers.

I inspect the situation at the back of the truck, tugging on the metal joint, assessing what could have gone wrong. "I think we'll want it when we can't go any damn place without this huge beast. So yeah. Let's try it again."

I put the car in neutral and push it forward until I'm close enough to hitch it again. Scarlett's watching with a little smirk.

"You know, that's why they make those things drivable. So you don't have to brute-push them around."

"Why waste the gas just to move it twenty feet?" Just that little bit of distance made sweat sprout on my forehead, and I swipe my forearm across it.

"Show off," she murmurs but watches with interest as I hook everything up a second time. I sense more than just *I want to see what's going on here* energy from her, but since there's no way in fucking hell she has even an eighth of the lewd thoughts that I've been having about her, I know she's just being nice. Providing moral support. *Being my guinea pig.*

"Yeah. I'm just showboating for you," I crack, even though I'm kind of not joking. "Look at how much of a man I am, in case you forgot."

"Don't worry—it's hard to miss, with how much dick swinging you do around any woman in her early to mid-twenties."

I scoff as I rig up the hitch a second time, double- and triple-checking the connection. "That includes you, you know."

"Oh, please. You'd never be desperate enough to swing your dick my way."

I grit my teeth. If only she knew how many times I've imagined swinging it in her general direction this week alone. But maybe I *am* desperate. Desperate for something I'm not sure I should have.

"Of course not. Tom would beat the shit out of me, for starters." I wipe my forearm across my forehead again, out of nervousness this time. Our footsteps crunch over the gravel as we walk to the truck door. I should add something about how we don't think about each other like that, because we're just friends and nothing more. Maybe it'll make it true again.

But I can't.

Scarlett pulls open the door and lets me go inside. There's a lot left unsaid between us, but neither of us picks up the threads to continue the conversation. The truck rumbles to life again, and this time when I hit the gas pedal, there's no ceremonious disaster.

We're free and clear.

And soon, we're on the open road. Route 2 east, then we're on I-90, gunning into downtown Cleveland. Scarlett picks the music—she came ready with various USB drives for my recently updated radio console—and we're singing along to Queen, Muse, MSI, and One Direction. She has varied tastes, what can I say?

Once we hit the convention center where the day one meet and greet takes place, my nerves are bundled tight like an international package. Because the line of professional-grade food trucks is the first thing I see. Four other trucks, lined up neatly in a row as if they were the first to get the invitation to the party. Not us, the slapdash eventual last-placers who are rumbling into spot ten minutes too late (even though we're technically on time).

"Fuck," I murmur as I pull into the parking lot. Suddenly, it's too much. The anxiety. The unknowns. The upcoming challenges. We haven't even started, but I've already had enough. My cup is overflowing, but not with the good feels.

"Mav. Don't freak." Scarlett's voice is an unexpected balm. She looks over at me, shrugging, acting like we're heading to the library instead of the jowls of a reality TV monster. "This looks cool, you know?"

I nod, easing closer to the gathering of food trucks and industry professionals at the back of the convention center. Hors d'oeurves are being served on small platters, and I'm pretty sure at least one of these guys is the producer, based on how importantly he walks. Cameramen clog the parking lot, some of them still setting up, others already filming from the sidelines.

"Yeah. It looks cool." And like well-documented embarrassment and failure, but hey.

All heads turn our way as we crest the parking lot. Applause erupts around us. Scarlett is beaming, and we've hardly stopped moving before all these strangers are clapping the sides of the truck with hollow *thup thup thup*'s.

"The last truck is here!" There's some hooting and hollering as I pull into place behind the fourth truck, Uncle Lobster. I can pretty much guess what their menu is—either seafood or close family relatives. Scarlett slides open the door and hops out. My legs are made of clouds as I float behind her. Once my feet hit the asphalt of the parking lot, there's a flurry of introductions.

First there's Hartley, who's the production coordinator and the person we've been emailing with all week. The producer Bennett, the director, whose name I miss entirely, and the competing trucks. By that point, though, everything has turned into a blur, because champagne glasses are shoved into our hands and we're led to a side table where paperwork awaits us—our formal waivers, now that we've arrived. The cameras aren't focused on this part, of course. The production crew looks polished and definitely from someplace that isn't here. The style of their eyeglasses is cooler than you see in Bayshore, their shoes trendier.

Once we've signed in—and signed our rights away—Bennett gives us a pep talk about the upcoming challenge, followed by Hartley with some of the ground rules of filming. Then, as if to demonstrate their point about filming a reality TV show, we have to do it all over again, so the cameras can get a second take.

"Do we have to do everything double?" Scarlett whispers into my ear.

"Everything including going to the bathroom," I tell her.

She shoots me a look. "Gross."

"It's in the contract you just signed."

"So that means every random girl you shack up with on the road, you'll have to bang twice so they can get it from different angles." She says it with a laugh and the usual playful nudge, but this time, it feels like she's needling me. I swear, she never used to mention my sex life half as much when she was dating Tom. But I can't tell her angle. Maybe she wants to have sex with me...even though that's about as likely as Uncle Lobster actually serving up a crispy fried family member for lunch. No, she's probably just joking. Which is what friends do with each other.

Because we're just friends.

"No, I won't be banging anyone twice, remember? We aren't allowed to bring interlopers into the company-paid hotel rooms."

She looks like she's about to add something, but Hartley gets everyone's attention. It's time for the official migration to our hotel rooms while the crew prepares the next segment of our meet and greet somewhere else within the property. Each food truck crew sticks to itself, small pockets of team members that betray us as the smallest crew. Every other team has at least three members. Panic begins spreading through me, a virus in the bloodstream.

We're led into the grand entrance of the hotel. I don't often come to swanky hotels in Cleveland, but I never realized we had a place like *this* so close to home. It's a level of fancy better fit for a United Arab Emirates brochure. Everything is gilded and gleaming, hues of gold, our reflections bouncing off decorative mirrors. Our footsteps whisper across the shining black tiles of the foyer. One entire wall is dripping with vining plants, and I'm pretty sure I hear a waterfall nearby.

The swankiness mixed with the industry professionals surrounding us, multiplied by the camara crew on our heels, compounded to the fourth power of *I just bought my first commercial-grade appliance last week* equals WE'RE FUCKED.

"Are we underprepared?" I ask Scarlett.

Her eyes are wide as she nods gravely. "Oh yeah. One hundred percent."

"That's the inspirational talk I like to hear."

She bursts into laughter. "All we can do now is hang on and enjoy the ride, Mav."

And oddly enough, that's all it takes to help the tension melt away. We get our room keys, and Hartley makes all of us agree to meet in the so-called green room in a half hour, which is just the hotel bar. Our rooms are on the eighth floor, and apparently they bought out the entire floor for the production. Scarlett puts me in charge of the room keys, and once the door clicks open, we're greeted by a sprawling suite with an actual living room attached to a separate bedroom. The bathroom has a hot tub, so there's that.

It's not like I'm disappointed when I see that there's two separate full beds in the bedroom as opposed to one luxurious queen or king bed that we'd be forced to share. No. I'm fine with sleeping alone. I haven't been harboring lewd thoughts about Scarlett for weeks or anything, so everything is fine.

Despite everything being fine, I'm frowning as I wheel my luggage onto my side of the room. It just seems wrong. My bed...her bed. There should be *one* bed. Doesn't that make more sense? We're a team now. We should be sleeping together.

Oops.

Scarlett comes out of the bathroom, her eyes wide. "I want to move in."

"I think we just technically did."

"I mean permanently. Can I live in this hotel? I would totally live in this hotel."

"You'd be too far away from Bayshore," I remind her. *And me.*

She shrugs, sighing. "Maybe I'm ready to leave Bayshore."

"Jeez, you come to Cleveland for thirty minutes and you're ready to leave everything behind." I say it as a joke, because I want it to be, but what if she's serious?

"Now that I'm out, I might just stay out," she says with another sigh, falling backwards onto her bed. "They don't know where I am, so theoretically they can't guilt trip me. Guilt can't travel that far, right?"

"I take it the convo with Florence didn't go well."

"Nope. I'm pretty sure she's praying every day that we get eliminated first, just so I can get back to Bayshore as soon as possible." She heaves another sigh. "She didn't even say 'congrats' or 'good job on landing your first reality TV show gig.'"

I haul my luggage onto my bed and unzip it. "I'm not surprised. Are you?"

"No." There's a long stretch of silence then, and the tension grows so thick that it pounds between my ears. "But is it so wrong to want her to care about my life?"

I know how she feels. Sort of, at least. Her Florence is my Dad, in the How Much They Care About Us department. I've never had to watch my dad's kids though, because I *am* the kid.

"Not wrong," I finally say. "Just...unproductive." Those words are for me, too. Another bitter pill to swallow, since I'm pretty sure my dad will never care about what I do with my life the way I want him to.

"At least the kids miss me," she finally murmurs, pushing up to a seated position. "Out of everyone in my family, I can count on Fifi and Louie."

"And me," I blurt, before I think better of it.

She glances over her shoulder. "I said in my *family*."

"Aren't we family yet?" I busy myself with locating my underwear, even though I don't need it.

"I guess we could go ahead and push the sibling adoption papers through," she cracks, which only makes my stomach pitch to my feet. That wasn't exactly where I was heading with this conversation, but okay.

"I meant you could count on me," I remind her.

"I know," she says, nodding, but facing away from me. All I can see is the rhythmic bob of her messy bun. "And you can count on me, Mav, you know?"

"I do know," I tell her, finally coming around the beds to sit at her side. The mattress dips as I sit down, our arms brushing. She's honey warm and inviting in a way that I cannot fucking think about, much less indulge. "That's why you're here, right?"

She swings her head to look at me. "Yes. It's for you. But I *want* to be here, too."

I get lost in the pretty green swirl of her eyes, intensely aware of the weight of the four walls pressing in around us. We're all alone in here. We can do whatever we fucking want. She wants to be here; I want to be on top of her.

Stop it.

I will not forget about the fact that the words *sibling adoption papers* just crossed her lips, even though I wish she'd fucking see me for the one thing she refuses to notice.

"Thanks, Lettie." I swallow the conflicting thoughts and cover her hand with my own. I give it a small squeeze. "Whatever happens, I'm okay with it. Because you're doing it with me."

And it's true. It will always be true.

Because over the past few years, one thing has become clear. If there's one thing I need in my life, it's Scarlett.

But over the past few weeks, I've learned something else.

I want more from Scarlett than I ever have before.

CHAPTER ELEVEN

When I awake the next morning, my body is humming. I can't tell if it's the fact that our first real, filmed challenge awaits us in mere *hours*, or if it's the fact that Maverick is ling half clothed, fully sexy, and totally, maniacally single just *six feet to the left of me.*

I'm going with a healthy combination of both. Either one of them will kill me from the pent-up tension, so it's imperative for me to do the only thing I know how to do: exercise the stress away.

It's just after seven a.m. I set my alarm for eight thirty knowing full well I wouldn't need it, because my body is trained to wake up before everyone else no matter what. Even after a night of drinking and mingling with the other food truck contestants while cameras lurked, filming our every move and gulp of wine. I might never get used to the cameras, but they at least kept me from drinking too much, because I was too scared of making an ass of myself.

And who wants to be reminded of that for the rest of their lives? This isn't *Love is Blind,* after all.

I roll out of bed quietly, wash my face in our enormous bathroom, and then start searching out the best spot for my morning routine. We have an entire living room in this suite, so the choice makes itself. I roll out my yoga mat and align myself so that I'm facing the sun-drenched curtains on the eastern wall of the room.

And then I move. And breathe. And move more. And breathe more. This is my unfailing safe haven, the only place where my thoughts melt away and stress begins to unkink and for a blessed blink of a second, everything makes sense. I lose track of time—as I always do—and by the time I'm pushing up into a brutal sequence of handstands followed by a mid-air cross-legged ab workout, I hear a groggy, "Holy shit."

My muscles tense but I know better than to wildly search out the source of the voice. Logically? A) It can only be Maverick, and B) if I lose my center of balance, which is my vision right now, I'm going to fall on my face and break my damn neck.

My arms wobble as I struggle to keep my center. I focus on deep breaths.

Maverick doesn't say anything else. I'm facing the window so I can't tell if he's still watching me or if he's excused himself back into his wing of the hotel suite. I can still feel his gaze burning on me, though. I slowly lower myself to the ground, unknotting my legs so that I pop back onto the tips of my toes into a plank position. A deep breath rattles out of me, and when I turn around, Maverick is sitting in one of the armchairs in the living room, facing me.

Wearing only his underwear.

My insides clench. I didn't expect him to be up this early. I didn't expect him to see this routine *at all* during our trip. And I certainly didn't expect him to be en route to his audition for *Hotties Gone Wild: Boxer Brief Edition.*

"Morning," I say.

He tips his head, propping it on his index and middle finger as he watches me. He narrows his eyes. "What the hell is this?"

"Um, yoga," I say slowly.

"No, I mean, this. You do yoga like this and you don't even tell me about it?" His words are usual Mav, but his voice lacks the usual oomph. He sounds groggy still, that just-woke-up grit scraping over me, sending every inch of my body into high alert. I offer a smile and make the mistake of looking at him for more than a split second.

I see the crinkle of his belly from how he's leaning back in the chair. The powerful muscles of his thighs. The dark hair sprinkled up and down his legs. The white band of his boxer briefs contrasting with the black fabric covering something I might actually donate an organ to see at this point. The flat planes of his chest that beg me to run a palm across the barely-tanned skin.

God, Mav, why didn't you put on clothes first?

"I don't see what the problem is," I say, sitting on the mat, stretching my legs out in front of me. Forward bends are a good idea. That way, I don't have to look at him.

"I just can't believe you never told me you do this," he finally says.

"Well, here's your formal notice," I crack, hooking my palms behind my heels. "I practice yoga."

"Not just yoga," he insists. "Like, *professional* grade."

I shrug, which is sort of hard to do when your chest is pressed to your knees. "Well, whatever."

"Why have we never talked about this?"

Because I don't want anybody to know. "Never came up, I guess."

"You don't think this is weird."

A laugh bubbles out of me. "Was I supposed to submit in writing my application for having a personal yoga practice? Damn, Mav."

He grumbles something I don't entirely catch. I'm still smiling to myself, because it's cute, and somewhere deep inside, it feels like something way more than it is.

"It would be like if I played rugby for an entire year and never mentioned it once," Maverick says after I've switched to wide-legged seated forward bends. "You'd be like, 'Wow, Mav, I can't believe you never told me you played rugby.' And I'd say, 'Yeah, well, did you want me to submit in writing my application for personal sports?'"

My forehead touches the floor as more laughter rolls out of me. "Are you done giving me shit about this?"

"Not yet."

I heave a dramatic sigh. "Well can you hurry it up? You're interrupting my routine."

"You have a *routine*?" He scoffs and gets up, heading back into the bedroom. "Are you practicing for something? It's like I don't even know you anymore." He continues griping but the bathroom door shuts a moment later, muffling his complaints. I continue with my practice, though my concentration is shot. My mind is irrevocably on Maverick—wanting him to come back out and continue griping at me in just his underwear, so I can catch the crinkle of his abs one more time. *Please, God.*

The bathroom door opens, but he doesn't come back into the living room right away. When he does, he's got black board shorts on and my favorite black tee. Black on black. Just how I like him. He folds himself into the arm chair again, swiping his fingers through his hair.

"Now where were we?" he says.

"You were complaining about the fact that I do something without your knowledge."

"Exactly. What the fuck, Lettie? I thought you were my home-girl."

I'm glad that my workout provides an excuse for why my cheeks heat up. I can just say I'm sweaty if he calls me out on the flush. "I *am* your homegirl. One who practices yoga."

"That's why you're so..." He squints at me like he can't find the word.

"What?"

"Lean," he finally says.

"It takes a lot of muscle to do what I do," I blurt, which I imme-diately regret. I don't want to get into silks right now.

"Which is what?"

"This." I gesture broadly at my body. "You know. Existing."

He doesn't look convinced. "Uh huh. I can't believe Tom never told me you do yoga."

I snort. "Why would he tell you I do yoga? He never cared, any-way. It's not a big deal."

Maverick is still somehow dissatisfied; I can feel it as I push off the mat and roll it up. He's watching me with narrowed eyes. I store the mat in the corner of the living room, and when I turn around, Maverick's standing in the middle of the room, sucking up all the air with his impossible attractiveness. He basically just rolled out of bed, threw on the easiest clothes, and probably brushed his teeth, but he could still pose for a photo shoot and win a damn contest with the way he's looking at me right now.

"We could have been going to the gym together all this time." Accusation lines his voice, and it just makes me smile.

"Could we? I thought you only took your little fuck buddies." The words slip past my lips before I can think better of it, and my neck goes hot. I'm talking about his sex life nonstop these days, and I can't help it. I'm so terrified that I'm going to have to suffer through another one of his gal pals during our trip that my anxiety is coming out sideways now.

"Excuse me?"

"If I went to the gym with you, that would mean I'm, like, you know, one of your playthings." The words are just spilling out now, and I can't control them. This is an active avalanche, people, and I'm both the cascading rocks *and* the unaware pedestrians below. "I mean, isn't that why you take girls to the gym? Just to get them into bed afterward?" I have no idea what I'm saying anymore. My heart is racing. Please, God, make me stop. Maverick's face is slowly moving from amusement to deep confusion, which only makes me *more* nervous. Now I need to reassure him that I don't want exactly what I'm implying, which is coincidentally also what I *very much want*.

"I'm sorry," I continue babbling, "but, don't you think we should preserve the integrity of our relationship by avoiding gym sex?" Everything inside me is groaning. Am I done now? Have I convinced Maverick I don't want him, even while my cells vibrate with nothing but desire for him?

"Nobody said anything about gym sex but you," Maverick says, an edge to his voice that I've never heard before.

He's not wrong. And I am most certainly not in my right mind. Still, goosepimples rise on my forearms, and I can't look away from his captivating, icy blues. "Well, my point is—" God, did I even *have* a point? "—that some things need to be kept private."

His brows arch. "Oh? Was *that* your point?"

"Yes." I sniff, avoiding eye contact with him as I brush past and into the bedroom. "I'm going to take a shower now, bye."

I stomp into the bathroom, defiant about something that is a mystery even to me, and once the door slams shut behind me, I bury my face in my hands. *What the fuck was that?* If I needed any proof that crossing the line with Maverick is a bad idea, there it is. Not only would I not be able to handle myself if things somehow turned sexual between us, I saw the look on Maverick's face when the idea came up, and it *wasn't* pretty. The confusion was as raw as if I'd barked a command at him in German. Therefore, the whole idea of him mounting me, penetrating me, turning me into a gym-sex plaything is as terrifying and foreign as an unplanned verbal assault in German.

Great.

So why do I still want to cross that line so badly?

I take a shower so cold that it makes Antarctica jealous. By the time I've washed away my impure thoughts and the crippling embarrassment of my not-sexy and not-funny conversation with Maverick, I'm ready to suppress everything that involves thoughts of his penis. I wrap my hair in a turban, knot my towel around my chest, and breeze out into the bedroom with my best *everything is fine here, I'm not still replaying that awkward moment in my head on repeat or anything, ha ha* vibes.

Maverick's not in the bedroom, but I can hear the low tones of his voice from the other room as I pick out my clothes for the day. We have to be downstairs in an hour and a half for our assignment, and then the official first challenge will begin. Maybe I can pretend *that's* why I'm becoming progressively more incoherent around Maverick. Let's just call it nerves and pretend it has nothing to do with the desperate nerve endings that lead straight to my pussy.

The main door shuts a moment later, and there's some clinking of silverware in the living room. Maverick calls out, "You decent?"

"Uh," I snag a pair of panties and a bra, "Isn't that subjective?"

"You know what I mean. I got breakfast for us."

"Aww." I drop the towel and hurry to snap my bra on. Not like he's interested in coming in here. He's been with so many sexy women in his life that the best word he could think of to describe me was "lean." Not exactly what I plan to feature in my eventual online dating profile. People use that word as a plus when talking about ground beef. Not women they want to have sex with. "I'm almost ready. Hang on."

I hurry to pull my clothes on, reminding myself to *suppress*.

We're here to win a food truck challenge. Not fuck up our decades-long friendship with some weird feelings that are better ignored.

And damn it all.

I need to remember that.

CHAPTER TWELVE

SCARLETT

Once we smash breakfast and leave the tense, crazy-inducing confines of our suite, I feel slightly more normal. Being trapped in a small space with Maverick's testosterone is clearly the problem. This must be why he takes so many lovers.

It's his fault. He's wooing me with his womanizing pheromones, so maybe I'll just ask the producer to give us separate rooms from here on out.

Great plan.

After we get the briefing on the day and film it three times over for content purposes, we're given our very first challenge: *create a menu that takes less than thirty seconds from order to serve time.*

"Jesus Christ," Mav mutters, hands propped on his hips as he mulls over the task. The other food truck crews are in similar states of deep thought. We're all released to begin our product hunting and to maneuver our trucks to the prearranged serving location. We have the afternoon to plan and must be serving from five to six thirty p.m. It doesn't seem like enough time. Our truck has *nothing* in it, save the equipment and some basic serving utensils like tongs and spatulas.

A cameraman follows us—each crew gets their own dedicated cameraman, *yay*—as we head to the truck and climb inside. Maverick has been muttering to himself the whole time. I glance at the newly-installed cameras and mics the production crew installed along the upper ridge of the food truck. They're to make sure our every curse and sigh gets documented.

"Maybe we could do something like empanadas," I finally suggest.

"I thought of that too," he said, "but I don't think I have time to make the dough for the shells. We'd need too many."

"We could probably buy some."

"I'm thinking...hot-holding some specially seasoned veggies. Homemade peanut sauce." His eyes flutter shut as he accesses whatever spirit realm exists for chefs. "Ramen noodles."

"I'm already hungry for it," I say.

"Crunchy ass broccoli," he goes on.

"Yes," I say then look at the camera man. "That sounds good to you, right?"

"Don't address the camera," Mav chides.

"Sorry, I just meant—" I look at the camera again. "I won't look at you again."

Maverick breaks into laughter, rubbing at his forehead. "Okay. Fancy ramen. Pre-mixed in a huge serving bowl. Serve time: five seconds. Sound like a plan?"

"I'm on board with whatever you say, Chef Mav!"

The smile he sends me as he turns on the engine makes that moisture arrive in my panties again. I wonder if the cameraman will let me buy the footage off him, secretly of course, just so I can watch that smile over and over again for the rest of my life.

The cameraman stops filming for a little bit during the ride, and we get to know each other. His name is Keith, and he's been working on this show for the past three years. He and his wife got married four years ago, and she does makeup for a children's show. They are real, functioning adults within the entertainment industry, and my *mind is blown.* Part of me wonders if I could ever actually pay my rent doing anything other than wait tables.

What if I could pay rent with aerial silks?

Once Keith starts filming us again, it's go-time. We must not only buy the food we plan to serve, but the rest of the accompanying implements that we never got around to buying in our haste: deli sheets, plastic wrap, enormous ladles, spoons. The list goes on. We hit up a discount grocery store that I found through my GPS, and then we head to the nearest restaurant equipment store to stock up on the rest. By the time we're done with all those purchases, it's nearly two p.m. and I'm starving.

But there's no time to rest, much less eat. We head to the challenge spot, which is nestled among the patios and tall buildings of the Flats in downtown Cleveland. It's a famous section of the city, set against the Cuyahoga River, where bridges cross overhead and warehouses butt up against gourmet restaurants and brick sidewalks. It's beautiful and gritty at the same time, and I'm torn between helping Maverick navigate and gawking at the sights as we wind along the streets heading to the river.

"Will you help me find the alley we're supposed to park in?" Maverick barks once I've gotten lost in inspecting the underside of a nearby bridge.

"Sorry. Yes." I snap to attention. "Did you see that bridge though?"

"Kind of focusing on the road here, *Scarlett.*"

Keith chuckles. "You two sound like me and my wife when we drive somewhere new."

My neck flushes, but I stare intently out the window. Keith *will not* have eternal evidence of my embarrassment when it comes to talk about Maverick and me as a couple, *so help me God.*

"We're basically married," Maverick mutters. "Just waiting on the ceremony to make it official."

I snort. "Not sure either of us would show up."

"You would," Maverick reassures me, and I glare at him, because he's right.

We find our designated location at long last, but we're a little behind because of how many laps we had to make around the Flats (yes, my fault as the bridge watcher). By the time we're backed into our spot on a sidewalk between tree-shaded resting areas full of benches and picturesque spots to pause and admire the river, nerves are taking over. Mav cuts the engine and we look at each other.

"Are you ready?" he asks me, and although his voice is steady, I catch the waver in his gaze. He's terrified. So am I.

"As ready as I'll ever be," I tell him, and then I pull open the door. We all pile out into the humid afternoon air. Keith wanders off to get footage of the truck and the scene. A little way down the street, the next truck is pulling into their spot.

"See? We're not the last one," I tell Maverick.

He fists the front of his hair, pinning me with an intense look. "I can't do this."

"Come on, Mav. We did *not* just get lightweight lost in the Flats for a half hour to bitch out now."

He draws a deep breath, looking back at the other truck maneuvering into their spot. "Okay. You're right. Let's fucking do this."

We kick into motion. It's not exactly flawless, because there's lots of fumbling and swearing as we get things situated in the kitchen, which of course Keith documents fully. But we're working as a team, at least. He starts prepping the food while I attempt to intuit what resources we'll need in what part of the process. I set out gloves, deli sheets, knives, while Maverick boils an enormous pot of water on the two-burner stove and starts snapping broccoli florets. Occasionally he has me help with a task—crack the eggs, mix this, *here wash this spoon*—but once he's got the food under way, I move to the next important task: making the menu board.

During one of our marathon planning nights at his apartment, we impulse purchased a chalkboard menu and decided that I would be the official menu-maker. I prop the A-frame menu board against the back of the truck, my collection of neon-colored chalk markers lined up next to me. I make elaborate swirls around the border, and then front and center: *Grab My Peanuts! Ramen Bowl.*

I frown, staring at it. No, that's too direct.

Maverick comes out of the truck a moment later, swiping his forearm across his forehead. "I think we're actually somehow on schedule."

I look up at him, pointing at the menu board. "Is this what you had in mind? I'm going to write the ingredients underneath, along with the price."

He's quiet as he reads, and then he laughs sharply. "I fucking love it."

I hurry to wrap up the menu board, and when I've dotted all the i's and crossed all the peanuts, I carry it around to the front of the truck.

A gasp ricochets through me. I stop in my tracks as I behold…people. A lot of them. Like, *a lot* of them.

Standing in line.

In front of our truck.

Waiting to *grab my peanuts.*

I clamp my mouth shut, trying to act casual and ignore the sky-rocketing anxiety. We have to feed all these people. The network did its job of letting half of Ohio know about this show. Holy mother of God. As soon as I set the menu board down, a few people clap, and a chorus of "*Oooh!*" ripples through the line. I hurry back into the truck, looking between Maverick and the amount of food he's cooking, trying to do the math.

"What's wrong, Lettie?" he barely glances at me.

"We've...got a line."

He stops pushing the veggies around on the flat top to look at me. "Are you serious?"

"Not lying."

"How many?"

"Like..." I'm not good at guesstimating head counts. I'm always way under. "Fifty? Let's say fifty to seventy."

"Fifty to fucking seventy!" He dashes past me, out of the truck. When he returns a moment later, his face is pale. "Fuck. Fuck fuck fuck."

"This is a good thing," I begin.

"We need to cook more food." He returns to the flat top grill, his jaw set. "Can you wash the rest of that broccoli? Give me four more onions. I'm gonna switch up the ratio so we can make what we have last."

"But the ramen—"

"We bought extra. Let's just hope it's enough."

The air is tense as we start an unexpected second round of food. We've got a half hour until the window officially opens. A half hour for the line to keep growing. Keith keeps dropping in to film us, and each time he does, we're silent and focused. No drama here—just working our asses off.

Once five o'clock rolls around, a voice through a megaphone slices through the air. "Hellooooo, Cleveland!" I'm pretty sure it's Hartley. Pumping up the crowd. Preparing us to get our asses handed to us. I've served fifty to seventy people during a work shift before, but never in a fatal crush all at once. My stomach flops as Hartley introduces the show, the trucks, and gets the crowd cheering.

And then he says, "Trucks, open your windows!"

Maverick's wiping his hands on a white dish towel. He jerks his chin toward the window. "Do it, Lettie."

I gulp. I push. The window opens.

And the sea of people presses toward the window.

I jump into serving mode because it's all I can do. Bright "Hello there!"s, big smiles, well-timed winks. I'm pumping through the line as fast as I can, placing the order slips in a neat line for Maverick to call out once they're ready.

Hector. Brian. Angela. Harlow. Missy. Jaret. They just keep coming. Endless faces, endless money coming in.

We're pumping these orders out faster than thirty seconds a piece. By the time we hit customer thirty, I realize something. I grab Mav's attention as he's serving another bowl.

"Did you even try this? How did it come out?"

Sweat's collecting at his temples, and he sears me with a deep look. "I have no fucking idea."

Better not to think about that right now.

We churn through the line, sending out bowl after bowl of our fancy peanut ramen. But we don't make it to the end of the line. We run out of food at six twenty on the dot, with about fifteen people still left in line. And ten minutes left in the challenge.

"We're so sorry, guys, but we're sold out," I call out to the remaining guests. There's groaning and a few complaints. I pull the window shut, and then it's just Maverick and me and the well-placed cameras. Alone together.

We stare at each other for what feels like a millennium.

"They're gonna disqualify us," Mav starts.

"We served the shit out of that line," I say at the same time.

He draws a deep breath. "We did a great job. But fuck. I didn't think that many would show up."

"All we can do is wait and see what happens."

We fall into a tense silence as we begin cleaning up. For not knowing what the hell we were getting ourselves into, I think we did a great job. We made almost nine hundred dollars in an hour. Nobody complained to our faces or vomited on the spot. All around? I call it a success.

Once everything is off and we're packed up, we drive back to the hotel. The elimination ceremony—what they do after each challenge to formally say goodbye to one of the food truck crews—will happen tomorrow, after we've all had a full night to sleep on our mistakes and fret over that which we cannot correct.

Maverick pulls into the parking lot. A few of the other trucks are already back.

"There's the post-challenge party tonight, don't forget," I tell him as he locks up the truck.

"Oh, I won't. I plan on getting drunk."

"I wish we had been able to eat some of your ramen," I tell him. "I'm starving."

"Next time," he says, slinging his arm over my shoulder as we head toward the hotel. There it is again—that platonic touch. All the adrenaline and focus of the challenge melts away under his warmth.

God, it's nice to have him at my side at the end of the day, too, in addition to at the beginning and all throughout the middle.

"I tasted the sauce," he adds a moment later. "It was fucking awesome. But that was it. You want me to make you a quesadilla?" He stops, half-turning back to the truck. "I'll do it."

"No, dude. We have room service. Remember?"

Except we never even make it back to the rooms. Hartley and Bennett herd us toward the pool patio, where a whole table of food and ready-made drinks are waiting for us. I grab quinoa salad, lasagna, and a whole handful of carrots, because I can. Topped off with a margarita, this is about to be the best dinner ever. The rest of the contestants are filing in, grabbing food, sinking into conversation. I select a table and wait for Maverick to join me.

But someone else joins me first. A redheaded guy from the truck named Butter Me Up where, surprise, they cook everything in butter.

"Hey. Mind if I join you?" He sends me a dazzling smile, one that makes me stop with my fork halfway to my mouth. He's got finger waves that fade down to shaved sides, tattoos licking up past the collar of his shirt and onto his neck. He looks bulky, too. Like the type of guy who cooks everything in butter *and* hits the gym three times a day.

"Not at all. Please do."

He sets his plate down and offers his hand. I shake it with the wrong hand, still holding my fork halfway to my mouth.

"I'm Davie. You're with the ramen truck, right?"

"We don't only do ramen..." I begin.

"I heard some awesome things about your menu today." He stabs at the potato salad on his plate. "Great job."

"Thanks." Maverick is the one who needs to hear this though. "I wish I had gotten to try your food. We were so busy..." Why isn't

Maverick here yet? I scan the patio for him. For only five food trucks, there are a *lot* of people here. Finally I spot him, standing near the food table, a plate in his hand. Liquid heat streaks through my veins as I gaze at him. And then that heat turns to ice as I spot the blonde who steps into view, nodding intently, looking up at him with eyes that say *fuck me now.*

Shit. Here we go again. Maverick's conquests will soon expand to a reality TV show, and all I can do is sit back and watch.

"So, tell me...that chef, what's his name?" Davie smiles, his eyes crinkling at the edges. "Are you guys...like..."

"Sorry?"

He wets his bottom lip. "Like, would your chef friend be upset if we got drunk later and made out?"

My eyes go wide, his meaning slamming into me like a freight train. "Well...Maverick and I...we're just friends."

Because why shouldn't I leave that door open?

I deserve to flirt with a man. I have no intention of taking it all the way to melted-butter status—or whatever Davie might call an orgasm on his food truck—but why not have some fun? Hell, it's my only shot at distracting myself while Maverick starts wooing the pants off every female in the hotel.

Besides, Davie looks interesting. He looks like he knows how to have fun. He looks like the opposite of Tom.

At this point, these are my only requirements for getting to know a new person.

"Good. No territorial fights then, right?" Davie looks extra pleased with himself as he takes another sip of his drink. "Not that he'd have a chance against me."

I assess his biceps, tipping my head to the side. "I don't think you have to worry. Maverick doesn't get like that with women."

"Oh, so he's into dudes?"

I reeeaaally dislike the *har har, is he gay* undertone in his comment, so I just send him a tight smile. "It doesn't really matter."

"I was just kidding. Come on." Davie elbows me with a cajoling smile. "Let me get you another drink."

Drinks come and go in a blur. I don't connect with Mav for the next hour and a half, we're both so wrapped up in our own worlds of socializing. Once the sun starts to set, people are talking about getting in the pool. I'm drunk and compliant, so fuck yes, let's get in the pool. I'm best friends with everyone at this point, even though Davie and I have been chatting almost nonstop with only a few interruptions from outsiders. Somehow, I drunk-admitted to him that I practice aerial silks, which opened up a whole world of conversation, because his ex practiced silks, too.

I manage to escape to the suite to change into my bathing suit, a black string bikini. It's quiet and desolate up there. When I come back downstairs, the patio is raucous with laughter, the sky streaked with crimson and orange. Davie somehow shape-shifted into his swim trunks while I was gone. Almost everyone is in their suits at this point, though now, I can't find Mav at all.

My stomach sinks. I force myself not to think the worst: that he's already escaped upstairs with the perky blonde, who I'm sure is *so* eager to give it up to him already.

"Want to get in?" Davie asks.

"Sure," I say, and I follow him with a pit in my stomach. The water is crystal clear and way warmer than expected. Everything is perfect tonight. Pure revelry, new people, comped drinks. So why am I missing Maverick?

Because you're too fucking attached and you need to fall out of love with him ASAP.

Whoa, there, Subconscious Sally! Didn't expect so much brutal honesty from myself after three margaritas, but hey, here we are. I force a smile for Davie as he leads us toward the deep end. Most everyone is hanging around the pool at this point, and one of Davie's crew shouts at him as we bob in the piss-warm water. I bet Maverick would think it was too warm too.

If only I could find him.

I float toward the edge of the pool, near where Hartley is sitting with his legs dangling in the pool. He and one of the cooks from the Crusty Bastard truck are discussing variations of olive oil. I hook my arms along the stone edge of the pool and float, taking it all in.

It isn't long before Davie and the other men start getting rowdy. More beers crack open as the sun sinks toward the horizon. There's shouting, horseplay, tons of splashing. Finally, I spot Maverick. He's at the other edge of the pool, black swim trunks on, and our gazes connect in a searing flash. I wonder if he can feel the question baked into my glance: *Where the fuck were you?*

The blonde is trailing behind him, so I don't even want to guess where he was.

Nothing against her—if I were anybody else, I wouldn't be able to resist Maverick either. I'm just the unlucky bitch who happens to be his platonic best friend.

Hartley offers me another margarita, which I accept. Hartley is lovely. Everyone is lovely. Everyone except Maverick. Every cell of my body is sighing as I sip at the marg. Davie and the group of men around him start chanting.

"Top-less. Top-less. Top-less."

It takes me a minute to catch up. Davie is waving me toward the slowly congregating group in the middle of the shallow end. Pretty much every single female in the show is gathered. We're all wearing string bikinis. We're all in our twenties. It's like they planned this or something.

"Topless challenge!" someone shouts.

I'm whooping and splashing as much as I can with a margarita in one hand. Why the fuck not? I'll take my top off, if for no other reason than to prove to myself—and to Maverick—that I'm single and do what I want. That's as far as it'll go—that much, I'm sure of. I'm not interested in meaningless sex or one-night-stands. Not even with Muscly McButter.

"The cameras will blur out the nipples, right?" Someone from the Crusty Bastard crew calls out to Hartley.

"Of course! We can't show that on television. It qualifies as soft-core porn," he says with a laugh.

"I'm in!" I say, adding my consent to the masses. Besides, I love my boobs. They're perky. They're cute. They should be appreciated by *somebody.*

A hand at my elbow makes me gasp just before I'm able to take a sip.

Oh, lookee. Maverick is here.

"Scarlett," he hisses, guiding me toward the far wall. "What do you think you're doing?"

His hair hangs damp, strewn across his forehead as if he swam at top speed to rescue me.

"Just hanging out." My head is spinning. He backs me up against the wall, his hands on the stone ledge on either side of my shoulders. Heat is pouring off him, and I swear to god, if he gets any closer, I'm going to break and wrap my legs around his waist.

It's a horrible idea, one that would only lead to a lifetime of embarrassment. Why did I drink so much? Why is Maverick so hot? Why is he *so close* to me?

"Those guys are fucking pervs," Maverick says, leveling me with his gaze.

"How do you know? I'm the one who's been hanging out with Davie all night, not you."

His gaze darkens. "I know. And I'm just saying, I know how to read the guy. He just wants to see your tits."

I scoff. "Well, let him. At least somebody does."

He lowers his chin. My nipples turn to tight points beneath my bikini and I pray Maverick isn't aware of this insane betrayal from my body. I don't want him to know that his simply standing a foot away from me is enough to send my pussy into spasms. That really, all I might need him to do for me to get off would be to whisper the right word into my ear while he brushed his knuckle between my legs.

Jesus, I've orgasmed to memories of him smiling at me. My desperation knows no limits.

"Don't fuck with those guys," Maverick says, his voice rough. "You deserve more than that."

I laugh, but it's humorless. "Right. I deserve a totally boring and stable relationship where I can count on one hand how many times I've been eaten out."

Oops. That's the margarita talking.

Mav's jaw flexes and he looks past me, to some distant point on the horizon, where he's probably fighting the urge to puke. When he finally looks at me again, he says, "You're drunk."

"No shit, Sherlock."

"Come on. Let's go up."

"No, I want to expose every inch of my body for these men," I say. Not because I want to actually do that. I want to see how Maverick will react.

His jaw flexes again. God, it's hot when he's trying to keep calm in front of strangers. It's almost like he's jealous. *Almost.* "Scarlett. Come on. We've got a lot of work to do."

I don't know why I'm being so contrarian. Oh wait, yes I do. *The margs.* "Oh, it's time for work, now that I'm having fun? Typical."

He guides me by the elbow toward the ladder. "You need water. And to eat something."

"I already ate dinner," I hiss as I climb out of the pool. I'll follow him because he's the only man I truly want to spend my time with. But I'm going to act like I don't want it every step of the way. "Or didn't you notice? Maybe you were too busy getting laid."

Maverick's silence is unmistakable. It's intentional. It's *thrilling.* I grab my towel from a nearby chair just as Davie hoists himself out of the pool.

"Scarlett. Talk later?"

"I think I'm heading to bed," I tell him.

"Well, show me your silks video tomorrow. I'm dying to see it. I wish I could watch you perform." He sends me a playboy smile and sinks back into the pool. I glance up at Maverick in time to catch the puzzled look slide over his face.

"And hey, Maverick," Davie goes on, jerking his chin toward him. "My buddy Frank thinks you're cute, so if you're into him..." He smirks as he lets the suggestion hang in the air.

"Thank you," Maverick says, the sarcasm so thick he might choke. "Oh my gosh. You are the sweetest." To me, he says, "Isn't that Davie such a thoughtful guy?"

I'm not sure whether I want to laugh or run away from the pending rivalry, so I just slip my sandals on. Maverick flips him off as we head back to the hotel, and then walks so close to me our hips touch.

"What was that about?"

"What?"

"Silks," he says.

"Oh, nothing," I say. Apparently the whole Frank-wants-you thing didn't even register on his scale of irritation.

"He said he wants to see you perform," Maverick says, and now I'm really in trouble. I offer a meek smile. He caught me. I don't offer anything up, and the silence is heavy between us as we walk into the hotel lobby and head for the elevators.

Once we're trapped in the tiny steel box catapulting upwards, Maverick turns to me.

"Why do I feel like you're lying to me?"

"Why do I feel like you're lying to *me?*" I shoot back, because I can think of nothing better.

"What the fuck would I be lying to you about?" The exasperation is evident in his voice.

"Oh, I dunno," I say. God, arguing is hard when you're drunk. "Like where you wandered off to for all of dinner?"

"I was at the pool!"

"Well you didn't come eat with me." I cross my arms and turn away, feeling every bit a petulant child and *not caring at all.*

"Did you want me to? You seemed pretty enthralled with Mr. Butter Face."

I laugh, but I suppress it quickly, because I'm supposed to be *mad.* "I was just being nice to him."

"Is that why you wanted to take your clothes off for him?"

Ouch. I frown, watching as the number on the panel clicks from 6 to 7. Good, we're almost there. So now I can stew not only in my drunkenness, but also my repressed sexual attraction.

"We're on vacation, Mav. I can take my clothes off for whoever I want."

Maverick is eerily silent, and the elevator finally clicks up to floor eight. Just as the doors begin opening, Mav jams his thumb into the *Door Close* button. His jaw is flexing like he's grinding his teeth.

"So let me get this straight. You want to show him the goods *and* confess some fucking deep secret to this guy after you've known him for thirty minutes. And I've known you for over ten fucking years, and I don't get the same consideration?"

I stare up at him, my drunk mind unable to focus on anything other than *so you want to see my goods?* It takes a moment for me to unravel what Maverick is saying. But I'm able to see through the fog. He's hurt.

Fuck, maybe he's right to be.

"Why does he get to waltz right up and get to know that about you, but I have to fucking stop an elevator and beg?" Mav asks. His eyes are sharp and brilliant, light catching in a gemstone. All of my margarita sauciness evaporates.

I heave a sigh, staring at the door. "I'm sorry, Mav."

He shifts, removing his thumb from the button. The door slides open a moment later. We start walking toward the room, the air still taut and weird between us. When we get to the door, I grab his wrist.

"I've been studying aerial silks for the past few years." I whisper it, like the walls might betray me. Maverick nods, his blue gaze crisscrossing my face.

"That's cool," he says. The door unlocks a moment later.

"I didn't want to tell you."

"I noticed."

He steps into the room, and I'm still holding his wrist as the door shuts behind us.

"I don't want anyone to make me feel like shit about it," I say, my throat growing tight all of a sudden. *Damn these margs.* "Tom made me feel like shit when he found out. He's the only one who ever found out. And I..." I can't go on. I just shake my head, feeling the drunk tears coming on.

"I won't make you feel like shit about it," Mav says, slinging his arm around my shoulders. He pulls me into him, my face smashed into his chest. My arms go around his waist, and I melt into the reassuring solidness of his chest. His warm skin that I've never had pressed to my cheek before. There's something raw, something visceral about this. I can feel his damn heartbeat through the apple of my cheek.

This is a space that feels like home in a way that Bayshore, my childhood home, and even my own apartment can't touch.

The emotions erupt like a geyser, and my breath hitches. *I will not cry.* Except I already sort of am crying, and *goddammit,* when will I fall out of love with my best friend?

"Let's get some sleep." Maverick rips away from me suddenly. He rakes a hand through the long part of his hair, avoiding my gaze. "We had a long day."

There's something electric buzzing in the air between us. I watch as he drags his hands down his face just before he heads into the bedroom. There's an unspoken question there, something I'm very curious to know about. The thumping of my heart wants it to be the question that I'm too scared to ask.

What about us?

"Yeah," I say, long after he's disappeared into the bedroom. I prepare myself to ask him to come back. Hold me again. Wrap me in his arms for the night, *please.* I struggle to find the words to ask him *what if we just kiss until we fall asleep?*

But instead, I head to the bathroom, where I can splash water on my face and grope for sobriety in the harsh lights.

Because I need to remember what it's like to simply be Maverick's best friend.

Somewhere over the past month, I forgot what that means.

CHAPTER THIRTEEN

MAVERICK

I wake up the next morning thinking about Scarlett's tits. That painfully hot black bikini. Her long almost-black ponytail plastered to her shoulders. Water droplets skimming the curves of breasts that I would actually sacrifice our friendship to swipe a tongue along and collect every droplet.

My eyes are closed—I'm not technically awake yet, even though my cock is fully awake—and I furrow my brow, angry that I even thought the words. Scarlett and I are friends. We've been friends forever. That's not going to change just because I can't see her in a bikini without getting a fucking hard-on. I turn onto my side, away from Scarlett's bed, and try to think about literally anything other than what sort of silken paradise I might find between her legs.

I might need to physically remove myself from her presence if she gets drunk like that anymore. Because all I could think the rest of the night was *So Tom never ate her out...*

Jesus Christ, I would eat her pussy so fucking hard. To the point of asphyxiation. I would die on Scarlett's pussy and not regret a second of it.

My brows furrow harder, and now I shift onto my stomach to trap my raging hard-on against the mattress. Like this might somehow convince it to go away. But after a few more minutes, it's clear that the only thing that's going to help me is an ice bath or jacking off. Maybe both, because I don't have much faith a cold shower is going to cure what I've got.

I roll out of bed and hobble to the bathroom. I'm positive that Scarlett is practicing yoga in the other room, so I absolutely *must not* go witness it in any way. I push open the bathroom door.

And there she fucking is.

Buck naked. Her foot propped on the side of the shower as she towels off all the way down to her ankles, exposing the graceful arc of her leg and those creamy Honeycrisps and the most delicious, plump shadows of her womanhood.

Fuck fuck fuck.

I'm paralyzed in the doorframe, my jaw dislodged and located on the floor. Some sort of choking noise escapes me, because she turns and gasps.

"Mav!" she cries out, whipping the towel around her. I hide my lower half behind the door so she doesn't witness the massive tenting in my boxer briefs. Memories of her bikini were enough to do me in. Walking in and glimpsing her pussy—it's fucking lighter fluid on a smoldering pile of wood.

"Sorry. Sorry." I rub my eyes. "Just woke up. Have to pee."

Yeah, right. If I try peeing within the next half hour, it's going to end up on the ceiling.

"Ok. I'm hurrying." Her cheeks are pink, and she floats over to the vanity mirror. I should let her get ready in peace, but I can't.

"You sleep okay?" I ask.

"Yeah. Still woke up at seven," she says with a little laugh.

"You were pretty drunk last night."

She sighs, squirting some girly stuff on a cotton ball. No idea what most girls use after showers, but whatever. I like it. "I know."

My throbbing cock reminds me of what it thinks my priorities are. Even this early in the morning. *Especially* this early in the morning. "So Tom really never ate you out, huh?"

Her mouth parts, and her gaze meets mine in the mirror for a split second. She's mortified. I'm just not sure how to let her know she shouldn't be. "Oh, God. I—can we just...not?"

"Just saying you need a man who's down to eat pussy." This conversation isn't helping my dick go soft, but when does logic ever rule in the minds of men?

"I wish guys were up front about those sort of things," she mutters.

"Oh, I am. I fucking love eating pussy."

Now her cheeks are beet red, and yes, I'm loving every second of this. I'm out of my mind horny. I just glimpsed Scarlett naked from behind, and I'd gladly ruin today's schedule just for a chance to fuck her brains out for the next three hours straight.

But we're just friends.

"I'm sure all the women you sleep with are very appreciative of that," she says, swiping the cotton ball furiously over her cheeks. "But some of us are accustomed to what we affectionately call 'selfish assholes.'"

"Sounds like you need to step up your game."

"Thanks for the recommendation, Mav." She squirts some moisturizer onto her palm. "But the truth is, I'm not even playing the game. Fuck the game. I'm celibate."

I snort. "That's not what Butter Boy thinks."

"I don't care what he thinks. I'm not down for casual sex. The next time I sleep with someone, it's going to be my fiancé."

Her words slam into me, reminding me of her angle. She wants the happily-ever-after. I just want to eat her pussy until she's screaming my name. Yet I also want her to be in my life until the day I die. We could be best friends with benefits.

But isn't that just marriage?

It's too much to think about right now, with this hard-on, with her so close yet so unattainable. She wraps up at the mirror and tightens her towel around her chest, squeezing past me. The amber and jasmine-scented trail she leaves behind doesn't help. I pace the bathroom for a few moments, then I finally opt for the cold shower.

When I come out of the bathroom, she's mostly packed. After the elimination ceremony today, those of us who remain are heading to Chicago. I toss on my standard uniform—black shorts and a tee, this time light gray—and find Scarlett in the living room, staring out the big window, bending one leg behind her so that the heel of her black Chuck touches her lower back. She's dressed in black skinny jeans with a tight gray tank top.

"We're twins," I tell her.

"I think at this point, we're just the same person," she says with a laugh. I'm about to contradict her, remind her that she's been hiding *an entire pasttime* from me for years now, which doesn't sound like being the same person at all. But no. I've got more research to do. She might have passed out immediately once we got back to the room last night, but I stayed up an extra hour looking into aerial silks.

In a nutshell? Holy shit.

If that's the type of shit Scarlett gets into when nobody is looking, we have some catching up to do.

But as Scarlett turns to face me, her smile warm and knowing, that familiar sparkle in her glittering green eyes, I realize there's just one small problem.

There's no fucking way I'm going to be able to keep myself off her for much longer. I'm a ticking time bomb, and when the explosion finally happens, nothing is safe.

Not Scarlett. Not her Honeycrisps.

And least of all our friendship.

Somehow, nobody gets eliminated in the elimination ceremony. We all did such a good job that they send us all off to Chicago with the promise that the next challenge *will* destroy someone's hopes and dreams.

Scarlett and I embark on our road trip to Chicago, except she takes the car and I drive the slow-ass beast. Keith is needed elsewhere for re-filming issues, which means my cameraman buddy is absent too.

So instead of a six hour trip to Chicago with my best friend and resident temptress at my side, I'm stuck at my max speed of sixty-five for seven hours, *alone,* listening to death metal and reminding myself of all the reasons I shouldn't lock us in the bedroom as soon as we get to the next hotel and fuck until sunrise.

I'm a horny motherfucker. I know it. Scarlett knows it. Everyone in Bayshore knows it. And even though I very much want to fuck Scarlett until sunrise, I'm still trying to be good. I remind myself of Tom, though I'm less in favor of them getting back together now that I know he's such a wimp in bed. I remind myself that I don't want to make things weird if it ever came out that I fucked his ex-girlfriend during our random reality TV show stint throughout the Midwest. Work would get awkward. I don't like drama in the workplace.

A week ago, that reason was enough of a deterrent. But now?

I don't even fucking care.

Tick. Tick. Tick.

Scarlett gets to Chicago first, of course. She sends me triumphant photos of our latest comped oasis. Modern silver towers, the encroaching sunset reflecting off the windows like a prism, the steel jungle of the city stretching out all around.

SCARLETT: It's another suite! Look at our view.

A photo of the cityscape bathed in the rosy hues of dusk comes through, but this time from a significant height. It's all cement and steel profiles, metallic reflections. We must be on the fortieth floor or something, because the hotel pool in the photo looks pretty far down.

SCARLETT: There's another mixer at the pool tonight.
MAVERICK: I bet you already told Butter Boy you'd be there.
SCARLETT: If I didn't know better, I'd think you were jealous.
MAVERICK: Why do you think you know better?
Tick. Tick. Tick.

She doesn't write back. She doesn't need to. Probably she can tell that I'm coming for her, but if she hasn't caught on by now, she'll know soon enough.

CHAPTER FOURTEEN

SCARLETT

You know that feeling in your body, like somebody is blowing a kazoo into your lungs, and every single inch of you is expectant, waiting, brimming with anticipation?

I used to feel that way before Christmas each year, waiting to see what my parents—or Santa, I guess—would rustle up for me that year.

This feeling, though...

I don't think I've ever felt like this. I could wait for a thousand Christmases and still not reach this level of anticipation. Waiting for Maverick to get to Chicago is like showing up at a buffet with an empty stomach and lead weights tied to each foot. I need to move faster toward my goal, which is Maverick *being with me*, but all I can do is trudge along and wait.

I head to the mixer without him, because I feel a particular brand of pathetic when my only plan is to wait, perched on Maverick's bed like an obedient puppy, until he shows up. No, I'm going to have some fun in the meantime. Eat some damn dinner. See if I can't coax some more of this jealousy out of Maverick, just for funsies.

I text Mav the room number and tell him to find me at the mixer when he gets here. And then I head up—all the way to the rooftop. The show has converted the entire rooftop lounge area into our personal reality TV oasis. Cameramen are stationed throughout the tiled and backlit paradise. Sashimi is laid out next to hand-battered shrimp poppers, and a whole portion of one table is dedicated to different sauces, each with a tiny, hand-written label on a stick in front of it.

And behind it all, Chicago gleams in the golden hour. Breathtaking and dazzling, both land and lake.

Before I'm even three shrimp poppers deep, Davie is at my side.

"How was the drive?" Cologne wafts my way, and he somehow looks more handsome today, more impeccable. But all I can focus on as I look at him is the wild red stubble shooting out of his chin; I wonder if it would hurt if it rubbed against my cheek and realize that I would take any amount of stubble pain if it meant Maverick would finally kiss me and put me out of my misery.

Because at this point, yes, I'm in misery.

I love him so much that I'd do anything for him.

Including forsake my own boundaries regarding our friendship.

"Drive was good." I send him a breezy smile. "It feels so good to be in Chicago, you know?"

His grin stretches ear-to-ear as he nods. "Yeah. Reeaallly good to be in Chicago." He takes a sip of whatever he's drinking, the breeze moving his strange red hairdo. "Where's your friend?"

"Oh, he's still on the road. His—I mean, our—the food truck is really slow."

He nods, his gaze turning serious. "So you never mentioned before. What restaurants has he trained at?"

"Oh, uh, none, actually." I laugh, fingering the fourth popper I really want to eat but, come on, I've already had three and there's still this whole table of awesome food left. "He's self-taught."

Davie's brows shoot to the heavens. "Self-taught."

"Yeah. His food is...fucking awesome."

Davie doesn't seem to hear me, and then makes a big display of noticing what's in my hands. "Do you need a drink?"

"I would love one."

Davie touches the small of my back before he disappears. I scarf the remaining shrimp poppers on my plate and scoop up two more. Fuck it. Shrimp poppers are officially my dinner. When he returns, he hands over a pale beer that, at first sniff, I can already tell is super light.

"I figured you'd want the light beer," he says. "Girls always want the light beer."

I force a little laugh and take the tiniest sip possible. Give me the hoppiest shit out there, please. Not like Davie knows that.

"So your chef...sorry, your business partner, he has no formal training?" Davie sips his own beer, shoving a hand into a pocket of his jean shorts. "Fascinating. I'm shocked he would even try."

"It's his passion, though." I toss my paper plate, eyeing my next conquest. "He makes the best quesadillas in the world."

Davie doesn't look convinced. "But you haven't tried *my* quesadillas."

He means it as a joke, but on the inside, I'm a little offended. How dare he imply that anybody's quesadillas are better than Maverick's? I take another sip of the awful beer. "Yeah, well, I guess we won't really get a chance."

"Tomorrow." Davie nudges me, and I get another waft of his cologne. Something nauseous slides through my veins. "I'll make you my best quesadilla after the challenge."

I nod, pretending to think about it. But the truth is, I can't eat another man's quesadilla. I made a sour cream oath to Maverick in his apartment. That shit is *serious*.

Something hot slides over the exposed skin at my waist. When I turn, all the air turns to stone inside my body out of sheer surprise. Maverick is there, his blue gaze waiting for mine, a cocksure smile on his face.

"Hey, babe," he says, his voice gritty and deep. My mouth parts in response to the logjam of questions forming inside my head: *Why does his touch feel so good? Why does seeing him feel like the deepest, most satisfying sigh? Did he just call me* babe? My veins fill with liquid fire. I am so desperate to have him around me, to fill me, that I stumble into his embrace.

"M—Wh—" Speaking is hopeless, so I give up.

His other arms slides around my waist and he gives me one, solid jerk at the waist so that I settle into place in his arms. His hands hook at the top of my ass and all I can do is gaze up at him in wonder.

"Did you eat already?" he asks, his breath coming out hot far closer to my lips than he's ever been before.

I nod. My arms naturally fold around him, until I can grab my own wrist. There is no remaining space between our bodies. I am plastered against him, wondering if he can feel how fast my heart is racing.

"You drunk?" he asks, softer. I haven't been able to look away from him, much less blink. I shake my head. And now, while I'm this close to him, pressed against the hard, unyielding length of him, I fucking get it.

Why women fall at their feet for him. Why he can have his pick of any woman out there.

Why his own best friend would sacrifice her whole damn friendship with him.

We just need a taste of this man. Maverick is simultaneously enigmatic and familiar. He's a whiff of Armani cologne paired with the dish your mom always made growing up. He's my best friend...and a fantasy lover that I never dared imagine.

But maybe I'm misreading this, after all. Maybe he's just being jealous for no reason, because Davie and food truck competition and the simmering need to win. He's competitive, after all. I can't forget about his older brothers. Maverick was born with an intense need to win, even when he doesn't want to be competing, and—

My thoughts fade away when Maverick dips down and captures—no, *consumes*—my lips in a kiss. It's not just any kiss. It's hot and seeking and elaborate, a kiss that involves tongue right out of the gate. Maverick wastes no time in fucking my tongue with his own. He plunges, dips, traces the contour of my lips. All of my thoughts evaporate, followed by the air in my lungs, followed by any idea of who I am or what my name is. And yes, my clit is throbbing immediately because *oh my god, this man knows how to use his tongue.*

He kisses me so deeply that I almost choke. He pulls back, his fingers digging into the flesh of my waist.

"You ready to go?" he says. I pinch my eyes shut and nod. I don't know where he plans on going, but I'll follow him anywhere.

Maverick straightens, looking over my shoulder at Davie. "Good to see you, bro." The statement is so devoid of warmth, shallow-sounding, that I would laugh if I could remember how to make noises.

"Might be our last chance seeing each other," Davie says, "once they announce who's going home after tomorrow. So, good luck with whatever you do after the show."

I can practically see Mav's hackles raising. He sneers, offering another middle finger over his shoulder as he leads me away by the hand.

"Bad luck to you too, buddy."

He grips my hand in his, guiding me past the food tables. I follow like a helpless doll. Am I supposed to continue living after that kiss? I'm replaying it in my head already, turning myself on more and more. Jesus—if that tongue—down there—

He glances behind us, slinging his arm around my waist. "You know he's a fucking douche canoe, right?"

"Uhh," I begin. Nothing else arrives to follow it. I do know that. I just can't convey that I know it.

"It's not worth fighting with him," Maverick goes on, as though I had actually replied with substance. "He gets off on being the bigger dude, but really, it pisses him off more when I don't engage."

I blink at the poppers as Maverick slows near some of the food.

"I would know," Mav adds. "The garage is actually a breeding ground for shit like that."

Blink once for *Oh, interesting;* Blink twice for *Hmmm, didn't know that.*

"What should I eat?" The answer seems obvious—*my actual vagina.* But I can't form words yet. I might not ever be able to.

Some of the fog begins to clear. "Ummm."

Maverick swipes a plate and begins loading it with shrimp poppers. "God, these look good. You want some?"

I shake my head. On the inside, beyond my paralyzed-by-the-kiss exterior, I am laughing about how we chose the same food.

He swipes a big handful of the poppers, pauses to scoop some sauce on the plate, and then he steers me toward the elevator shaft. My arm is slung around his waist as we navigate the circuitous path that leads through trellises dripping with vines. Once he presses the Down button, my gaze shifts to the burnt orange panorama backing the skyscrapers of downtown Chicago. My mind clears just as he pops the last popper in his mouth.

"Um, Mav?"

He swallows his food. "Yeah?"

"What just happened back there?"

"I kissed you." He sets the plate down on a stand nearby. "Really fucking well, I might add."

My eyes flutter shut, but I remind myself to focus. "Right, but like...why?"

"So he fucking knows you're off limits."

His words are both thrilling and dismaying. He did it to *mark his territory*. It also means I was very wrong about Maverick: he'll apparently mark his territory for *me*.

"That's not necessary," I tell him.

"Yes it is. You shouldn't be wasting your time on him."

"I wasn't wasting my time. I was having a friendly conversation." And poking the beast a little, but come on.

"Babe, I can already tell he's just trying to get laid. Trust me on this. He thinks you want to have a good time. Did he get you a drink tonight? He's trying to score."

"Why do you care?"

His eyes widen. "Are you serious? That's like asking me why I eat food every day."

"Well?"

"We're here together," he says, but that's not the whole story. The falter in his voice betrays what he's leaving out.

"Yeah. As friends," I say. "I let you go and do what you want."

"Which is what, exactly?" He steps closer, but I steel myself against him. "Why don't you just admit it? You think I fucked that girl last night."

"It's what you do."

He scoffs. "We were talking about graphic design. I showed her the wrap on the truck." When I'm silent, he adds, "And what's it matter *to you*? You jealous?"

My throat catches. I'm so jealous I could break open, but I refuse to become part of that drama. I refuse to become one of the girls that gets burned and cast to the side. "I could ask you the same thing."

"Then ask me," he growls, a fire in his eyes that I've never seen before. We've never spoken like this to each other. So intense. So convoluted. This is new territory and I, for one, did not bring my fucking map.

I swallow a knot in my throat, because here it comes. The moment when Maverick finds out I'm the poor fucking sap who's in love with the playboy but too scared to do anything because of our friendship. Somehow, it will come out that I've been in love with him for months. Possibly much, much longer. I draw a deep breath, focusing on the distant honking from the Chicago streets below before I force the words past my lips.

"Are you jealous of Davie?"

"Yes!" He barks it out, raking a hand through his hair, just as the elevator door slides open behind him. But I ignore it; I need to hear this. "I can't fucking see you with him, okay? It drives me nuts."

My mind is spinning now. "Why?"

"Because you shouldn't be wasting your time on him." He's standing a few feet away from me now, his hands propped on his hips. "What's the point? He's going to be eliminated soon, or we will. And then we go home and what then? You'll just get hurt."

I scoff just as the elevator door slides shut, empty from its fool's trip to the rooftop. "So you don't want me to talk to anyone who might be interested in me on the trip. You want to just keep me for yourself, huh?" I'm trying to make it sound like the joke I think it is. Because there's no way Maverick truly *wants me*. But in the back of my head—all through my limbs, actually—the truth is buzzing. The realization is cresting.

"Yes." The word falls like a hammer. Definite. Unequivocal. He's watching me with that icy gaze that can crack me into a million pieces. The meaning slams into me so hard I can't even understand it at first. Being jealous of Davie is one thing. But this...

I try to laugh it off. Because I don't want to be the girl who somehow missed the fact that her painfully hot and single best friend was interested in her. No. I can't be that girl. Those girls are always the first to die in sci-fi movies, and if I'm that girl, it means we're going to be eliminated first on this show, too.

"Just lock me up like the little sister you never had?" I ask, unable to ask the question that I desperately need to: *Do you actually want me?* "Keep me tucked away so no man can possibly find me until I get back home to Tom and he can make me a good wife. Sounds like a great plan."

His gaze darkens. "Don't fucking bring up Tom."

"You love bringing him up like he's my long-lost soul mate."

"I don't see you as my little sister," Mav spits, his jaw back to flexing as laughter from the mixer drifts our way. "I see you as my best friend and a bombshell. And as far as I'm concerned, Tom's never coming near you again."

There's a strange cocktail of emotions sliding through me, threatening to swallow me whole *and* send me into outer space at the same time. I'm delirious. Dizzy. Absolutely, unforgivably turned on.

I need more of those kisses, but I know that getting them will lead to more questions. More confusion. More despair.

"Are you that hard up you need to come my way?" I can't stop defaulting to weak jokes, but this time, my voice falls flat. Maverick drags his hands down his face and groans.

"Scarlett! Do you not fucking see yourself?" When I don't respond, he gestures broadly at me. "You're sexy as fuck, babe. Can I be real about that?"

My mouth opens, but the air in my lungs disappeared again, so no more talky talky. Just stare-y stare-y.

"You don't believe me," he says, stepping closer. This time, his slides his hand over my shoulder and up around my neck. He guides me closer to him, back within tongue-fucking distance. My entire body lights into pinpricks, and I'm pretty sure my feet leave the ground from how high I feel right now. "I'm not trying to make this weird. But I want to show you how sexy I think you are. Let me tell you how many fucking nights I haven't been able to sleep because I'm thinking too hard about you. Because I cannot stop imagining peeling off these skinny jeans"—he hooks his fingers suddenly in the belt loops of my pants and brings me crashing against him—"and having my way with you. Lettie, I've got a million different ways I want to light you up. But only if you'll let me."

My breath hitches, and I squeeze my eyes shut. It's too much. It's exactly what I want, but it's too much. Because it's only a *part* of what I want. Yes, I want the sex, but I want the relationship more. And am I actually, realistically considering a relationship with Maverick? My brain is fried. I can't handle all the inputs because only one thought is ruling right now: *Oh my God, Maverick actually wants to have sex with me?*

"Mav," I start, trying to remember what my objections were to this plan. Fucking seems perfectly fine right now. I've only been imagining it for months. "I don't...I'm not..."

"What?"

I force myself to pry the words from their burrows inside my throat. "I can't do that with you. I...I'm not like that. I don't have meaningless sex."

His laughter is incredulous. "You don't think it would mean something?"

"How could it, when by the time we get back to Bayshore you'll be on to the next girl?"

Something dark slides over Maverick's face, and he releases me, nodding. "Okay." He rubs his face, backing away from me. He jabs his thumb against the Down button of the elevator again. "Got it."

Now that he's standing over there, cold air whooshes around me, reminding me of how much I need his warmth. Even though it's a warm summer night, I need Maverick.

"Do you, though?"

"Yeah. It couldn't possibly mean anything. Because it's with me. Got it."

"That's not what I'm saying." Emotion cinches my throat. Holy shit. Wasn't expecting to get so worked up about the possibility of sleeping with Maverick becoming a reality, but here we are. "You say you don't want me to get hurt? Well there's only one man here at this hotel, in this entire fucking country, who could hurt me. You. And if we take this any further? I'm going to get hurt. Everyone knows it, Mav. You don't date." I mark the words with exaggerated air quotes. "So if we do anything, and I mean *anything* at all, I'm going to end up like all those other girls in your history. Ghosted. Forgotten. Just one more pussy on your eternal scroll of conquests."

I'm in love with you. They're the words I cannot say. Because if I do, I will start crying.

And if there's one thing our first-ever dispute doesn't need, it's my tears.

The elevator door slides open for a second time, waiting for us to enter. Maverick's jaw works back and forth as his stare bores through me. He looks neutral, but I can see right through it. He's fucking seething. But I don't regret what I said. Because he's been proving his inability to commit for the past five years.

"Glad you think so highly of me," he spits. "Thought maybe two decades meant something, but I guess I was fucking wrong."

Maverick spins on his heel and storms into the elevator car, leaving me in a stunned silence. I watch him until the doors slide shut, and then I wait until I recover my ability to move. Except I don't push the button again.

Instead, I go to the farthest reach of the rooftop patio. Away from the beer and the cameras and Davie and conversation. I need to sit and stare at the city for a while. See if the tangle of humanity might help me unravel my own knots.

Losing Maverick is my biggest fear, but I might have been the one to ruin things.

CHAPTER FIFTEEN

MAVERICK

The next morning, I sleep through my alarm. It goes off so many times that a pillow is launched against my head.

"Turn it off!" Scarlett groans.

I grunt, groping blindingly for the phone. I can't open my eyes yet. My mouth is dry as sandpaper, and I've got a sunflower of headaches—one big main headache with side shoots, all blossoming with their own headaches.

I'm not going to say that I got depressed and drank all my sadness away last night, but...

Well, yes. I did exactly that.

Not the brightest idea, but I'm not what you'd call proficient at dealing with the storm of emotions that ruined my fucking day yesterday. Jealousy? Possessiveness? Stormy emotions were why I stopped dabbling in relationships in the first place, but apparently I fell into a sexless relationship with Scarlett somewhere along the way. She's my girlfriend without benefits, which is the actual worst fucking arrangement on the planet, in case anyone was considering trying it.

Except now that I'm trying to add sex into the mix, she ran like the guinea pig I was supposed to see her as.

I'm so confused. Nothing makes sense. And she's five feet away from me, probably bent over with those off-limits ass cheeks just waiting to wink at me.

Great.

I haul myself to sitting and finally turn off the alarm. I spend a long time sitting there, gathering my willpower to stand up, trying to remember the details from the end of the night. After excusing myself from Scarlett so I didn't say shit I regretted, I came to the room, realized I needed to be literally anywhere else, and then went straight to the bar.

But there was one good thing in drinking away my sorrows.

I got to know the bartender, as well as one of the other food truck participants. Turns out, I befriended Uncle Lobster himself. He's a flat-billed ballcap-wearing, half shaved–half long-haired punk with facial tattoos and gauged earrings who goes by Kru. By the end of the night, I had my arm slung around his shoulders crooning "True Kruuuu." Curiously enough, he is not a lobster in disguise, but he *is* an uncle. The name came from the fact that his youngest niece always called him Uncle Lobster due to the sheer amount of lobster bisque he'd bring to family gatherings.

That's enough for me to call him a best friend already.

Something hard hits my low back. I twist to find a water bottle lying behind me. Scarlett wordlessly disappears from the room.

"Thanks," I croak. If I were even slightly less hung over, I'd be able to register the sheer amount of tension between us. But right now, I don't care. I'm pissed and hurt and hungover. Worst combo ever.

Our challenge assignment is at eleven downstairs. I have two hours to get functional. I start with some ibuprofen and a cold shower, cursing myself every second of the way for drinking those last shots of rum. Why does it always seem like a good idea at the time? They need to start serving the shot glasses with a sticker that says "THIS IS NOT A GOOD IDEA, DRUNK ASS."

By the time I'm dressed and I've chugged that first bottle of water and refilled it twice, Scarlett and I still haven't exchanged a word. But I'm not going to be the first to budge.

She's the one who told me what she really thinks about me. Made it more than clear that I'm not capable of protecting her. Not worth going farther with, because I'm such an uncontrollable dickhead or whatever she didn't say but was absolutely thinking.

Waves of hurt crash over me again, and I fight them back as hard as I can. I need to be focused today. I can't be distracted by this bullshit. This is exactly why I don't do relationships, yet somehow my closest, most important friendship still got fucked up.

It's 10:55 when I'm finally feeling like sewn-together crap. Functional, at least. Definitely featured in the discount bin but will probably fall apart on the first use.

"You ready?" I ask as I double check for the important things: phone, room key, the black-billed ballcap I wear when I cook. I pull the hat low on my head and avoid eye contact, since I still have no fucking idea how to feel about the nosedive our friendship took last night. I didn't just put myself out there with her. She watched me take that leap, watched me reach for her, and then let me fall on my f ace.

I should have known that was going to happen. Fuck, I *did* know at one point that I needed to avoid crossing that line. Somewhere between all the boners and Honeycrisp slips, I forgot.

And now look at us.

"Mm-hm." Scarlett is apparently also feeling just as weird. She's got on black shorts and a loose black tank top over a black sports bra. Every time a tiny breeze flutters by, it flutters up and allows a tantalizing glimpse of her bra. I would know, because she's worn this shirt before, and I love it.

Except today I don't even have the heart to look forward to it.

We ride down the elevator in silence on opposite sides of the car. At least we're in agreement that this is fucking awkward and we should just fester in it until it kills us. Isn't this exactly why people avoid this shit? I guess it's my fault, since I was the one who got possessive and tried to throw Davie off her tail. I pull the ballcap lower, my stomach churning again but for different reasons altogether this time.

The doors slide open, and Scarlett walks out first. I follow her, careful not to look too hard at her lest I notice her ass or any other part of her that will remind me of what I cannot have. Because she does not want me.

Bennett and Hartley are in the sprawling conference room, which is already decked out with cameramen, interview pods for all those fun solo camera confessionals, and snacks. We run through the assignment once—the menu feature must involve chutney—and then three more times for additional angles and reaction shots.

And once we're released on the world with the clock ticking and Keith trailing behind us, it's go time. Scarlett and I head to the garage where the trucks spent the night. I'm trying to focus on what I plan to cook, but all I can think about is the pulsing ache in my chest.

Why do I feel like Scarlett and I broke up?

"So," Scarlett ventures once we're situated in the seats and I'm navigating out of the garage, "what are you thinking of making?"

I clench my teeth. I don't even want to hear her voice, because it makes me soften, and I need to be angry at her. "I don't know. Something with chutney."

She snorts. "Coulda guessed that."

"Got any ideas?"

"You're the chef, not me."

"Then what exactly are you?" Uh oh. The snark is approaching terminal velocity. This isn't going to be a good day for us. We should probably just not speak.

Her mouth forms a thin line, and she crosses her arms. "Just trying to help out a friend."

I clamp my mouth shut before this escalates into a category 10 spat. When I come to the first intersection, I realize I have no idea where I'm going. "Did you put in the address?"

"I don't have one," she says.

"Jesus. They sent it to everyone." I fumble with my phone, but she snatches it out of my hand.

"Let me do it. You drive."

I grumble to myself as I pull off to the side and flick on the hazard lights. First she puts in the challenge location, but then two blocks later I remember we need to go to the store first. After pulling over for a second time, we scout the nearest wholesale food distributor, and I remind myself to get my damn head in the game.

The rest of the morning and early afternoon goes the same way. I'm two steps behind every decision that needs to be made, and every action is wrapped in sludge and fog that I just cannot shake. I can't tell if it's the hangover, or the wham-bam heartbreak, or the fact that this is the first time Scarlett and I have been upset with each other.

I get to Lower Wacker Drive just in time to get the last spot in the line-up of trucks. We're all butted up together today, instead of sprawled out like we were in Cleveland. The windows open toward the sidewalk, which backs up against a thirty-story office building, and the plan is to be serving from one o'clock to two, for a quick lunch service. Bennett promised us this would be more than enough time to make our money and sell out, because Chicagoans are used to food trucks lining their streets, and the five of us won't even make a dent in their appetites.

It was that warning specifically that prompted me to buy four times as much food as last time, just in case. And with the menu I have planned—an Indian-Mexican fusion burrito that might be either the best or worst thing I've ever conceived of—I'm gunning to sell out.

Once we're set up, I give Scarlett some prep tasks while I start making a mango chutney. She stops chopping cilantro after a while and shouts, "Ah ha!"

I glance back at her but say nothing.

"I know the name." She abandons the chopping and heads for the menu board. She wipes it clean from the Cleveland dinner and then starts scrawling. When she's done, it reads: *Mexi Mango Wild!*

I nod. It'll do.

We continue prepping in silence until I realize that I need music to drown out my thoughts. I pair the Bluetooth speaker, turn on the death metal music that soothes my nerves, and we work.

It isn't long before it's time to open. I've barely had time to let the mango chutney cool after I cook it before Scarlett pushes open the serving window.

A sea of people awaits on the other side. The previously sparsely-populated sidewalk is now crammed with people. Bennett set up railings to help guide people into lines, but the line for each food truck has spilled far beyond the preset confines. My stomach tangles into a nervous jumble, and I turn to the flat-top grill, trying to do some quick calculations.

"Mav..." Scarlett begins.

"I got it," I snap. "Just take orders." I toss an entire pan of backup chopped ribeye onto the grill so it can start cooking while I begin putting together burritos. Scarlett begins greeting each customer, but only I can hear the forced brightness in her voice, the waver that betrays the tensions pulling at us, tighter every second.

The orders are rolling in, and I can't keep up with them. Beyond that, every damn order is coming with restrictions: half onion on one, extra chutney on another, one of them is hold everything but double the steak, sub ketchup for chutney. It's a fucking mess, and by the time I make it through the first batch of orders, my ribeye is scorched on the grill.

"Fuck fuck fuck." I hop away from the prep station to try to salvage the meat. I scoop everything into a pan and try to assess the situation, but my heart is racing a mile a minute and all I can think about is the curling line of people outside. *Please, God, make this end.*

But there might not be a line ever again if this is our last event. If I've fucked this up because Scarlett and I had a fight and I can't get my shit together.

This, right here, is proof that I'm not fit for the long haul with someone. What might happen if I actually committed to her? I'd lose my fucking mind. I wouldn't be able to go a day without worrying that she'd leave me. If I'm this much of a possessive jerk after quietly imagining fucking her for a month, then what would happen if we actually started fucking?

Because here's the problem. She's mine, but in my head only. I can't lay claim to her. I can't give her what she wants. She wants a signed fucking contract of marriage, and I can't think past next week.

She's right. I'd only end up hurting her, even though I don't want to.

So now I just have to keep swallowing this bitter pill until the day I die, I guess. Like a prescription from the doctor. I'm going to stew on the fact that I laid all my cards on the table and she pushed them back toward me.

I'm able to salvage only some of the rib-eye chunks, but supplies are running out and the line isn't any shorter. I'm trying to keep an eye on customers as they wander away from the truck and eat. One guy throws the burrito in the trash, which makes my gut twist. Anxiety level 1000 activated.

We're done. We'll be the first truck to be eliminated. The chutney didn't even have time to cool. Who were you fucking trying to kid?

"Sure, sure, just give us a minute or two…" Scarlett is saying to a customer with a bright smile. When she turns to me, the smile is replaced with a severe look. "I need a redo, right now. She's allergic to onions and her burrito had double."

"Fuck." My head is spinning. I scramble to remake a burrito, but I'm braindead and on autopilot, so I add onions again. This day needs to end. And now, I don't care if it ends with us being eliminated—I just want off this truck and away from these burritos.

"No onion," Scarlett hisses.

"I fucking know." I toss the whole thing into the trash and start from scratch. This time, I get it right. Scarlett wraps it for me while I move on to other orders.

The eternal hour of the lunch session drags on like this. Constant mistakes. Unhappy customers. More complaints than wind in the Windy City. By the time two o'clock rolls around, I pull the window shut myself, even though there are still easily fifteen people in line.

"We're fucking done," I snap.

"Yeah, no shit. You don't even want to serve them?"

"Serve them what? This bullshit burrito?" Outside, there are some shouts, a few people clapping the side of the truck to say "I want a Mexi Mango!" I'm not consoled. I shove the unused tortillas away from me. "It doesn't matter. We're done after this challenge. There's no way in hell we're gonna make it through to the next round."

"Well maybe if you'd stopped sulking for thirty seconds," she bites back.

"I'm not fucking sulking. I'm pissed. There's a difference."

"Is there? All I can tell is that you're being insufferable."

Anger zips through me, hot and wily. I slam the prep table cover open and try to focus on clean-up, but I can't actually see anything in front of me.

"There we go. More low blows. You've got a lot of those coming these days. Why didn't you tell me before we started this that you actually think I'm a piece of shit?"

She lets out a sharp laugh. "A piece of shit? Maverick, I think *the world* of you. Except your head is so far up your ass you can't even tell."

I grab the griddle spatula and turn angrily toward the grill. "You clean the prep station. I got the grill."

"Fine," she says.

"Fine," I retort. Our bickering has released a tiny fraction of the tension, but I need more release than that. The scraping of my spatula over the grill is the only noise for a few moments as we focus on our stations. My head is full of so much noise I don't even notice when she's talking to me.

"Maverick? Now you're ignoring me?"

"What?" I snap.

"I said why can't we just talk about this like adults?"

"What do you want to talk about?" I turn, exasperated. The cutting board of the prep station is lined with all the small pans that normally sit inside of it: the chutney, the diced onions, sour cream, and more. Scarlett has a cleaning rag in one hand and a huge squeeze bottle of ketchup in the other.

"Oh, I don't know...the enormous elephant you let loose in the room?" she says.

"I didn't let loose an elephant—you did."

She sighs exasperatedly and slams the ketchup bottle against the edge of the cutting board. She says something, but I don't hear it, because the cap of the bottle goes flying off. Ketchup sprays everywhere: into the prep station, all over the cutting board, into the diced onions.

All over her. All over me.

Her eyes go wide, and we stare at each other for a moment. And the only thing I can think to do next is get her back.

I scoop up a handful of my homemade chutney and fling it at her. Her eyes go wider, but there's something else in her gaze. Amusement, maybe. Hurling the chutney at her was therapeutic—I can't even lie. Some of the accumulated tension trickles out.

"Seriously?" she asks and then flings more ketchup at me.

Now it's on. Bona fide food fight. We scramble to raid the prep station, laughter leaking out of me as well as my frustration. She elbows me as she dives for the mustard. I manage to shove a handful of diced onions down her tank top, which elicits a round of giggles.

Scarlett squeals as we fumble with the pan of diced tomatoes. Half of them go flying in the air. I shove rice in her mouth as she smashes tomatoes into my cheek. I grunt, spinning her in one deft movement so that she's pinned to the side of the countertop.

I grab her wrists, pinning them to her sides. We're staring at each other, chests heaving. Her hair is wild and dotted with cilantro and diced onion. But more than that, I see the rawness in her gaze. The question marks dancing there. Her green eyes dance across my face.

I know the question she's asking me. I thought I knew the answer. But after last night, I'm not going there.

Scarlett's gaze drags down to my lips.

"You happy?" I ask.

She shakes her head. And when her gaze meets mine again, I know exactly what she wants. What she's asking for.

But this time, instead of saying a damn word, she closes the distance between us. Her lips land on mine, needy, hungry. And I have to respond. I'm built to respond to this; the tightly wound desire that's spilling out of her is only awakening my *fuck-it-all* instinct. As in, fuck all the consequences. I do not care.

Because there is one thing I need, and it's Scarlett.

If her first kiss is seeking, the second one is confident. I'm letting her lead the way, because now I have no fucking clue what's going on, but yes, I'm here for the ride. I squeeze her wrists as she deepens the kiss. My cock is hard as a rock already. She can probably feel it, given that it's pressed to her hip.

When she whimpers, all bets are off. I hoist her onto the cutting board countertop, right along with the spilled onions and chutney slop and every other remnant that we should be cleaning up but aren't. One of the prep pans goes clattering to the floor. I cup her face in my hands, and this time, I press my tongue in to find hers.

She's willing. Pliable. She's fucking desperate for this. I can taste it in her kiss, beyond the smear of chutney—which tastes great, by the way—and the lingering taste of the rice I shoved into her mouth. She squeezes her knees around me, bringing me closer to her. I inhale sharply after we break the kiss.

"What the fuck are you doing, Lettie?" My hands drift to her hips, fingertips pressing past waistline of her shorts. "I thought you didn't want this." I drag my fingers over the exposed skin at the small of her back and down lower, dancing over the top of her ass cheeks. Her breath catches and she arches against me.

"I never said that," she says, her voice thick with lust. I've never heard it from her before, and my horniness skyrockets to level eight billion. Like I'll ever be able to erase *that* voice from my memory now. All future fantasies are stained. Forever. *Thanks, Scarlett.*

"I want this so fucking much, Mav, I can't even explain." She grips the sides of her head, squeezing her eyes shut. "I've wanted this for so long. Longer than I can even—" She stops abruptly, and I can tell she's about to get emotional. Fuck. She rolls her lips together and runs her palms over my shoulders.

"Then how can you say it wouldn't mean anything?" I'm watching her so intensely I wouldn't be surprised if she burst into flames. My attention is like a magnifying glass and there is a *lot* of heat being funneled through to her right now.

"That's not what I meant," she whispers. "I know it would mean something. But for how long? That's what you don't get, Mav." Her throat bobs, and she hides her eyes with her hands.

"It would always mean something, babe." I brush my lips over her chin. She sniffs hard, and when she drops her hands her eyes are watering and she's shaking her head.

"Maverick, I'm in love with you. Okay? That's why I can't just...*fuck you.*" She draws a shaky breath.

For a moment, the words don't hit me. They linger pleasantly in the air, like clouds drifting past a sunset. But once they hit me, oh God, those clouds turn into a tornado. But it's not a bad feeling. No. Instead, it feels like someone coming in and making sense of the tangle of nerves inside me. Like I hired an organizational consultant, and she's come in and filed away all my feelings and emotions into their correct spots.

Things make so much more sense now.

Because I'm in love with Scarlett too.

The truth trickles through me, illuminating the dark parts of me. The jealousy, the anger, the need for her to be with me, to go on this adventure with me. I've been in love with her longer than I can even articulate. And recognizing it allows it to blossom and swell and make everything else in my life seem right.

I didn't want a relationship, but we've been in one all along, without even fucking realizing it.

"I didn't want to ruin our friendship," she goes on shakily, "by making things weird. But I can't avoid making things weird, because I'm in love with you. But I can't have sex with you, because it would ruin our friendship. So I'm just waiting for there to be some loophole I'm unaware of that means I can be in love with you and still have everything be okay."

"Babe," I whisper, my voice sticking to my throat. I squeeze my arms around her waist, eliminating the last bits of space between us. "We can do all of those things. It'll be okay."

Her body shakes with a sob. "Maverick, I can't do friends with benefits. I can't stand the thought of you being with anyone else once we end the show. I—"

"I can't stand that either, as I've demonstrated," I say, guiding her chin up until her watery gaze meets mine. "So what if the loophole is you become my girlfriend?"

She rolls her lips inward. I'm not going to lie, my heart is pounding. I didn't see *asking Scarlett to be my girlfriend* on today's to-do list, but I'm not upset about it. It makes sense. It feels *good*. And honestly, this is the missing piece to the giant puzzle of my life.

I'm in love with Scarlett, and I need to fucking claim it.

"Are you..." she begins.

"Yes, I'm serious. Babe, let's be real. You already fucking are my girlfriend. And you have been for a long time."

I cup her face again as disbelieving laughter rolls out of her.

"And just so your loophole knows? I'm in love with you too." I guide her lips to mine. This time, we kiss so deeply, so passionately, that she's crying through the kiss but urging it just as much. Our kisses are tinged with salt and ketchup, which is definitely a more positive combo than I would have expected. I shift against her so that my cock slides right between her legs. She squeezes her leg around me and bucks. Oh Lord. She's not just desperate for it. She's dying for it.

And I'm going to give it to her as much as I possibly can.

Fuck whatever it was we were fighting about. Fuck the competition. Fuck everything. Because it's time to fuck Scarlett.

"Ohh my God," she moans when the kiss breaks. She presses her forehead to mine. "We need to go back to the hotel room."

"Do we?" She's on board. *Finally.*

"Yes. And guess what I just realized?" She looks up at me, the familiar sparkle returning to her eye. "All of that was just recorded for the show."

"Then we need to get out of here, because if you move like that against me one more time, I can't promise I won't take you right here." She shivers in my grip as I drag my teeth along her jawline.

She sighs. "Maverick..."

"Let's go *now* and clean up *later*," I tell her.

I've never seen a prettier grin blossom on her face.

CHAPTER SIXTEEN

My body becomes a puddle in the copilot's seat as Maverick tries to get back to the hotel through the midday traffic and the fact that we keep getting lost on Wacker Drive. Once we're heading into the underground bowels of the city for a second time, he lets out a frustrated groan.

"Jesus Christ, how did we come back here?"

"You can't see past the ketchup on your face," I tell him, though it might be more due to the fact that the GPS signal disappears every time we descend into the labyrinth. All of the tension that followed us for the entire morning and afternoon is gone. Those kisses—not to mention a well-timed declaration of love—cured everything. And now, I'm curious to see how much else will be cured once we take things further.

Because yes. I need this man, and we're going to make love. It's not fucking. It's making love.

I am in love with Maverick, and I said it out loud, and *oh my god, is he really my boyfriend now?*

My pussy is *throbbing*, and I'm not sure I can wait until we get back to the hotel room. I need him now. I'm not going to think about the future or potential heartbreak. I'm going to accept that he loves me enough, that this is meaningful, and that we will end up exactly where we should.

Besides, now that these kisses are in the mix, it was only a matter of time before I cast aside all my morals and qualms and gave in to whatever this man wanted.

Using both of our GPSs and extra vigilance, we somehow emerge from the underground labyrinth of Lower Wacker and back up to sunlight and the right roads. The food truck rumbles into the garage, where all the other trucks are already parked. We'll get the results tomorrow. I have no idea what to expect. Today's service was the complete opposite of yesterday's, but all we can do is wait.

No, scratch that.

Make love, wait, and make love some more.

Maverick locks up, and then he strides toward me, ketchup-stained and handsome. He scoops my hand into his and brings my knuckles to his lips.

"What do you say we shower first?"

"Yeah. You can go first, if you want." I nudge him. "You got the worst of the ketchup, after all."

"No, we're showering *together*." His heated look sends desire barreling through me. I'm so excited that I trip. He catches me, laughing, his icy blues glittering.

"Don't get too excited," he warns, his voice gritty. "After all, it's just shower sex. It doesn't count until I get you laid out on the bed."

Pinpricks erupt all over my body. They erupt on my organs, too, because *that's* how excited I am. "I wasn't aware there were varying levels of consummation."

"Mmhmm." He slings his arm over my shoulders like he always has. But now, I recognize the possession in his grip. He's always pulled me tighter to him when others are around. My chest tightens as some more of the pieces begin to click together. How long has he been showing me that I'm his without saying it?

"And we're going to explore every last level there is," he adds, his breath hot in my ear.

We bolt through the hotel lobby, hand in hand. Once the elevator doors close, he pins me to the mirrored wall, kissing me so hard, so deep, that I moan, and I don't even care. I've never been kissed like this. Not even once. It's the type of passion that makes me willing to throw everything to the side. I'd fuck him in public if he asked me to, that's how convincing these kisses are.

When the doors open, he doesn't break the kiss immediately. Only when someone clears their throat does Maverick pull away, looking love-drunk and kiss-bitten. *By me.*

Unknown hotel patrons are waiting to step in. Maverick offers a smile. I offer a meek "Sorry" as we scoot by. When I look over my shoulder, I notice the mirror is imprinted with the smear of his palms.

Our passion is marking the hotel, now, too.

He leads me by the hand to the room, swipes us in, and immediately tears his shirt off. He looks over his shoulder at me, his gaze dropping to my chest.

"Come on."

"I'm coming." I feel a blush creeping to my cheek. I tear off my tank top first but pause before I release the twins. "Is this weird?"

His grin is equal parts goofy and sexy. "Yes. But also no. So like, half weird."

We both laugh, which takes the edge off the half-weirdness. We've never intentionally crossed this line before today. Well, yesterday. So yes, it's destined to be weird. But I've known this person for almost twenty years. If I can share this with relative strangers who are now my exes, I can share it with the one man who knows me better than they ever could.

Besides, the flat, muscular planes of his chest help convince me to keep going. I tear off my sports bra and toss it aside. Something goes flying and bounces off his arm, but he doesn't even notice. Diced onion. He wets his bottom lip, gaze stuck on my tits.

"Damn, Lettie."

"They're just boobs."

His half-cocked smile makes moisture surge in my panties. "But they're the best boobs."

"Stop it." His words warm me, even though deep down, I'm sure he's just saying it because we're inches away from boning. "Don't forget, your laptop password is 'ilovehugetitties.'"

"As soon as we get home, I'm changing it." He backs up toward the bathroom, unbuttoning his pants as he goes. When he crosses the threshold of the doorway, they drop to his ankles. His black boxer briefs are tented wonderfully. My mouth parts. "New password is 'ilovelettietitties.'"

I laugh, because thank God—even though we're broaching this strange, new reality, it's still us. The same *us* that we've always been.

"You ready for this, babe?" His gaze sizzles on me, something serious floating in the air between us as he adjusts himself. When his hand falls away, his cock is poking out past the waistband of his underwear. Bulging, veiny head. Shiny, somehow slick. My gaze is glued to his wonderful, erotic, absolutely-better-than-imagined appendage.

"Because once we start…I can't promise I'm gonna go easy on you," he warns.

And then he pushes his boxer briefs down, allowing his cock to spring free. It bobs heavily in the air between us. It's framed by trimmed, black hair. Heavenly thick, long but not fit for a circus. And you know what?

It isn't weird. It just feels right. And I need him immediately.

I swallow hard, floating toward him without even making the decision to walk.

He catches me, bringing me hard against him. My boobs smash against his solid chest. I wrap my arms around his neck, and he fumbles with my pants as our lips crash together in a sloppy, desperate kiss. Our teeth are gnashing, tongues swirling. We're kissing like this is the end of the world and we're about to part ways on some epic voyage. Except no, there's no epic voyage awaiting us, unless you count the reality cooking competition we may or may not be continuing in. This is simply the natural next step to acknowledging months—years?—of repressed attraction. It's bubbling out of me, like an active volcanic eruption, and there's no way to tell how long this rumble will last or how many towns will get scorched in the p rocess.

At this point, I don't even care.

He pushes my shorts down, along with my undies. I'm buck naked, and he's hoisting me against him. A loud moan escapes me once he's got me in his arms, his fingertips digging into my ass cheeks, my pussy pressed against the hard steel of his cock. That went from teasing to fatally sexy in ten seconds flat.

He backs me up against the tiled wall, which is cool and smooth against my back. He buries his face in my chest, lips skimming my collarbone, his cock throbbing hot and dangerous against the lips of my pussy.

"I need to put you down," he says, "and get a condom. But I can't."

I arch my back, urging more, urging *anything*. "Please, Mav."

He grunts, snagging my lips in another air-stealing kiss. And then he lowers me gently to my feet and storms out of the bathroom. Chest heaving, I try to remember what else we were doing before his penis came out to play. Was it a shower? Oh yeah. I stumble toward the shower, everything feeling new and strange, like I'm waking up to the world after a thousand-year rest. I can barely remember how to work a shower. When the water shoots out from the showerhead, it surprises me. Maverick's kisses aren't just passionate and deep; they're memory-erasing and debilitating.

Give me more.

Soft kisses up my spine tell me that Mav is back. I inhale sharply and turn. He's got the wrapper in his hand, and with his other hand, he guides my palm to his cock. I wrap my hand around his girth and gasp. He's big—there's no doubt about that. Possibly the largest I've ever seen in my life, including that one weird porno I saw when I was twenty.

"I've had so many fantasies about you, Lettie," he growls, scraping his teeth along my collarbone. "Of fucking you in the food truck. Of convincing you to put that red lipstick on again and wrap your lips around my cock."

His naughty words thrill through me, turning my nipples into stiff peaks. He drags his thumb over my swollen lips, just grazing my clit. I cry out and crumple from the unexpected jolt of pleasure. I always figured he'd be able to make me come just from dragging his knuckles against me someday. I just didn't realize it would be this close to happening in a hotel room in Chicago.

"I've had fantasies of fucking you in the shower, too. So many fucking shower fantasies." His voice scrapes through me as he dips down and takes a nipple between his teeth. "But this is already a hundred times better, and we haven't even hit the water yet." His tongue flicks against the hard point like a serpent, his hand covering my mound as he allows his middle finger to dip into the dampness between my legs.

This time, he captures my clit between the knuckles of his index and middle fingers and squeezes. I moan loudly, indecently, as if my fantasies are coming to life because they fucking *are*. He slips one finger inside of me, his palm creating hot friction with my clit just as he takes my other nipple between his teeth and—*BOOM*.

Fireworks.

Heat and thunder.

Hello, orgasm.

My knees buckle, and I crumple again, my fingernails digging into the ridge of his shoulders. This time he catches me. The smirk on his face is all-knowing, so fucking smug and satisfied. He made me come during the warm-up, while he was just considering putting the condom on. It's inglorious, at best, betraying how unsatisfied and hard up I've been, at worst.

Maverick presses a soft kiss to my lips, at odds with the heat and need pulsing through me. "Number one."

"We can't count that one," I protest weakly. "That was just the bilge pump."

He laughs. "Just letting off the accumulated exhaust, huh?" When he gathers me against him again and I'm back on my feet, he pins me with a tender look. I've never seen that from him before, and my gut tells me it's not something any of his former gal pals have glimpsed either.

He looks at me like he's serving his heart up on a platter. Like we're about to go someplace that we can never recover from. Someplace we might never want to recover from.

"God, look at you," he murmurs, his gaze searching my face, and then down between our bodies. "I'm not dreaming, right?"

"That bilge pump orgasm was very real, so I'm thinking no, we're not dreaming."

He grins, tears open the condom, slides it onto his cock and then backs me up into the shower. Warm water hits my shoulder as he hoists me against the wall. And this time, when his cock slides into place, his eyes go hooded.

"Do you want me to go slow, babe?" He presses a lazy kiss to my shoulder.

"No," I say. Because I need him to fuck me as hard as he can. To make up for the days and weeks and months that I've been needing it without getting it from him.

He tugs at my bottom lip with his teeth as he eases himself inside. A groan rasps past his lips as he sinks inside. I'm moaning like an animal soon enough too. He slides into me, thick and hot and confident, filling me in a way I've never been filled before.

Each new inch brings a body buzz and sparkles at the edge of my vision. I can't tell if I'm tripping or just ascending to Heaven. Maybe this is what it feels like to make love with someone you're truly head over heels with. Maybe I was never in love with Tom. Maverick makes me question everything I thought I knew. I just know that it's never felt like *this* with anyone else.

He clenches his teeth as he sinks all the way into me. I arch against him, inviting more, my head swirling. My nipples are pebbles, scraping against his chest as I wriggle and writhe against him.

"Fuucck, Scarlett." His voice is jagged. Completely bathed in passion. I am so close to orgasm already, which comes as *no* surprise to me. After all, I am the girl who orgasmed while imagining him chopping carrots. He cups my breast, his breathing labored as he eases out of me and then pushes back in. He does it again, pinching at my nipple. I squeak in response. When he crashes into me a third time, much more forcefully than before, my entire body quakes.

"Ohhhhhhhly fuck!" I cry out. Everything is going taut inside me. My thighs turn into a vice around him, and my head falls back against the tiled shower. Maverick dips and kisses along my neck.

"Yesss," he hisses, pumping himself in and out of me. He hoists me again, the base of his cock pressed against my aching clit. But he's not just fucking me. He's grinding, rolling, rocking against me. It's like he's trying to make it awesome for me in every possible way. There goes the possibility that sex with Maverick would be a letdown.

Another graceless noise escapes my throat. This time, I sound like a dying animal. I can't even help it. He's unlocked something in me that has apparently been dormant for my entire life. There's a cauldron in my core, and he's tossing in exotic ingredients, cranking up the heat, casting warlock spells.

"You feel so fucking good, Lettie," he growls. His lips brush mine as he talks. "Do you have any fucking idea how sexy you are?"

"Nooo," I moan.

"Then you have no idea how hard I'm trying not to come right now." His voice is strained, his pumping getting faster. My limbs are liquid fire, every cell of my body expectant, awaiting the orgasm. "How hard it is not to blow my load every time you make those noises."

In my head I say, *Oh, the noises that sound like a rhinoceros dying?* But since that's too many words for this state of mind, I just moan.

"Come with me, babe." His voice falters as he drills up into me, rolling in a slow circle. The move puts delicious yet fleeting pressure on my clit. "Give me number two." He does it a second time; my fingers curl into his shoulders. And when he does it a third time, the fireworks explode in my limbs and my vision goes black.

"Ohhhhh my...Maaaaav," I cry out. My pussy and thighs and belly and every soft part of me goes tense as my orgasm wreaks havoc on my body, pulsing and pummeling through me. I'm pretty sure I scream, if not in real life, then absolutely in my heart. Maverick's lips are buried in my chest and he's groaning, giving one last weak thrust.

We don't move for a while. Instead, I cling to him, chest heaving like I ran a marathon. He's buried inside me. His breath comes out in hot puffs on my collarbone. It isn't until he shifts that I remember the water. Warm and steady against my arm. God, we were supposed to be showering in here. How am I supposed to do that now?

Maverick slides himself out of me, and then slowly lowers me to my feet. It takes me a minute to stand. I sag against the wall and he catches me, a soft grin on his face.

"You got it?"

"No. You fucked the equilibrium out of me," I croak.

The heated gaze that licks over me while he rolls the condom off his dick is one that will live in my memory for eternity. He is so handsome it hurts. Familiar to me as the Mav I grew up with, but also this sex god I never counted on.

And even though it's crazy and hard to wrap my head around, for now I just want to bask in it.

CHAPTER SEVENTEEN

The next morning, I don't exercise.

Because I physically can't.

Turns out, Maverick has a medical condition called *cockus enormous.* What he affectionately referred to as rearranging my organs once we got to round two on the bed last night could probably be verified by a doctor. I'm pretty sure I need a chiropractor after all the pounding my pelvis took.

And I couldn't be happier about it.

Soft kisses trail up my spine. I grin, burrowing back into him. We spent the night interlocked somehow—me in his arms, or our ankles touching, the occasional arm thrown over each other—and waking up to this today sends yet another wave of bliss crashing through me.

This is perfect. It's so much better than I imagined it could be.

"Morning, babe." His gritty voice at my ear has me pressing my thighs together. How could I still be horny after the incredible orgasms he gave me yesterday? We're barely into day two, and we've already lost count.

"Morning," I whisper, wiggling my butt into his lap. He lets out a low hiss, his hot palm trailing over my hip and down the side of my leg.

And a moment later, I feel the hot steel of his cock pressed against my ass cheeks.

"I think I'm gonna have breakfast in bed." He kisses the hollow of my neck, and before I can ask what on earth he wants to eat so early in the morning, his hand slides around to my pussy. Ahhh. *Yes.* My legs part for him as his fingers slip between my folds. I gasp.

Because last night, we only focused on the pounding. There's still so much left to explore.

"What do you think?" He presses a kiss to my shoulder as he squeezes my clit gently. "I'm fucking starving."

My eyes flutter shut. "Mmhmm." Rendered speechless already, and I haven't even gotten out of bed.

Maverick throws the covers off us and eases me onto my back. When he gets into position between my legs, spreading them apart, I'm relieved that he didn't actually mean ordering room service at seven a.m. In the gauzy light of early morning, sunlight streaming in through the delicate white curtains, he looks somehow rough and raw. The stubble on his jaw, the bulk of his shoulders as he lowers himself between my legs. He's wide and powerful and attentive. I'm not sure there's ever been a sexier combination.

I press a hand to my forehead as he spreads my thighs even further apart.

"Why are you wincing?" he asks.

"Because you're just *staring* at my vagina."

He laughs, nuzzling the crease of my leg. "Well, it's fucking gorgeous."

"It's battered and bruised, after what you did to me yesterday," I tease.

"Are you sore?"

"Yes." I cover my face with both hands. "Is *this* weird?"

His laugh is guttural. "No. Absolutely not." He covers my clit with his lips, swiping his tongue across for good measure, and warmth fills my veins. My thighs open further, of their own volition this time. "This is what I've been fucking waiting for."

He nuzzles my pussy, pressing slow kisses around my clit. He's taking his time, being slow and thorough, which is just as hot—if not hotter—than our passionate, fiery, desperate grinding the night before.

"Mmmmm." I melt back into the bed. Yes. This is nice. This is the nicest thing that's ever happened in my life. "Have you seriously been waiting for this?"

"Oh, my God." He flattens his tongue over my clit, his ice-blue gaze pinning me to my spot. "You have no fucking idea."

I laugh weakly but trail off as he nicks his teeth against my needy nub.

"The other day, when I saw you bent over in the bathroom." He slurps at my pussy, and I arch my back, needing more. "I almost ate you out on the spot."

"I wish you would have." I pinch my eyes shut. It feels so strange yet so good to finally be admitting these things. "I've been dreaming about it for months."

He pauses, his brows drawing together. "Are you serious?"

I nod. God, he looks good down there, buried between my legs.

He grunts and returns to his work. He covers my mound with his lips and flicks his tongue back and forth over my clit. A low moan escapes me as I melt against him.

"Fuck, Lettie. We could have been doing this for months?" He slips a finger inside me, his tongue drawing circles. The fact that he's staring at me, intense as hell, only pushes me closer to the edge.

"I—I didn't know..." It's getting harder to talk. "I thought you..."

"Well, now you know." He eases a second finger inside of me, searing me with a devilish grin. "I've been dreaming about fucking you for too damn long. You're mine now, babe."

He buries his face between my legs again, lavishing my clit with all the slow, swirling attention that I've been missing for my entire life. I rock against his face, a maneuver I have *never* done before with Tom, or my other ex, Brayden, who I dated for six months but never had sex with. But with Maverick, it feels right. It feels good to let loose, to dive headfirst into this naughty, thrilling swirl.

He slides his hands underneath me, squeezing my ass cheeks. It keeps me pinned to his face as he eats me out, faster now. I'm moaning and grinding against his face, completely uninhibited now. I am fucking his face, and oh my god, it's wonderful.

He sucks at my clit again, and I lose it. My orgasm goes *POP*, and heat floods my limbs. I scream, locking my thighs around his head. He breaks the suction and plunges his tongue into my pussy, which is a soft and sexy thing I had not yet considered. I turn into a puddle of satisfaction and unyielding loyalty.

Because here's the truth. I'm in love with him. And now that he says I'm his?

I'm fucking his.

When Maverick pulls away, his mouth is glistening and he's grinning like he knows a secret. I know the secret too, now. The secret is that Maverick can eat pussy like a legend.

I try to speak and fail. I reach for him, but my arm falls limply to the bed.

He just smirks and pushes off the bed. He gives me a sloppy kiss on the lips—tainted with my own juices and everything—and then walks off to the bathroom with a massive tent in his boxer briefs.

Is this real life?

The water runs in the bathroom for a moment. When he comes back out, the bulge in his underwear has reduced slightly, but not completely. He rejoins me on the bed and scoops me into his arms.

"That was a wonderful breakfast," he says into the shell of my ear.

"You are too good," I say, swatting at him but missing.

His biceps bulge as he squeezes me against him. "No, you."

I laugh, and my eyes flutter shut. We lie like this for a long time, wrapped in a cocoon of arms and heat and a beguiling sense of perfection. Eventually, his alarm goes off, reminding us of the day ahead. As he reaches to shut it off, I remember my own phone. The fact that I have a life outside this bed. I wonder what's happening in that world.

I yawn, reaching for my phone, slowly trying to reconnect with anything that isn't Mav's head between my legs. As I swipe through screens, bits and pieces of what I left behind, pre-sex with Mav, comes trickling back to me.

Namely the fact that yet another day has gone by and my sister still hasn't written to me or updated me on the kids.

I open the message thread. I'm beginning to stalk it, but it never changes from the three unanswered texts I've sent over the past week.

SCARLETT: Hey, Flor! Miss you guys already. Hope all is well.

SCARLETT: Any pics or updates of the kids? Miss them so much.

SCARLETT: You guys doing okay? <3

I also initiated a video call two days ago, which she declined. At this point, I'm pretty sure she's not speaking to me.

My Maverick-induced high bumps down a few notches. I don't expect her to care about what I'm doing out here. I don't even expect her to ask how it's going out of a pretend display of caring. I *did* expect her to at least keep me in touch with Fifi and Louie.

I send a quick text to my mom:

SCARLETT: Hey, Mom. How you doing? We're in Chicago now. Just wondering if you've talked to Flor? Been trying to connect, she won't write back.

My mom was distantly intrigued by the competition when I told her I'd be leaving, about as interested as my boss as E. Lago, in fact. A sort of distant confusion mixed with slight disdain but needing to appear at least marginally supportive. So really, a disgruntled layer cake.

My mom is always awake this time of day so she writes back fast.

MOM: Just saw her last night, they're doing good.

On a scale of one to supportive, my mom is about a three. She prioritizes Florence and her grandkids, which I'm used to. Ever since Louisiana was born, my mother and sister have made their position clear: I don't have kids, so my life is not as important.

I check email and dick around on my phone for a little bit. Then I get another text.

FLOR: Sorry been super busy.

Her response tells me Mom probably reached out and told her I was asking about her. But her response is as good as not responding at all. No acknowledgement of my questions. No updates. No questions about the fact that I'm in the middle of a reality TV show.

I sigh and push the phone away. Maverick rolls toward me. "What's wrong?"

"Nothing."

"Come on." He nudges me. "I just bathed my face in your pussy juice. You can tell me."

A laugh rockets out of me. "God, Mav! When you put it like that…"

"So? Why are you sighing?"

"Flor finally wrote back. I've been texting for days. I even tried to video call her. I just wanted to know how they're doing. See some pictures of the kids. And she wrote just now: 'sorry, super busy.'"

Mav rests his chin on my biceps, his crystalline gaze searching my face. "Are you surprised?"

"No. Not at all. Just can't figure out why I'm still hurt by it."

"Because she's your sister, and that's a shitty way to treat your sister," Mav says.

"I'd give her the shirt off my back. I skip shifts at the restaurant so she can go take her boyfriend to court. I've literally handed her money, the keys to my car, food out of my own fridge. Yet I still feel like she's punishing me for daring to leave. Like she's judging me for making the wrong choice."

Mav shakes his head. "Babe, you're not doing anything wrong. If she's judging you, it's because she's unhappy with *her* choices. Not yours. She's unhappy. She wants you to be, too."

I heave a sigh. He's right.

"I just wish we could be *sisters* again." I pause, thinking a little deeper into it. "I wish she'd fucking leave their dad."

"It's not your mess to fix or figure out, babe." He presses a kiss to my forehead. "You gotta do you."

Maverick's words make the world feel right again. I hobble to the bathroom—both of us laughing about how hard it is for me to walk—and wash my face, brush my teeth, and start getting ready for the day. When I walk back into the bedroom, I notice the waste basket, filled with spent condoms.

The sign of an amazing evening.

Maverick pulls on a black tee with the logo of his favorite death metal band. He's got varied musical tastes, but death metal is one of his not-so-secret faves. With dark shorts, black tennis shoes, and his dark brown hair falling into his eyes, he's dark and intense and handsome and provocative all at the same time.

He's Mav.

He's *my* Mav.

He notices me smiling at him, which causes a goofy grin to break out on his face.

Soon, we're smiling together, hugging, rocking back and forth.

It feels like we've been doing it for years...I just hope this fantasy doesn't end when the competition does.

CHAPTER EIGHTEEN

MAVERICK

Later that day, the points are delivered in the elimination ceremony.

And this time, one of the food truck teams goes home.

But it's not us.

Somehow, we weren't the only team to royally fuck up. The Crusty Bastard served a dish that absolutely crumbled under the weight of their extra-juicy mint chutney. Turns out, their bread bowl was not designed to sustain a watery chutney, and so most patrons' meals ended up bursting through their bastard bowl and plummeting to the sidewalk.

Oops. Oh well. Better luck next time.

The producers give us an extra couple of days in Chicago, partially for footage, and partially as planned down time in the production schedule. They peg us to re-film a few shots on the inside of the truck—random reactions or cooking angles—which don't take much time at all and leave us with two full days of Chicago ahead of us.

And the first thing on my agenda? The surprise for Scarlett.

Each night before I go to bed—yes, even the night I was depressed and drunk—I've been researching and learning more about aerial silks. I didn't have a plan until last night, when I realized that Chicago is a hotspot for aerial silks gyms.

Scarlett can't just confess this secret passion once and then continue keeping it hidden in the shadows. I *need* to know everything about this part of her life. Even more now that I've learned a few new things about her, namely that she fucking loves having her pussy eaten, and she moves like she knows how to climb those silks. And I'm not going to miss a chance to see her Honeycrisp ass in action.

Once we're done filming our redo spots and we've had lunch at one of the Chicago-based food trucks right outside the hotel, I begin my surprise attack.

"Hey. I have an idea." I toss my napkin in the trashcan nearby. The sun beats down on my shoulders, warming me through my favorite black band shirt. Scarlett's just taking the last bite of her fried fish taco. She pulls a funny face as she chews, and we both burst into laughter.

"You wanna go bang some more?"

"No. Well, yes. But I have a different idea before that."

"Lay it on me."

"I can't tell you. You trust me?"

Her eyes sparkle as she cocks a hip. "Yeah, I suppose. As long as it doesn't involve the Lower Wacker labyrinth again."

I scoop her hand in mine, pressing her knuckles to my lips. We amble hand in hand to the garage to find my parked car. She's got her big black sunglasses on, along with a loose black tank top and super short black shorts. And somewhere between the taco truck and the inner-city garage I realize, from the outside alone, we look like we're made for each other.

But it's the same way on the inside too.

Why has it taken me so long to realize it?

We roll down the car windows and enjoy the boisterous city air while I follow the GPS instructions as closely as possible. By the time we're pulling up to an unassuming warehouse that simply says AIR on the other end of downtown, Scarlett looks suspicious.

"Mav…" she begins.

"Yes?" I snag a lucky street spot less than a block away, hardly able to keep myself from cackling evilly.

"Is this what I think it is?"

"That would depend on what you think it is."

Her throat bobs, her hand on the door handle as she looks out the back window at the building. When she looks at me again, her eyes are shimmering.

"Okay, it's what you think it is," I admit with a little laugh. I didn't think she'd get this emotional. She swipes at her eye quickly then leans across the car to wrap me in a hug.

"Thank you," she says. "Unless this is some sort of HVAC facility, in which case, no thank you."

I press a soft kiss to her forehead. I'm surprised by how easy it is to do it. How natural it feels. How much I want to keep kissing her, for as long as I possibly can. "Let's go in and find out."

We walk hand in hand again to the aerial silks gym. Her face lights up once we're inside and the gleaming floors and spacious practice rooms confirm that it is, in fact, not an HVAC company. There's time for her to drop in on the next class, which starts in a half hour. When she mentions how she doesn't have the right clothes for practice, I buy her the company's branded leggings and practice-friendly tank top on the spot. Problem solved.

"Only one request," I tell her as I pass the clothes off, after I've paid for her session. "I want to watch you practice."

Her cheeks flush, and she glances at the lady behind the desk. "Is that allowed...?"

"Not for the classes. But you can purchase a private practice room for after the class," the receptionist offers.

I slide my credit card back across the desk. "Add that on for me."

The class is an hour long, which I spend roaming the front room, chatting with the receptionist, and jotting down menu ideas that occur to me every time my mind wanders. When the big doors to the gym open, red-faced and smiling students file out. There are women of all ages and body shapes here. Behind them, in the high-ceilinged practice gym, silky strips dangle from reinforced bars. This repurposed warehouse has been turned into a performance art wonderland. Dozens of aerial silk rigs dangle from the ceiling, and an entire wall is dedicated to props for other performance arts: hula hoops, staffs, boomerangs and more. There's a stage, curtains pulled back, along one side of the room, where two black silks dangle from above.

Scarlett bounds up to me, her face flushed, sweat glistening on her chest. She looks like she's never been happier to see me in her entire life. She throws her arm around me, wrapping me in a damp hug.

"How was class?"

"It was *amazing*!" She plants a big kiss on my lips. And then another. "Oh my *god*, I've been missing practice." The other women have filed back to their belongings in cubbies on the other side of the foyer, but we're parked in the doorway. "It was like no time had passed at all. And I haven't been to the Cleveland gym in over a month!"

My cheeks hurt from how hard I'm smiling, watching her gush like this.

"They had me demonstrate some moves," Scarlett adds in a quieter voice, wrapping my hand in both of hers as she leads me into the gym. The instructor is lingering near the front of the room, putting away fitness blocks. "The teacher asked me if I'd ever considered doing the training to become an instructor! I was just...so honored. My teachers in Cleveland hinted at the same thing but, I dunno, maybe I'm ready?"

"Damn, Lettie. That sounds amazing." I squeeze her hand as we come up to the teacher, a short, curvy woman in the same branded leggings that I just bought for Lettie. She's beaming at us as she approaches, her shiny blonde hair in a bun at the back of her head. Scarlett joins her, and it's not hard to imagine her in a similar position: cleaning up after a class, instructing eager women how to lift themselves up into the air via strips of fabric.

"This is Maverick," Scarlett says, presenting me to the instructor. "And this is the teacher, Dawn."

"Nice to meet you." I offer my hand, and Dawn grips it much harder than expected. Probably stems from the fact that she can climb silk.

"I'm so happy you get to witness Scarlett's practice! She's such a natural."

"Ohhh, now, I don't know about that," Scarlett says, batting away the compliment. But I can see how much it warms her. How much it's making her day, her week, her *life*.

"She's been practicing in secret for years," I say, shoving my hands into my pockets. "And I am so ready to see this."

"What do you think about doing a part of that routine we were talking about earlier?" Dawn asks Scarlett. "I can turn on the sound system and pump the music through, as long as you have the song."

Scarlett's eyes go wide. "You mean, like, do my show?"

Dawn grins. "Of course. And you can use the main stage."

"Well, you—I was just thinking about showing him some of the basics," Scarlett says. "I mean—we don't need—I can use one of the little—"

"Let's do it on the stage." I squeeze her elbow. I love how nervous she's getting. She wants to do a good job, and I already know she will. And she better know that I plan on filming the entire thing.

She sends me a deer-in-headlights look. "But I—"

"We bought the extra practice session, remember?" I knock her with my hip. "This is your extra practice."

She draws a deep breath and nods. Dawn drifts off to turn the speakers on, and Scarlett walks in a slow circle, looking like she's counseling herself.

"Where's the best place for me to sit?" I call out to Dawn. "I want a front row seat, but I don't want to distract the performer."

Dawn laughs, pointing out the floor in front of the stage. "You'll get the best pictures from there. Because I know you'll be taking pictures."

Scarlett sends me a warning look. "Please don't."

I shoo her away. What I do with my camera is none of her business. For every bit of nervousness Scarlett has, I'm equally salivating for this performance. Dawn calls her over when the sound system is ready. Scarlett joins her, their heads together as they select the music. I get my phone ready, pressing record just as the smooth tones of an electronic song floats out of the speakers, filling the gym with a sexy, lounge-y feel. Scarlett looks back at me, gives me a look that says *here goes nothing*, and approaches the two black bands of silk and hauls herself up.

Her feet are only a few inches off the ground as she swings in a wide circle. She bends her legs behind her, looking up at the silks like maybe she's waiting for them to pull her up on their own. And then she kicks her knees up and pushes herself up, hands knotted in the silks.

I'm unsure what I'm seeing. Has Scarlett managed to defy basic laws of physics? She steadies herself, hands fisted in the silks, piked at the waist so her legs are parallel to the floor. Then she lifts one up, wiggles her foot between the two silks—completely upside down, mind you—and drops her other leg back.

It's an upside down half-splits. I'm sure there's a more technical name for it, but at this point, I don't care. She's hanging in the middle of the damn air, and I've never seen anything that looks as fucking awesome as this.

My jaw makes a slow trek to the floor. As her performance progresses, it gets harder to remember my camera, to make sure it's filming her and not the ground. When she needs to go higher, the silks create mesmerizing lines around her legs as she wraps, wraps, wraps the fabric around her. At one point, she hoists herself into multiple somersaults. Up. Up. Up. Just as the music is at a crescendo, she tugs at the fabric and plummets downward in an orchestrated fall. Even Dawn cannot contain her glee. She is clapping and shouting while Scarlett continues her synchronistic movements to the music.

I am transfixed while Scarlett slowly comes back to the ground. No, transfixed is an understatement. I am painfully head over heels for this woman, so proud of her I could crack open. I am Lettie's number one fan. And anyone who wants to fight me for that title can meet me outside. Today and forevermore.

Once Dawn erupts into applause, I tap to stop recording and join in. Scarlett looks bewildered, almost dizzy. I come to the edge of the stage, pinning her with a serious look.

"Scarlett." I cover my heart with my hand, because I'm not sure it's functioning normally yet. "Next time, you need to warn me you're going to unleash so much badass onto the world."

She laughs weakly, nibbling at her bottom lip. "Did you like it?"

"Like it?" I scoff exaggeratedly. "I'll be dreaming about it for years."

"Scarlett. That was fantastic!" Dawn oozes as she flips off the music.

"Did you see where I missed the silk going into the flip?" Scarlett rattles off some details about a particular part of the performance, but I can't even follow. The entire thing was perfection.

"Now when are you taking this show on the road?" I slap the stage floor for effect. Dawn grins as she floats toward us.

"Pff. Yeah, right." Scarlett rolls her eyes.

"You can't just do all those flips on a piece of silk dangling from the ceiling and not show it to the world."

"Actually, I can," Scarlett replies.

"He's right. You're a natural performer." Dawn looks over at her with a conspiratorial sparkle in her eye. "There are a lot of performance troupes that travel the world, and they're always looking for new members."

"See?" I tell Scarlett.

Scarlett opens her mouth as if to bat down the idea, but a grin erupts on her face instead. I can tell she likes the idea. I know this woman too well, and she knows it, which is why we're locked in a staring match with cocky looks on our faces.

"I actually applied to one in late May," Scarlett says slowly, in that way that conveys equal parts embarrassment and pride.

"You did?" I ask, at the same time that Dawn says,

"Which one?"

"Momentum," Scarlett tells Dawn. And then to me, she says, "I didn't want to make a big deal about it. My instructor in Cleveland took care of it, and I'm trying not to think about it, honestly. It doesn't sound like it'll work out, anyway. I just kind of gave her the green light and forgot about it."

"Wow. Momentum is a *big deal*," Dawn says, leveling us both with her gaze. "Probably the biggest deal in the US."

"What if you get accepted to the biggest deal troupe in the US?" I ask Scarlett, enjoying the too-big-for-her-face smile that erupts.

"I can't even think about it," Scarlett says.

"You better," I tell her. "Because from what I've seen, you've got a good shot."

Dawn sends us a knowing smile. She winks and says, "I like how you support this endeavor for her."

"Well, she did the same for me not too long ago," I tell her.

To Scarlett, Dawn says, "This one is a keeper."

Scarlett's cheeks flush, and when she looks at me, there's a whole world of emotion written across her face. My chest gets tight, fingers curling with the need to touch her, wrap her in my arms. Scarlett is a keeper too. But I already knew that. I just didn't realize I wanted to keep her in my life like *this*.

Dawn walks back toward the speakers. "Any other music needs before I turn this off?"

"No, I think I'm done for today," Scarlett says with a laugh. "My biceps are jelly." She sits at the edge of the stage and then hops to the ground. I hook my hands around her waist and bring her against me, smoothing my lips along her hairline.

"So I'm serious about the performing thing," I say.

She grins up at me. "I can tell. I see the crazy in your eyes."

"I am feeling crazy. Crazy inspired. Crazy good. Crazy about *you*." I dip down and press a kiss to her lips, another wave of emotion wrenching through me. Things went from zero to serious between us in no time flat. But I'm not sure what I expected. We've known each other for a lifetime. What else was there left to explore other than our anatomy?

Because, this right here, this intimacy, this type of support? It feels normal. It feels like a natural extension of our friendship. Feels like what I should have been doing from the beginning. Since the second she set foot in my apartment after breaking up with Tom and we started to hang out more regularly after nights at the bar.

"I'm crazy about you too, Mav," Scarlett whispers, dragging her fingertips up the sides of my arms.

"I want to be with you when you go on tour," I say. "And after your first official performance with whatever amazing troupe that hires you, I'm going to propose to you on the spot."

She blinks about a million times. "Are you—what—"

"I told you. I'm feeling crazy."

The grin is blossoming. "Do you have a fever?" She presses the back of her hand to my forehead. "Maverick Daly just suggested marriage of his own volition. I think we might need to go to the ER."

"I can see it now. Food truck and aerial silks tour. We serve food during the day, and then you perform at night. We'll travel the entire country."

She doesn't look convinced. "That's if I don't get laughed out of the room once Momentum reviews my performance."

"Oh, we'll have to change the food truck name," I go on. "Silks and Spoons. New concept."

She laughs. "You're too much."

"I say once the challenge is over, we launch the tour."

Scarlett heaves a sigh. "There are a million reasons why this plan won't work out."

"Say yes anyway," I say, and then press a kiss to her lips. "Let's dream and be wild together."

Her eyes flutter shut, and she answers with our lips pressed together, butterfly-soft. "Yes."

CHAPTER NINETEEN

Here's a riddle.

How many times can a girl get eaten out before she gets bored?

The answer is: Infinity plus five. Because it's a trick question. There is no amount of pussy-eating performed by Maverick Daly that can bore me.

And I never thought I'd say it, but so far, I've had more orgasms in Indiana than I ever had in Ohio. But I know that'll change once Maverick and I get home and start having orgasms near Lake Erie.

Our third stop—Indianapolis—went by in a sex-crazed blur. And whenever we weren't fucking or cooking or filming, we were hanging out with Maverick's new food truck buddy, Kru. The two of them are like long-lost best friends to the point that their instantaneous inside jokes make me a little jealous, but hey, I guess he's allowed to have *other* best friends.

After all, I'm the only one having sex with him.

Thai One Off is the next truck to get eliminated, because they weren't able to hang with the third challenge, which was a BBQ-sauce centric theme. They gave it their best shot. But sometimes, green curry just doesn't mix well with a South Carolinian barbecue sauce.

But that's not the only big event from the third challenge. Somewhere in the mix, Butter Me Up launched a formal shitstain campaign against us. Well, not *us*, but rather Maverick. Personally, I think Hartley is behind it. The crew is getting weird now that we're further into the show, and part of me thinks this is their way to drum up entertainment—and clashes—by secretly goading teams against one another. Whatever the reason, Davie had no problem loudly urging customers to choose his truck over ours because, in his word, "self-taught cook is just another way of saying shitty."

Shots fired, Davie.

Reality kitchen drama aside, it's when we're en route to the fourth challenge that it hits me. *This is it.* I knew I was in love with Maverick; I knew I was wildly attracted to him. I just never knew how *good* it could be between us once we finally addressed that scary and potentially fatal next step.

I know he feels it too. He doesn't just love me, he supports me.

And after last week at AIR? It feels like we exchanged vows already. He helped unknot a tangle that had been holding me back. Maverick believes in me. He's one of few. But for the first time in my life, I'm imagining a wild future with reckless abandon. I'm not weighing myself down with the *but how*'s and the *well maybe not*'s. I'm just opening myself up to the brilliant rainbow of *what if*'s.

We're somewhere in the plains of Iowa, en route to Omaha, Nebraska, for the fourth challenge, when Maverick decides he has to pee for the billionth time. We started our trip from Indianapolis with a carafe of to-go coffee, sans Keith, since he had a personal stop to make between cities. We've already stopped twice in four hours. We're hauling the car behind the food truck instead of the more practical option of me driving it, because we want to spend more time together.

That's right. Twenty-four/seven isn't quite enough for us.

I believe this is what they call *head over heels.*

As he's pulling off the side of the two-lane highway bordered by unending corn fields, I ask, "Seriously? Again?"

"What? I'd rather tinkle now than think about it for the next forty miles."

"You're worse than a woman who's pregnant with twins."

He sends me a sharp look. "How would you know?"

"I don't know. It's just baked into my ancestral genetic data."

He snorts. "Okay."

"I mean, I saw how Flor was with both kids," I tell him as he parks the truck and turns on the flashers. "Twins would just be double the bladder pressure. You've got two of them in there."

"I've got a different set of twins in here," he says with a smirk as he pushes to standing. "With a different type of pressure." I'm opening my mouth to correct him when his meaning hits me, just as he's squeezing past me toward the door.

"Oh, you mean your testicles," I say when his crotch is roughly at eye level.

"Mmhmm." He tugs open the door, looking me up and down. "You should meet me in the car after I'm done pissing in the corn."

I laugh to myself, both because of the concept of him pissing in the corn in Middle Of Nowhere, Iowa, and because I know exactly what he's getting at. No amount of sex is enough. I'm definitely not complaining, though part of me wonders if this is how it might be for him with all the girls he hooks up with.

Scarlett. Stop.

The doubts creep in here and there. How could they not? Things are too perfect. Too fun. Too absolutely what I've always dreamt of without realizing the perfect man was at my side all along. There has to be a loophole somewhere. I thought I'd been able to predict the loophole—*Maverick isn't serious about me, he could never be serious about me, he'll bolt as soon as we get home*—but the longer we stay infatuated and tumbling down this tunnel of love, the more I realize he's still the same best friend I've always had.

He's Maverick. I'm Scarlett. There's nothing new here. Except, of course, the sex.

Once he's finished his cornfield meditation, he looks back at me then jerks his head toward the car. He's serious. I hurry out of the truck, ready to follow wherever he leads. Even if it's into the damn cornfield. He tugs open the passenger side door and when I'm within reach, he slides his hand behind my neck and brings me against him, hard.

His kisses are always urgent. *Deep.* This is one of the new things I know about Maverick. He kisses like he's pouring his soul into me. Like if he doesn't do it deep enough, then some of that passion will leak out past our lips and evaporate into thin air. Sometimes, the emotion bubbles up and gets so thick that tears drip down my cheeks as we kiss.

Maverick unlocks something inside me that I didn't know was there, a passion that feels both familiar and terrifyingly new. When we're kissing like this, teeth gnashing, whimpers escaping, arms clutching at each other's bodies like this is the last time we'll ever embrace, it's hard not to float off into the stratosphere. He is equal parts drug and grounding rod. He enlightens me to the carnal pleasures of life on Earth as much as he sends me straight into Heaven with these fatal kisses.

And God, I need more.

He's groping for the door handle behind me, trying and failing to open the back door. We disconnect long enough for him to tug it open. He assesses the back seat briefly, shuts the door with his foot, and then pulls open the front passenger door.

"Here." He leans in and reclines the seat back as far as it will go. Then he sends me a kiss-drugged grin. With his mussed hair and his intense eyes, I'm rooted to my spot.

"Right here?" I ask with a small laugh. "On the side of the road?"

He makes a big display of looking up and down the abandoned highway. "I'm pretty sure the neighbors aren't going to complain."

"Just don't be loud," I warn him.

"Why's that?"

"Because the corn has ears." I wait for an outrageous groan, and when he launches it, it is *so* satisfying.

"All right," he says, digging in his front pocket. "Just for that? You have to be on top."

"Have to, huh?" I can't keep the grin off my face. "What if I don't want to?"

He digs in his other pocket. "Don't act like you don't want to. I know things about you now, Lettie. And I know that you are one bona fide sex kitten who loves to ride on top."

My cheeks flush—the corn is listening, after all.

"Don't be embarrassed," he says, pressing a kiss to my lips as he hunts through his back pockets now. Then he drops his hands. "Fuck. I thought I had one last condom."

"Didn't you put the box in the car?"

"No. We used the whole box, but there was one left," he says.

"But what about this morning right before we left?" We're having a lot of sex, so it's blurring together. "Our quickie in bed. Was that the last one?"

He sighs. "Yep."

We share a heavy look, one that contains an entire conversation without saying a word. I push at his chest.

"Why don't we just do it without one?"

He cocks his head. "Really?"

"I'm on birth control." My gaze falls to the passenger seat. I didn't have sex with Tom without a condom until after the first year had gone by, because I wanted to be *sure* that Tom might be The One. With Maverick, it took one week. "I'm down if you are."

Maverick clutches the sides of my head and presses his lips to mine. When he breaks apart, he climbs into the passenger side seat, unbuttons his pants, and fishes out his cock. He's half hard, his gaze stuck on me as he fists himself a few times.

"Take your clothes off, babe," he says, his voice husky.

"No! If the cops or Farmer John show up wanting to help us fix a tire or whatever normal thing they think is happening here, I'm not going to be topless."

He wets his bottom lip. "Fine, just your shorts."

I look around one last time—the road is dead, the sun is beating down on me, and we're still in the middle of Cornfield, Iowa, about to have sex in broad daylight. It's now or never. I shove my shorts down and he groans.

"Fuuuck, I forgot you were wearing the thong." He lets go of his cock, reaching for me. "Get over here, you gorgeous woman."

I climb into the car, delicately positioning myself on top of him. The seatbelt latch is in the way. The center console is also annoying. "I don't know—I can't—"

"Shush. If you can climb silks, you can climb onto this cock."

I dissolve into laughter. "Fair enough." I find the right place to squeeze my bent knees in beside him. My pussy slides up against his fully stiff dick. There's nothing to separate us this time. The big, swollen head of his cock pushes at my clit, and I inhale sharply. I swear I can feel his heartbeat through the tip of his dick.

"Yessss," he hisses into my ear, his hot palms sliding up into my shirt. He rocks his hips, pushing into my clit again. A liquid wave of pleasure courses through me, making my eyes flutter shut. I could come from this sensation alone. And Maverick knows. He has to know.

"Fuck, Lettie, I love when you're on top," he says, then sinks his teeth into the side of my neck. While he's got me snagged there, his hands slide hot and possessive down my back, over the curve of my ass cheeks. He palms my whole ass, gripping me tight, guiding me back and forth along the shaft of his cock. My arousal is leaking out, juicing him up as he slides back and forth, back and forth. He bites his bottom lip and moans low.

"God, Mav," I gasp out, and buck against him. Desire swirls hot and stealthy in my core, begging for all of him and then some.

"You're so fucking wet, babe." He sounds drugged. A million miles away, yet perfectly present here with me as he snags me with his gaze and tugs at my bottom lip with his teeth.

"It's you, Mav." I drag my pussy up his length again, then grind into the hot steel of him. "You turn me on like no one else."

He grunts, squeezing his arms around my waist. "Oh god, Lettie. You have no idea." He inhales sharply and shifts beneath me. His eyes are swirling with intensity as he pins me with a look and slowly, slowly eases himself inside me.

He's been inside me what feels like hundreds of times already in the past week. But this? This is all new. The unsheathed, raw feel of him, pure heat and passion, sinks into me. My jaw drops as he pushes me down by the hips, his cock starting a slow, slick slide into my core. A choked noise escapes me. His head drops back to the seat.

"Ohhhh my god." His voice is pure grit. He's panting already. I've never heard him sound like this before. "You feel so fucking incredible."

"Mmmmrrmghh," I say, pressing my hands against the top of the seat, trying to brace myself. But it's hard. My limbs want to turn into jelly. I want to collapse on top of him and live here forever, Maverick buried balls deep inside me.

"Lettie." The harsh hiss of my name on his tongue sends chills up my spine. This is deep and raw in a way I've never known before. Never even knew was possible. We look into each other's eyes, and I see everything there. The shock of this connection. The bone-deep knowledge that what we have here is surreal. Powerful. Life-changing.

I move against him, barely, because I am liquified and useless. He groans and drills up into me. I whimper and collapse against him. He squeezes my ass cheeks, as if checking that I'm alive.

"I'm gonna come," he says, chest heaving. "You feel too fucking good."

"MMMrrgh," I reply.

"Ohhhh, Lettie." He squeezes his arms around me, squashing me against him. My hips are wide open, knee pressing into the corner of the seat belt buckle, which will surely tattoo me with indentations. But I don't even care. Because I'm receiving every inch of him as he thrusts up into me. Again. And again. I draw a shaky breath, feeling my own orgasm lurking near the edges.

My fingers snake up to the back of his head, knotting into the long hair there. He hisses, drilling up into me again. Our eyes lock, and emotion cinches my throat.

"I love you," he whispers, his lips brushing against mine. My head is spinning, entire body buzzing down to my fingertips.

"I love you too, Mav," I say, spilling forward into another kiss. I move against him as he drills up into me, filling me to bursting with his penetrating heat, his soft and urgent love, this passion that threatens to consume me entirely. When he thrusts and grinds up into me again, it's all I can do to hold on. The warm bliss starts a languid path through my veins. "So fucking much," I breathe out, just as the fireworks explode.

I cry out, and he buries himself again, so deep that his cock could come out my back. Light dances at the edges of my vision as the pleasure expands, balloons, swallows me. He pushes my hips back and forth on top of him, which just adds more friction to the fire between my legs. I've never been so fulfilled. So utterly fucking orgasming. Every way I turn, I'm still coming. Maverick lets out a gruff cry and his head pitches back.

His moan bleeds into my name. His abs jerk. When he comes, I can tell, because heat fills me and the moan turns guttural, the grit scraping over me, sending shivers through my spent and sated body. I struggle to catch my breath and my mind, lying limp against him. Our chests are heaving. We're silent. Drifting in a different realm. Together.

"Holy shit," he finally whispers. He's been clutching me at the hips ever since he came. He's still buried inside me, and neither of us shows any signs of moving soon.

"Mmmgghrhg."

He shifts slightly, pressing a kiss to the top of my head. "That was unbelievably sexy."

I can't talk, I can only tip my head to the side and try to look him in the eye.

"You are," I finally muster.

His arms squeeze tight around me. Bringing me back down to Earth. Right here on top of him, wrapped in his musk and leather.

Right where I want to be forever.

CHAPTER TWENTY

MAVERICK

Three teams are left on the morning of the fourth challenge.

Uncle Lobster, Butter Me Up, and yours truly, Fork Off.

Things are getting tense. Kru and I are brothers from another mother, so I don't want to see him go, but I also don't want to be the one to go.

Butter Me Up, however, can shove that stick of butter right up his ass.

Davie comes into the morning briefing that day looking like an electrocuted rooster. He's bright red—no sorry, that's just his hair—and sneering, which is typical. His gaze immediately settles on me, a warning baked into his creepy stare.

Apparently, he didn't like it when I took Scarlett off the market. Boo hoo, buddy. She's mine and has been for a long time, even if I didn't realize it until recently. Davie has made me his personal target over the past week, which I've mostly been able to ignore. After all, he's got the rooster look going on. Everybody knows that people with that type of vertical hair are not to be listened to.

But we're not five seconds into the briefing for the fourth challenge when he specifically looks my way and says, "Man, aren't you tired of limping along?"

"Excuse me?" I ask.

"You've gotten lucky at every challenge so far, bro. It must be exhausting trying to act like you fit in with the real chefs."

The hair on the back of my neck stands up. Scarlett's hand finds the small of my back. "Just ignore him."

You can tell Bennett and Hartley are eating this up. Hartley covers his mouth with some papers, but he's grinning like a fool behind them.

"Dude, he's just as much a chef as you are," Kru pipes up, his big black frames sliding down his nose as he reaches over to slap me on the back. "Don't let him fucking get to you."

"He's not," I say, crossing my arms. "Doesn't even register."

"Such a fucking novice," Davie mutters.

I steel myself in case he adds anything else. "Can we move along? Really curious about the challenge today so I can continue being a novice in the kitchen."

"When were you planning on not being a novice?" Davie asks, his cronies gathered around him snickering amongst themselves like it's the dirtiest comeback in the world. "Like, it's gotta happen sometime, right?"

"I don't know, *bruh*," I say, dropping my arms. I don't have much in my arsenal against the fact that I don't know nearly as much as they do. I can't defend against it. So all I can do is lean into it. "Not sure it fucking concerns you, either."

All the cameramen, including Keith, have fanned out around us, recording this from all possible angles, because this is the shit they can't afford to lose.

"I'm shocked this show even fucking let you on." He runs his tongue along the inside of his bottom lip. "After what I've seen come out of your truck? Pathetic."

"Real classy," I say. "This is why the fans love you. Criticizing people for enjoying good food. You know, those people you call pathetic like what they like. They don't give a fuck about your resume. And you might win this competition if you fucking learned that lesson."

He scoffs, crossing his arms. His forearms bulge. Not gonna lie, the dude and I aren't even in the same weight class. Still, I'd fucking take him down.

"Like there's anything you can teach me," he says, his voice lined with a snarl.

"First lesson of the day: keep your fucking mouth shut when they're trying to tell us what to prepare for," I say, jabbing my finger toward the crew. "I'm trying to fucking concentrate, and I can't when you're yapping about how fucking sucky I am."

He scoffs again, his jaw flexing. I can tell I'm getting under his skin and pushing him off balance at the same time. He wants to provoke. He wants me to lose my shit and come after him.

But while most of the Daly brothers are prone to fist fighting at the slightest provocation, I need a damn good reason to fuck up my knife hand. Being the shortest—and previously scrawniest—brother has meant I need to be judicious with my dick swinging.

Even though my dick is usually the biggest in the room.

"Seriously. I'm ready to COOK," Kru adds with a groan. "Can you stop being a stick of fucking butter, my Davie dude?"

Scarlett snickers, and I bite back a grin. It doesn't make sense, but that's why it works. Kru is a gift to humanity.

"Don't you fucking start with me," Davie says, pointing at Kru.

"Okay, okay," Scarlett chimes in, slicing her arms through the air. "I'm ready for the challenge. Come on, guys."

The female voice of reason silences us all, and we receive the fourth challenge: grits must be the menu feature. Additionally, we need to collect one hundred reviews on our social media profile from this one dinner service alone.

Given that usually fewer than ten percent of our customers have left reviews on our profile since the challenge started, that means we'd need to serve a thousand mouths this evening, which is absolutely not going to happen. I'd need to clone my truck six times over.

Time to hustle.

We escape the briefing without a physical altercation, but Davie's words linger with me as Scarlett and I put our heads together. He's not wrong. I'm the one with the least qualifications, the least knowledge, the least experience. What *am* I doing here?

"You know," Scarlett is saying as we fumble with the GPS and agonize over side streets in yet another unfamiliar big city, Keith's camera lens practically burning a whole in the side of my head as he quietly films the tension. "I think I know the trick to the review part."

"Yeah?" I'm struggling to merge into the turn lane without knocking out a few construction cones in the road.

"Something like, if they leave a review today only, they'll be entered to win a gift card for the truck for the future."

"We're never coming back to Omaha, though."

She crumples slightly. "Right. Well what about another incentive? Like, an Amazon gift card."

I smirk. "That feels too much like begging."

"Aren't we though?"

We stew in our own thoughts as we head to the wholesale food store, Keith in tow. As we're browsing onions and fine-tuning the menu I plan to serve—a cheesy gruyere-and-bacon shrimp and grits that is going to snap buttons off people's pants—Scarlett lights up.

"I know what we can do! If we say that people who *check in* to the food truck online are eligible for a discount today, then we can respond to each person who checks in with a personal request to review."

"Oooh." I set down the giant yellow onion I'd been weighing in my hand. "I like that."

She grins so hard that dimples flash. I lean in to kiss her perfect lips, and we whoosh off to continue purchasing for our menu. We run into Kru while we're out, brainstorm a few tweaks to each other's menus, and give each other a sidelong bro hug before parting ways.

"I'd like to cook with him someday," I tell Scarlett as we're pushing the overloaded cart back to the food truck. Keith opted for a bathroom break while we unload our purchases.

"Maybe you could be a guest chef on his truck once he gets back to selling his food in Wisconsin," she suggests, looking over at me with a glittering smile. I get caught in her gaze, as I tend to do, smiling at her like a dope as I memorize the lines of her face for billionth time. And still it's not enough.

"Mav." Her voice cuts sharp. A second later, my cart crashes into the food truck and she's giggling.

"Sorry. I was distracted."

"By what?" She's pulling open the back doors of the food truck, but she already knows by what.

"By the most beautiful woman I've ever seen in my life."

She hops into the food truck, taking her place to receive the goods we just purchased. This is our routine, which, after so little time, already works like a well-oiled machine. Further proof that she and I are destined to do this. Together.

"Oh, stop. You just think that because you know my silky secret," she teases.

"Well, that's part of it. Silky pussy is another reason." I send her an evil grin as I hand things to her from the cart. "But mostly your silky face and personality."

She snort-laughs as she receives the enormous pack of grits, followed by the four ten-pound bags of frozen jumbo shrimp. Once she's brought everything into the truck, we both make quick work of putting things in their right places.

Keith comes back soon after, and then we're off, heading to today's challenge spot, which is set against the backdrop of the Missouri River in a park in downtown Omaha. We're cruising through downtown, flanked by tall buildings and a distinct sense of spacious, Midwestern glory—something unique and almost more present here than in Indianapolis or Chicago. I pull up to a stoplight when we're less than half a mile away from the challenge location. Scarlett's staring out the passenger side window, and then suddenly rolls down the window.

"What's that?" she asks into the traffic. A car has pulled up beside her. I can't see who she's talking to or hear what they're saying. But when she turns to me, her face is pale.

"Mav, this guy says our truck is leaking something."

"Say what?"

"Leaking. Something." She turns back to the window, nods, and then rolls it up. "He says it's coming from the inside. We better pull over."

I blink at the packed, rush-hour traffic surrounding us. "You want me to pull over *now*?"

"Well, we're leaking! We better figure it out!"

The light turns and traffic presses forward. I cruise along, gnawing on the inside of my cheek, until I find the chance to merge over. I find a spot nestled between a McDonald's and an apartment tower to pull over, turning on my hazard lights. Scarlett pulls open the door and we tumble out into the commotion of the city, tainted with exhaust fumes and random shouts from a nearby conversation, heading straight for the back of the truck. Keith trails behind, filming everything.

Scarlett gets there first and gasps. A moment later, I see it too.

Our truck is dripping from beneath the back doors. I don't know with what. But one thing is certain: it shouldn't be leaking.

"Mav..." Scarlett begins.

"I'll get it," I say, fishing the keys from out of my pocket. Except, I'm spooked, so I drop them—twice—in my attempts to open the back doors. And as soon as I do, a gush of amber liquid rushes out.

The tipped-over fryer in the middle of the truck explains everything.

"It's fry oil," Scarlett hisses, sidestepping the stream that is now running down Douglas Street. Cars are whizzing by the truck. We're mere feet away from a debilitating car crash, and now there's oil in the mix. All I can do is watch it dribble away, striking out its own sinuous path in downtown Omaha like a drunkard determinedly trying to stumble off. "What do we do?"

"I have no fucking clue," I admit, watching the oil pool and then diverge in front of a parked car's tire about two spots down from us. I blink, looking at Scarlett. "Can we get fined for this?"

"By who, the fryer police?"

"Like, by Omaha. This is an oil spill."

"I hardly think the EPA is going to come after us for a little fryer grease," she says, running her palm over her topknot. "Unless the EPA *can* come after us for something like this."

"We gotta clean it up." I pull at the side bars of the truck to help hoist me inside, but it's too slippery. I grimace, heading for the passenger side of the truck. "You stay here. And quit looking like you just spilled fifty gallons of fry oil into rush hour traffic."

She sputters as I walk away, but I catch her say, "I'm pretty sure *you* spilled fifty gallons." Inside, I right the fryer, noting that only a pathetic slosh remained inside. Great. I gather as many paper towels as I can and approach the back doors helplessly.

"This isn't gonna do shit," I say, looking at the river of lost fried snacks twisting away from the back of our truck.

"Give them to me anyway," she commands, and I pass them off. She starts swiping at the back of the truck, but it isn't long before she sighs and crumples the paper towels. "This isn't doing shit."

"We need water. Water and soap." I turn to begin rummaging through the truck. We have no water connection here. I'm not even sure if my water tank is full. Without our generator running, we wouldn't be able to pull any water anyway. My heart is thumping.

"Maverick, people are looking at us," Scarlett informs me in a low, urgent voice. Because of course they are. We're dealing with an oil hazard in rush hour traffic with a personal cameraman filming every second of the debacle.

"As long as it isn't the fryer police, we're fine."

I look back just in time to catch the smile on her face. I'm not sure how I'd be handling this if I were with anyone else. But she and I, we balance each other. When I freak out, she reels me in, and vice versa. Just more proof that I can't do this with anyone else.

It's always going to be Scarlett.

I grab the dish soap, a squeegee broom, and when I'm at the back door looking lost, Scarlett suggests, "The water bottles!"

Bingo.

Thirty spent water bottles later, we've managed to squeegee the majority of the oil mess out of the truck and onto the pavement below, where we further disperse it with more water—and more soap—into the gutters.

It's not ideal, but when is an oil spill ever ideal?

We make quick work of buttoning up the truck, check one more time for the fryer police, and climb back into the truck. We're only a half hour behind schedule.

By the time we reach the challenge site, the other two trucks are lined up, which means we get the last spot, at the very end of the pathway. Because there's more space this time around, we're given a wide berth between trucks, and the path ends with us.

"Wow. We're the last forgotten truck back here," I tell Scarlett once the production crew has waved us into place. There's a dumpster off to the side, which is not appetizing either. "You think they staged this so we'll get kicked off?"

She deflates, looking back at Keith, who only shrugs. "We're in a reality competition. Anything is possible. So, let's say yes. That, or it's Davie's black magic finally kicking in."

I turn off the engine, and we clamber outside. I walk around the front of the truck to inspect how I lined up. It feels like there's a half mile between trucks, and the parking lot empties out right at *Butter Me Up*. Davie's got the advantage, pure and simple.

Not just because of his location. He doesn't have floors slicked with fryer grease, either.

"Let's get to work," I tell Scarlett. There's too much to do to concentrate on whether people will choose to wander down here. We have to serve 100 mouths minimum, no matter what. And then convince each one of those 100 to leave a review. Also filing that in the *Do Not Think About* category for now.

We grind forward with prep, though doubts are swirling, thick and hearty like the worst stew I never asked for. Time melts away under anxiety-riddled focus. I've got an enormous vat of buttery, cheesy grits in the warmer, caramelized onions working on the grill, shrimp about to go on next, with the bacon popping, lending its grease to *everything*. By the fourth challenge, we've learned to take time to pause and taste test the concoction, and the gruyere touch is to die for.

We're as ready as we can be. So here goes nothing.

Scarlett makes a sign for the side of the truck that promotes the check-in and discount offer, so people have time to do it before they order. Once she pushes the serving window open, we've got a long line stretching out from the truck. But it's not as long as the other trucks. In fact, there's a notable pattern between the trucks. *Butter Me Up* has the longest line. Then it's *Uncle Lobster.* Then us, with a measly forty people or so.

But there's no time to freak out. We start slapping together the dish and sending it out window. Ticket times are flying. Customers shriek with excitement when they get their dishes, which brings more people over. And without fail, Scarlett is shouting out reminders to the people in line to check into our social media page to snag the discount. Explaining how much we need reviews for this challenge. Telling them they're going to loooove what they're about to eat.

Every single person opts for the small savings, which means that we've got ten, twenty, fifty, and then seventy check-ins racking up on my notifications screen, which I'm trying to check between platings. It's clear that our dish is a hit. I just can't tell amid the fervent cooking and plating if it's the biggest hit, nor how many people will go on to review.

By the time our service ends an excruciating three hours later, we're completely sold out. The last bowl of grits went out with a measly one shrimp in it. Scarlett pulls the window shut—we still have to turn away at least five eager people—and we face each other.

We're exhausted. Sweating. Covered in flecks of grit.

And yet, I've never seen a more beautiful sight in front of me. Her black ballcap, cocked to the side, her long, dark ponytail flowing out and down her back. The skintight black tank top, showcasing her elegant and unexpectedly strong lines. When she sends me a shy grin, I can practically hear the question hanging in the air—*What are you staring at me for?*

It's all I can do lately. How long has she been right in front of me and I never fucking realized that *this* could be our future together?

I rush forward and wrap my arms around her, hoisting her by the waist. She giggles, folding into me, clasping her hands behind my neck. I spin her in a slow circle.

It doesn't truly matter whether we win or lose today.

In fact, the competition doesn't matter at all.

I got Scarlett as my sidekick, lover, and business partner.

I've already fucking won.

CHAPTER TWENTY-ONE

SCARLETT

The next twelve hours are tense.

A new breed of uncertainty has cropped up, which is unfortunate, because I thought I already had enough doubt and anxiety in my life. But no. There's a mutant offspring, and it's the uncertainty that is born in the post-challenge lull.

The judges tabulate. The producers contact test audiences. The crew awaits formal tallies. And this time, we're waiting, hoping, and praying for the review count to continue creeping upward.

By the morning after the challenge, our review count sits at eighty. I've been commenting on people's check-ins like crazy, doling out the gentle reminders, crossing my fingers, my toes, and my split ends that we'll reach 100.

Maverick wakes up after I've already finished my workout. He yawns loudly, flinging out his arm across the bed like he does every morning now. Checking that I'm not there, and subtly calling me back to bed with him.

And like a good little soul mate, I sneak back under the covers to snuggle with him.

"Mmmm." He welcomes me into the warm home that exists in his arms. It is actually the warmest, most perfect, most secure place I've ever been. It is his familiar leather and musk scent but multiplied by a billion. When I die, I want to be buried in his arms, which is creepy but also a fact.

I'll wait to bring up these small details until later in the relationship, I think.

I bring my knee between his legs, and he hooks his ankles behind my calves. We are a perfect, cozy pretzel.

"I love you, Mav," I whisper into his ear. Tears prick my eyes, because they always do when I talk about how much I love him. I'm *that* girl, now.

"Love you more, Lettie." He squeezes his arms tighter around me, and a few more moments of silence drift by—languid, dreamy perfection. I don't know much about what he's shared with the women who came before me, but I do know one thing.

It wasn't like this.

It couldn't have been like this.

I didn't share these tender, perfect moments with my exes. Not even after pining after, searching for, chasing after exactly this.

"I was thinking yesterday," he says, his voice gritty and extra-deep, "how good we are at all this."

My eyes drift shut as I nestle into his chest. "Mmhmm."

"Even if we don't win, we're set up now," he goes on. "We got this, for when we get back to Bayshore and open up over there."

My eyes jolt open, and I'm blinking rapidly, trying to digest his words and the unsavory cocktail of emotions they provoke.

It's not that I don't think we'll win. It's not that I don't want to help him out.

It's the fact that somehow, somewhere...the understanding that I was just helping him out so that he would take the leap and participate in this competition *for himself* has now turned into something much larger. Much more permanent.

And I don't know how to correct it, because the last thing I want to do is disappoint him when he's riding high.

After all, what do I have waiting for me after this except the same things I've always had? Part of me thinks it's wrong to not want to do this full-time with Maverick if he's offering and I'm able. But there's still a very significant percentage of my innards that are pulsing in wait for something else.

It's not E. Lago. It's not babysitting my beloved Fifi and Louie until they're 18.

A slightly smaller percentage of me thinks that maybe it's related to silks and that ridiculous application my teacher sent in, but I absolutely, positively *know* that cannot be true.

I must have been silent too long after Maverick shared his idea about opening up the food truck back in Bayshore, because he squeezes me gently. "Right?"

"Right, yeah." I hate how hollow my response sounds. And I'm not sure how to make it sound *not* hollow. Why do I feel like I'm lying to Maverick?

Even though I love the expression of silks, the physical challenge, the sinuous ballerina dance that emerges when I'm climbing into the sky suspended on two elegant yet strong pieces of fabric, there's no way that I could abandon my life in Bayshore to pursue that.

But when I think about it, I'm not sure why.

"I think Bayshore will *love* the truck," I add, trying to convince him—and myself—that I'm not a horrible friend. "I'll have to talk to my manager about splitting shifts between the restaurant and the truck." I swallow a knot in my throat. "Hopefully they'll be okay with me going part-time."

"You'll make more with me anyway," he says.

I open my mouth to respond but nothing comes out. All I can focus on is the sick knot in my gut. I wish this conversation felt lighthearted or happy or exciting.

But it doesn't. It feels like I'm making another sacrifice, which is ridiculous, because I'd be going home anyway, back to my regular job. What's the difference if I help Mav out at the same time?

The thoughts churn, sickening and fiery. I extricate myself from Maverick's embrace and kiss his forehead. "I'm going to take a shower. I had an intense workout this morning, and I stink already."

"You smell fine to me." He reaches for me as I slip out of bed, a lazy smile on his face. I worry that he can read my thoughts. That he can sniff out the fact that I am less than thrilled about the idea of continuing the food truck adventure in our hometown.

Once I'm in the quiet, spacious bathroom, staring at the immaculate white tiles of the shower while the water slowly transitions from cold to warm, I vow to figure this out.

Right here. Right now.

Do I like helping on the food truck? Yes. Do I like working with Maverick? I actually love it. What about food service? It's second nature to me.

So what is the big fucking problem, self?

This feels like a riddle without an answer. I am the helpless traveler, stuck at the important bridge in the middle of my quest, trapped because I can't answer the weird, snaggletooth elf's riddle: *Bacon, mushroom, you love him so! Grits and shrimp, why don't you know?*

I don't get it either, snaggletooth elf.

I take a lazy shower, mulling over the problem at hand, which is that 1 + 2 = WTF. Just as I'm finishing up, Maverick stumbles into the bathroom to brush his teeth. We grin at each other in the mirror. Once he spits out his toothpaste and rinses, he's tugging at my towel, urging me to drop it. I giggle and give him what he wants. My towel crumples to the floor, and he replaces it, wrapping his warm arms around me, my damp skin sticking to his.

"Mmm." He takes big handfuls of my ass, grinding against me. My nipples stiffen, that familiar heat winding through my veins. The ridge under his navy boxer briefs showcase how much he wants it, wants *me*, already. And I can't help but respond.

He's the only one who can light me up like this, and I love falling headfirst every time. Which means that if we want to be together, and he wants to open the food truck in Bayshore and work with me, then I should do it. One hundred percent.

He dips down and snags me in a minty kiss just as his phone starts ringing. He grunts, deepens the kiss, and then pulls away to answer the phone.

"H'lo?"

I can overhear just enough of the vibrant greeting to know it's Hartley. Maverick's cock is still pressed into my bare belly. I run my fingertips back and forth over his balls through the underwear, enjoying the stern look he sends me.

"Yeah. Yeah." Maverick clears his throat as I push my fingers past the waistband of his underwear, revealing his bulging cockhead. I never knew such a dick could fit inside me, but we have so many instances of proof now that I can't even keep track. He bites his bottom lip and thrusts against my hand. "Oh," he says to Hartley.

I drop to my knees as Maverick clears his throat again. I tug his underwear down, and his cock springs free. It bobs heavily, looking straight at me. Encouraging me to keep going, even though this is one of the wilder things I've done in my life. Right up there with having sex on the side of a road in an Iowa cornfield.

But Maverick does that for me. Where Tom used to keep things just this side of boring, Maverick awakens passion and lunacy in me.

He brought me on this crazy road trip. Encourages me to pursue my silks dream.

So why not suck his dick during a phone call?

I cover his bulging cockhead as he's listening to whatever Hartley is saying on the phone. He covers his eyes with his left hand, his head tipping back, as I swirl my tongue up and down, up and down his thick shaft. I love his smell, even between his legs, which feels like a weird, almost primitive, confession. But I do. I love his musk, his manhood, every last corner of this man. For how good he makes me feel, I want to give it back to him double.

I swallow the length of him as he clears his throat for a third time. "No," he says to Hartley, his voice raspy, "I'm okay. I just swallowed wrong."

A moment goes by.

"Yeah, no, I'm fine. So what time do we need to be there?"

I swirl my tongue up and down the seam on the underside of his cockhead. His free hand drifts to the top of my head, knotting his fingers into my hair. All the hair on the back of my neck stands up, and I dip down to swallow the length of his cock.

"Oh...you...you're coming now?" Now he sounds far away. Strained. "Great. See you soon." He swipes the phone off and tosses it to the ground. I watch in shock as it bounces off the small rug nearby.

I disconnect from his cock with a loud *pop*. "Maverick! Your phone—"

"I don't fucking care," he rasps.

I grin devilishly and dance my tongue over the slit of his dick. "But you cracked your screen."

"When your mouth is around me, I don't fucking care about anything else, Lettie." He knots his hands in my hair and bucks his hips, grunting softly. I love seeing him like this. He's primal and raw when we make love and get intimate. It's thrilling in a way I didn't realize would turn me on so much. Just as I swallow the length of him again, knocking sounds from the door to the hallway.

He groans, gritty and low. "It's the crew."

I pull back. "What the hell did Hartley say? Are we supposed to be doing something?"

"It doesn't matter. I want to fuck you on the counter, babe. Can I?"

I admire his perseverance. I'm not the type of girl to not immediately answer the call when someone knocks, so this seems scandalous. "But Mav—"

"We'll be quick," he murmurs, pulling me up to standing. "And I promise you'll come."

He hoists me easily onto the bathroom countertop. My squeaky-clean butt cheeks stick to the cool marble surface. He pushes my legs apart and eases himself into the space, the furnace of his groin meeting my pelvis in an erotic jolt. His mouth meets mine, inviting a sloppy kiss, just as he pinches the hard bud of my clit and pushes into my core.

His pace is languid yet brimming with urgency. It goes from sexy to intolerably hot in one second flat. He's stretching me, filling me, and now rocking against me. He holds me by the back of the neck as he pushes into me, over and over. He's fucking me with abandon on the bathroom counter, and as promised, with all the friction and naughtiness layered in—after all, Hartley is *outside waiting for us* while we snag a quick orgasm—I peak in a minute, just as he starts groaning, abs jerking, and scoops me up against him.

I melt against him. My thighs are tense, body sated. When he pulls out of me, his juice dribbles out of me. He wets his bottom lip, squeezing the tops of my thighs.

"Love you. Let's go rock the day."

That's the type of go-getter attitude we need. We share secret smiles, hurrying to clean ourselves up and get dressed.

Maverick has dissolved my confusion, because he's good at that. Even when sex wasn't involved, he could always melt away my bad mood or anxiety with just one joke, one look, and now, one pelvic thrust. The warm fuzzies overtake me, and I'm floating in heaven as I pull on my T-shirt.

And then one single thought crashes through me.

If you go back to Bayshore to work the food truck, you'll be there forever.

My smile fades. Maybe this is the clarity that a good orgasm brings, but as Maverick opens the door and welcomes Hartley into the small sitting area of our hotel room, more of the pieces begin to click together.

Maverick got to chase his dream.

Now I want to chase mine.

CHAPTER TWENTY-TWO

MAVERICK

We don't get the results for a few more days, since they're giving seventy-two hours for reviews to roll in. We work like mad behind the scenes to encourage as many people as possible to leave reviews, but it's impossible to guess what might happen next.

So we bop around Omaha, most times with Kru and his right-hand man, checking out breweries and art installations and parks. This is the type of shit I love, but usually never do. And with Scarlett at my side?

I'm in fucking Heaven.

There's no doubt about it. She and I, we're attached at the hip now. Because I get it, finally. What it means to fucking love someone. What it means to have *fallen* in love, to actively *be* in love. Because if I think about it, I fell for Scarlett so long ago. A quiet accumulation of all her quirks and bits and laughter and flyaway hairs and secret Honeycrisp ass cheeks. I thought she was a tomato, but she turned out to be an apple so juicy that I forgot about the rest of the damn fruits in the salad.

And now, I'm actively in love. Because falling is a moment, whether you notice it or not. But *being* in love? That shit is forever. It's something ongoing, continuous, renewing. It's a livestream that refreshes automatically, no buffering or lags. And slap my ass and call me a hopeless romantic, but I'm in it for the long haul with this one.

She made me fall. And guess what, Lettie—I'm yours for the rest of my damn life.

And once this competition is over, it's time for a life that we're going to start building—no, merging our independent lives—in Bayshore. And not only that. I'm ready to leave my dumb job at the garage once and for all. Tom can suck my dick. I've got Scarlett and a fledgling food truck empire.

What more do I need?

It's Wednesday when we finally get the call to assemble in the conference room at the Omaha hotel we've been camped in since Friday. Kru and I are sending each other encouraging looks as the judges begin their terribly dramatic discourse about the food, the setting, and the happenings. Once it's time for the big reveal, they preface it with the fact that only one team managed to hit the review counts.

Fork Off.

The news takes a moment to hit. Scarlett gasps. "Wait, did you say us?"

We fumble through processing the good news, and then are asked to continue fumbling for second and third takes, and then finally we are collectively ready for the elimination ceremony.

"You all performed admirably," the celebrity judge says, sending perfectly drawn smiles our way. "But one of you has to go home today." She bites her bottom lip, looking at each team heavily. Gravely. "And that team is Uncle Lobster."

"Fuck," I say, wincing as Kru sinks slightly. The judges go on to explain what eliminated him. Not only did he not hit 100 reviews, but his grits recipe missed the mark. The lobster-infused grits was beautiful in theory but failed in execution.

He's going home. And now it's just us against Davie and his squad of goons.

I give Kru a big hug after he gets the news. "You did a fucking awesome job," I tell him. He nods sadly, looking like he might be crying behind those thick black glasses.

"Yeah, well. It had to happen sometime, man," he says.

I do the best I can to cheer him up. Since Kru and I spend so much time talking after the ceremony, it allows me to ignore Shithead Davie while he stalks around, glaring at me. I've had retorts and insults burbling inside me for Mr. Stick O'Butter himself, but I'm trying to be good. I'm trying to keep quiet. But on my way out of the room, something slips against my better judgment.

"Man, Davie," I tell him as Scarlett and I are leaving hand-in-hand. "It's really gonna suck when you get beat by a self-taught cook, huh?"

"It's so cute you think you have a chance," he calls out. I don't stop walking. "What's it gonna be next time? Another fucking burrito? Your creativity amazes me."

I turn to face him, but I'm walking backwards, still technically leaving. "At least my customers don't need to visit their doctor for cholesterol issues afterward. Fuck, man. Butter soup is *not* an appetizing main course."

I spin around and grab Scarlett's hand again. Davie says something, but I don't catch it. I wave as condescendingly as possible over my shoulder as we cross the threshold and spill into the lobby. We take a few steps before either of us says anything.

"Well at least that didn't end up in a fistfight," Scarlett says.

"I'm not interested in throwing fists. Just making him choke on a butter burrito," I say, slinging my arm over her shoulders. When we hit the line of elevators, I pause, looking over my shoulder. "You gonna head back to the room?"

"Yeah. Aren't you?"

"I kinda think I should go talk to Kru a little more," I tell her.

"I'll go order us lunch to the room," she says with a wink. "They have ravioli on special."

"You do that, and no kisses for you, one week."

"You could stop yourself for a week?" she teases as we stop in front of the elevators.

I brush my hand over her temple, absorbing all the soft lines of her face, her smart-ass smirk, her brilliant green eyes. "No. I'd last a half hour, at most."

We kiss softly before she calls an elevator. I head back to the conference room and find Kru and his team chatting with Bennett. I hang around until they're done, and Kru pulls me into a bro hug.

"Dude, you're the fucking best," he says. "Promise me you'll come visit in Wisconsin?"

"Of course," I say. "Shit, we're all heading there for the last challenge anyway. Scarlett and I will come by no matter what after the last show."

Kru nods, sniffing. "Yeah. I can show you my smoker, too." Because Uncle Lobster isn't just a seafood fanatic; he claims to smoke a crazy good hog.

"Deal. You guys need any help packing up?"

He shakes his head, clapping me on the shoulder. "Nah. I'll see you in a week or two, bro. Lobster out."

We hug one last time, and I head for the elevators again. This is our last night in Omaha, and then tomorrow it's full speed to Minneapolis. Between today and the last challenge, we've got another week, so my plan is to concoct a miniature road trip. Maybe get lost somewhere cool along the way, with plenty of cornfield stops to enjoy the view.

The view of Scarlett riding my cock, that is.

I'm humming—actually humming, like I'm in the happy credits of a goddamn rom-com—as I make my way back to our room. I'm excited to see what Scarlett picked for lunch. I'm excited to see her face again, after fifteen minutes apart. I'm excited to see what Minneapolis brings, and Bayshore, and the rest of our lives together.

Because that's the key. *Together.*

I thought I *didn't* want the happily-ever-after. But now I want nothing more.

When I get back to the room, Scarlett is over by the windows, staring at her phone with wide eyes. She's got her palm pressed to her forehead. I can't tell if this is good news or bad news. I enter cautiously, and when the door shuts, she notices me. She inhales sharply as she looks over at me, eyes like saucers.

"Lettie?"

"Mav," she whispers, stumbling toward me. She holds out her phone, pressing it into my hand. My brows furrow as I try to digest what I'm seeing.

RE: APPLICATION FOR MOMENTUM TROUPE – WEST COAST – BURLYBOY TOUR

I squint. Burlyboy? None of these words make sense to me. I read it a second time, still don't understand what I'm seeing, then read on.

Dear Ms. Weaver,

Thank you for your energetic and enthusiastic submission to our troupe! This is exactly the kind of energy we like to feature in the highly interactive shows that the Momentum Circus Troupe is famous for. We think you would be an excellent person to fill our most recently vacated understudy position for our BurlyBoy West Coast Tour.

When I look up at her again, I see the tremor of shock fraying her edges. The sparkle in her eyes mingling with fear. She's cracked open and waiting for me to lead the way.

"Dude," I say, pressing the phone into her hands. "This is fucking incredible."

"Right?!" She shrieks and throws her hands into the air. I catch her, pulling her into a hug. Something heavy pulses in my chest as we hug. I bury my face in the crook of her neck. "I'm so excited I could melt. I'm going to turn to liquid and you'll have to mail me to California in a water bottle."

California. The weird jerk in my chest returns.

"I can't believe it," she gushes. "I honestly didn't think—it just seems so—like, how?"

"Babe, you're amazing. I told you."

"But like—they actually want me?" Wild laughter rolls out of her. "What if I can't perform in front of people? Like, I miss my footlock and just fall?"

"Then you get up and finish the performance." I set her back gently onto her feet. "Simple as that."

There's so much emotion dancing in her eyes as she looks up at me. I'm not sure if she even heard me.

"I'm going to have to start training double hard," she says. "Like I should find a gym *tomorrow*. I might google some over lunch. Oh—lunch should be on its way." She's pacing now, lost in her own world. "If I can get into a gym every morning and start working on the routine, then I should be ready by the time they want me to start."

That part of my chest that feels heavy drops to my stomach, settling in there. Getting comfy in its bulkiness. "When does it start?"

She doesn't look at me right away, but she does stop pacing.

"Lettie?"

She starts nibbling on her lip, and this is when I realize something is very wrong. When she looks up at me, all the happiness on her face has been replaced with guilt.

"Soon," she says.

"Like...how soon?"

Her throat bobs. "Next Friday."

It takes me a minute to remember what day it is (Wednesday), where we are (Omaha), and what this means (she wants to leave).

Wednesday. Omaha. Leaving.

The words clank together inside me. I'm dumb and fumbling. Because a few additional details aren't clicking into place, and Scarlett can't actually be serious about what I think this means.

"I don't understand," I finally manage to say. "Where is the troupe based?"

"California." Her throat bobs again as her gaze drops to the floor.

And now I begin to understand the cold fear snaking through me. The pit that has lurked at the base of my rib cage whenever I try to fix the plan moving forward. Scarlett is open to not returning to Bayshore. She's okay with heading west when I want—*need*—her to come home with me.

"Next Friday." I'm saying it as a test. Just to make sure my reality isn't crumbling to pieces around me.

The shock and awe she had when I came into the room has been replaced with furrowed brows and a frown. She turns from me, slipping her phone into her back pocket. "Yeah."

Silence forms a gulf between us. My brain is running at half-speed, flickering and unstable like an iPhone left too long in the sun. I'm about to power down from overthinking. I grope for the missing pieces of our conversation in the recesses of my mind.

"Next Friday is the challenge," I finally say, not devoid of accusation. The decision seems simple to me. We planned on this. She's not going to bitch out in my time of need. So why are my palms sweating?

Scarlett stares out the window, hugging herself. She doesn't respond for so long that it allows thoughts to fester and multiply.

It takes me even longer to be able to form the words.

"You're coming to the last challenge, Lettie," I say, my tongue sticking. "Right?"

CHAPTER TWENTY-THREE

SCARLETT

I didn't have enough time to process this news.

All I was able to do in the small span of time that I was up here, alone, ordering tuna salad wraps with bacon and eggs on the side times two, extra sriracha, was reread the congratulatory email no fewer than fifteen times and drown in the blossoming disbelief.

I haven't thought anything through. I don't know what I'm supposed to do.

All I know is that Maverick is asking me a question I can't answer.

"Lettie," he says again, more forcefully. I can hear the urgency straining his voice. The quiet desperation he is not able to hide from me. "Are you listening? You're coming to Minneapolis with me, aren't you?"

I swallow hard, tears already brimming in my eyes.

"My head is spinning." I swipe at my eye to hide the tear that escaped, and then turn to face him. He looks aghast, as if I just told him I planned to cut off all his fingers in advance of the last challenge. "Can I just sit on this good news for a minute? I—I'm not—"

"I need to know if you plan to come to Minneapolis with me or not," he says, his voice firm. "If you plan to fucking ditch me or not."

"No. No. I'm not ditching you. I just—" I sniff, my gaze falling to the floor again. It's too hard to look at him. He's brimming with intensity, his blue gaze turning into the sheer wall of a glacier. "I need to work out the details. I just got this news. I—"

"What is there to work out? You come with me or you don't."

"I'll see if I can change the start date," I blurt, a shaky breath escaping on the heels of the words. There. It's something. Forward movement. A possible path to follow so that I can claim my dream *and* fulfill a promise I made.

He sinks a little, raking his hand through his hair. "Okay. See if you can change the start date." He expels a sigh and walks into the bedroom, leaving me with a tangle of emotions.

This had started out so nice. So exciting.

And now I'm feeling lower than ever.

It reminds me a lot of my sister, in fact. Facing down this choice between what I want and what a loved one wants. Like all of Maverick's success and happiness hangs on this one decision that requires me to forsake my dreams, *yet again.* I swallow the sour knot in my throat and collapse into the arm chair nearby. My legs can't sustain my weight anymore, not while I'm buried under thirteen tons of uncertainty and confusion.

Earlier this morning, I was certain that I'd be motoring north to Minneapolis tomorrow.

Now? All I want to do is hop on a plane and head to California.

I can't possibly be both places at once. So maybe I can stack them. Minneapolis first, California second. It seems logical. Feasible.

Except as hard as I try to latch onto this as a solution, I can't find the grips. My feet are slipping no matter how hard I try to haul myself up with different projected possibilities.

A knock on the door sounds a moment later. Room service. I scurry to answer it, so lost in my thoughts that I can barely focus on what I'm doing, whether or not I even say the appropriate things to the hotel employee as I receive the food. I take the big tray over to the small breakfast nook. Maverick appears a moment later and slips into the chair across from me.

I still can't look at him. Not a good sign.

I pop off the lids and two tuna salad spinach wraps greet us, along with big plates of bacon and eggs. His brows shoot up.

"Okay. An interesting approach. I like it."

"I was hungry," I say weakly. "All this worry about whether or not we'd make it to the final round has been taxing."

I expect a laugh, but he doesn't give it to me. He forks some eggs into his mouth first, leaning back in the chair. His gaze slides to me, and he watches me as he chews.

Still no idea what the fuck to say to him. So I bite into my tuna wrap and try to get used to the silence.

He crunches on some bacon. Still watching me. We eat like this—me under scrutiny, him doling out silent judgement—until my wrap is half gone and I can't take it anymore.

"Will you stop staring at me?"

"I'm not staring. I'm thinking."

"Well you're thinking at me too hard," I tell him.

"Can you hear my thoughts?" His words are joking, but the tone is not. It's a subtle dare.

"Basically, yes. We are connected at the hip, remember."

He nods, grabbing another strip of bacon. "And you want to go in for an elective surgery now."

I drop my chin, finally daring to meet his gaze. "Maverick."

He shrugs, chomping on the bacon. "Am I right?"

"No. You're not right." But even as I'm talking, the icy fear I've been avoiding diving into returns with a flourish, coating my insides, pushing me back into that awful, anxious place that Flor has shoved me into too many times to count. I hate being in this spot. I don't know how I keep getting here or why it's happening with the one person I thought was supposedly exempt from that. "I'm not trying to detach us at the hip. This is just an email. Besides, you encouraged me to go after stuff like this. Can we not jump to conclusions?"

He chews and watches me some more. "So it's my fault because I want you to perform?"

"I didn't say that!" The words leap out of me, much louder than I intended. But now frustration is leaking out. Accumulated anguish from years of *this*. Not with Maverick, but with everyone else in my life.

"So what are you saying?"

"I haven't said *anything*," I remind him. "You're the one pushing for me to say something right now."

"Well, shouldn't I? I mean, I kind of fucking need to know if you plan to hand first place to Davie on a silver platter."

My stomach pitches downward so hard that it exits my body and splatters on the floor. This is the worst. The actual worst. Because it becomes clear now.

If I leave, Maverick loses. If I stay, I lose.

"Jesus, Maverick. Can't I just eat my fucking wrap in peace?" I take an angry bite.

He bites at his wrap the same way. "Fine."

We chew in agitated silence. Once I finish and have cobbled together a semblance of a plan, I say, "I'm going to call them and see about changing the start date. Today."

He nods, wiping at his mouth with the napkin. "Okay. And if they don't agree to it?"

The question is a spear to the heart and reveals my plan for what it is: a stall tactic. Because I still can't answer his question with any certainty.

"Then we'll figure it out," I tell him, piling my dirty plates on the tray exactly like I would at E. Lago. Server to the bone. Once Maverick is done, I clear the table and place the tray outside the door. Maverick is standing, running his hand through his hair, looking at me so intensely that I could crack in two.

"I'm gonna head out," he says. It's not an invitation. That much is clear.

"Okay. Where to?"

"I don't know. I need to think."

"So you'll just leave me stuck here?"

"You're not stuck. There are ride shares. You can walk places. Besides, sounds like you have some calls to make." The way he's watching me makes my insides sink. He's goading me without jabbing too hard.

"Okay. I guess just let me know when you plan on coming back."

"I will." He snatches up his room key and phone from the front table, looks back at me once, and then leaves.

Without a kiss. Without a hug. Without so much as a goodbye.

I frown at the door for a long time, working things over in my head. I haven't even made a decision, and Maverick is pissed. I don't get it, and I'm exhausted already.

It's a good thing Maverick left, because I need the time to myself. I lie on the bed and stare at the ceiling, gathering the courage to make the phone call to receive the news that I already suspect. Before I muster the energy, I scroll through the email one last time. Absorbing all the details that my shock-high brain might have missed the first fifteen times around. And at the end of the email, I read:

This is a highly coveted position! You were selected as the top candidate out of over one hundred eager silk stars. Your participation as an understudy will be compensated with both experience and a stipend. Please know that we have a runner-up in line in case you are unable to accept this position for some reason. We are excited to work with you but understand if the sixteen-week tour is not ultimately feasible for you at this time. Normally our turnaround time is much longer, but due to an emergency with an existing troupe member, this is a short notice vacancy that must be filled immediately. We need to know by FRIDAY if you plan to accept this position with our troupe or not.

Two days to decide. Sixteen-week tour.

Every cell in my body wants to go to California right now. And if it weren't for the challenge, I'd be looking up flights from Omaha right now.

Sixteen weeks is nothing in the grand scheme of things. And now that I've been pushed off the ledge, all I want to do is soar.

What are the chances something like this will come up again?

I start brainstorming all my options. Turning them down now and reapplying at a future date. Maybe postponing my internship with the troupe until the fall or winter. Or turning them down all together, and then applying for a different troupe and a different tour, in some other part of the country. Or maybe some other part of the *world*.

The possibilities feel endless. I start a fervent search on my phone, pulling up information about the west coast Momentum troupe. It turns out they're the most elite troupe in the country. *Great.* That'll be hard to top. I find other troupes in other creative hotspots—Madison, Wisconsin, and Austin, Texas—but they're smaller operations. Nothing as full-fledged and widely-scouted as Momentum.

I fall down a performance arts rabbit hole. I flip between circus videos from Momentum's last appearance in Montreal and instructional videos hosted by former Momentum stars.

And at the other end of the rabbit hole, I'm breathless. Exhilarated.

Not only is Momentum an incredible opportunity, it's a launch pad.

I can see the country, if not other parts of the world, while getting paid and doing something I love. And once my tenure ends? I'll be better poised to continue doing what I love.

The ideas are flowing now. I could start teaching at the aerial silks gym in Cleveland, for starters, once I'm done with Momentum and ready to come back to Bayshore. I could even open my own gym in Bayshore. Hell, Maverick could park his food truck outside my performance arts gym. We could spend all our days together, doing what we love.

Tears come to my eyes again. How could Maverick not fall in love with this vision too? It seems impossible not to. I convince myself that he'll love it because it involves what we both want: to be together, in Bayshore, living our passions.

Because the choice is increasingly clear. I should take Momentum up on this offer.

Fighting nerves, I dial the number that the acceptance email lists as an information line. I'm gnawing on my bottom lip as it rings, and then a smooth-toned lady answers.

"Momentum! How can I help you?"

"Hi. Hi. I—uh—I'm sorry. My name is Scarlett—"

"Oooooh, are you Scarlett from Ohio with the hella good audition video?"

Something warm and oozing slides over me, nearly choking me with how fulfilling it is. Tears sting my eyes again and I nod, even though she can't see me. "Yes. Yes, that's me! I had no idea you'd know who I was."

"We have been talking nonstop about that video since we got it! Oh my gosh, I'm so excited to meet you! My name is Maya. You had a *killer* kite split sequence!"

I wipe away a tear. I wasn't expecting this at all. Like I'm someone impressive. Like I have any idea what I'm doing. The bitterest part of me laughs and thinks: *Could you tell my sister that?*

"I'm so excited to meet you too," I blurt, really meaning it. Suddenly, I can glimpse this whole new world. A world where circus arts is the norm and casual work chatter involves critiquing the new fire hoop routine and whether or not so-and-so should have introduced the butterfly lock into the silks show. This stranger in California complimented me on my kite split sequence, and I'm silently crying now, because this is a world I've been longing for without even realizing it.

My instructor in Cleveland helped push me here.

And now I have to plunge forward and go all the way.

"I just wanted to call and check on something," I go on, rubbing my palm over my cheek. "I am thrilled and shocked and amazed that your troupe accepted me and I—" *I'm ready to show up tomorrow.* "I saw the start date is next Friday and I was wondering if that had any wiggle room in it?"

"Ahh," Maya says. I hear the rustling of papers. "You know, the start dates are firm because the schedules are so packed. I'd have to check with the big boss, though. That's Gemma, of course. She personally selected you. Are you thinking you might get here the day after...?"

My heart sinks a little. I'd probably need a few extra days because of filming. "Max three."

Maya tuts. "I doubt she'd be able to agree to that, but I can always ask."

"Check for me," I say. "But if she can't, don't take that as a no." I pause, observing the words bubbling up from my heart and up through my throat before they finally spill out. "I'm going to make something work no matter what."

"Oh, that's *killer*," Maya gushes. "God, what great news! Listen, I'll chat with Gemma and get back to you ASAP. Ciao, babe!"

I swipe the phone off, feeling more fulfilled yet more torn than ever.

I'm going to make it work.

I just have a feeling Maverick isn't going to like it one bit.

CHAPTER TWENTY-FOUR

I spend hours at the hotel gym, running on the treadmill, using weights to improve my lunges, cycling through the exact words I'm going to use with Maverick so he can become as excited as I want him to be.

I need to be prepared. This is big news. And for every ounce of anxiety cycling through me, one truth remains constant beneath it: I have to follow this dream.

I head back to the room around dinner time, sweaty and ready to eat. Maverick still isn't there, so I shower and continue the self-coaching. Dipping out of the competition before it's completed isn't ideal. I feel like an asshole for even suggesting it. But who would have known my own window of opportunity would open right as we'd finished climbing through Maverick's window?

Besides, I'm brainstorming ways to replace me. Maverick doesn't need *me*—he just needs *somebody*. It won't be hard to contact local restaurants in Minneapolis and see who might be interested in a quick gig with a food truck for a reality show. Hell, we could put up a craigslist ad and make it real interesting. He'll fill my spot in no time flat. I'm positive.

And then the idea hits like a lightning bolt: *Kru.*

Uncle Lobster went home today. What if he diverted and just *went with Mav* instead?

I never wanted—or planned—to leave him up shit creek, and I would feel like an awful friend if I went after my own dreams only to leave Maverick drowning in his own. I hunt down Kru on social media and send him a message.

SCARLETT: Kru, are you there? I need your help. I had a last-minute call to come to California and I can't go with Mav to Minneapolis for the final challenge. Is there any way you could help our friend so he can beat Davie's ass?

The message doesn't log as read for a while, so I decide to stop staring at it and toss my phone on the bed. This could be the Hail Mary pass from me to Mav so he can win this thing. I try not to get too excited—after all, what if Kru has other plans, his own regular job to get back to?—but it makes too much sense. I want this to work out for Maverick so badly that if I can't find a replacement, I won't accept the troupe understudy position.

It will hurt like a bitch, and I might scream and cry and complain into my pillow for a few weeks afterward, but I love Maverick enough to give up the opportunity of my dreams if I can't make his own dream come true. And I can always reapply. There's only one final challenge.

Still, my nerves are jangling through the evening, no matter how much reason and logic I throw at them. Just as my stomach is beginning to rumble—bordering on panic and hangry now—the lock of the front door lights up and Maverick comes through.

All it takes is two steps for me to tell he's drunk. Or at least properly tipsy. He grunts as his elbow hits the doorjamb, and he shuts the door slowly behind him.

"Hey," I say cautiously. He took the phrase "it's five o'clock somewhere" pretty seriously. "You drunk?"

"Naaah." He smiles, but it's edged with tension. The dark cloud I've been battling for the entire afternoon returns and sits its fat ass on the ground between us.

"You check out a brewery or what?"

"A couple," he says.

"Nice." I run a hand through my wet hair, and he drags his gaze up to meet mine.

"So we breaking up or what?"

His words land like a hammer. I step backwards from the unexpected blow of them. "What are you talking about?"

He laughs, but its humorless. His boots clunk as he walks past me toward the bedroom. "You know what I'm talking about."

This is not the open and free-flowing dialogue I envisioned while exercising compulsively upstairs. "I don't. Breaking up was never even an option. Why are you bringing it up?"

"Because isn't it obvious?" He toes off his boots, facing away from me. "If you leave, you're leaving *me*."

I cross my arms, leaning against the doorway of the bedroom. He sits on the edge of the bed, resting his elbows on his knees.

"That's not true," I tell him. "I don't know why you think that, other than that you got drunk at two p.m. and started telling yourself stories."

"I'm not drunk," he spits. "I'm being realistic. You had your decision written all over your face earlier, Scarlett. I already know what you're doing."

"And what is that?" I ask him.

"You're leaving me high and fucking dry right before the biggest moment of my life," he says, his voice loud enough to make me step backwards. His jaw flexes as he watches me, waiting. And then he adds, "You think I wanna be with someone who would do that?"

My throat clenches. All bets are off. Any possibility of a positive conversation has been blown out of the water with that little gem. Maverick came back with guns blazing while I was preparing us a pretty little fantasy picnic.

Because once again—my life and decisions are the reason that someone else's life can't function.

I'm so tired of learning this lesson.

"Maverick," I snap, exasperation and anger and guilt forming a toxic stew inside me. "You were dreaming about this right along with me in Chicago. You helped me see that it might be possible in the first place! I didn't choose for the dates to coincide—it just *happened* that way."

"Then wait until the challenge is over before you go."

"I looked into it like we talked about. And guess what? There's no wiggle room. I forfeit the opportunity if I wait."

He throws his hands up. "Great. Then your decision is made." He stands up and brushes past me, leaving a roiling trail of displeasure as he heads for his luggage tucked away in the far closet.

"Not necessarily," I say, "but I love how you're acting like you know everything right now."

"Scarlett," he barks, pressing his palms to the closet doors. "Don't forget I fucking know you. Better than you know yourself."

"Then you know how much this means to me," I tell him, my voice cracking.

He slides open the closet door and it crashes open. He tugs out his suitcase angrily and throws it on the bed.

"It's not the only fucking opportunity in the world," he spits. "But me? I'm a week away from the biggest opportunity I've ever seen, and you want to fucking bolt to California. Gee, how helpful. How considerate. How fucking *sweet* of you."

Tears fill my eyes as he starts to rummage through the loose clothes he'd stored on the shelves in the closet. He's throwing things in haphazardly, not bothering to fold anything.

"This isn't the biggest opportunity for you, actually," I tell him, wiping away the tears as I talk. "The biggest opportunity was getting into the competition itself. Which I helped you do. Don't you see that? I still support you, even if I do leave. I helped bring you here, Mav. I've believed in you for so long, when you didn't even believe in yourself. And I thought you'd done the same for me."

"This has nothing to do with believing in you." He turns to jab his finger at me. "But you lied to me, for years, about this. You confided in *Davie* before you confided in me. So really, it sounds like you *didn't* believe in me that much. Not when it comes to this. So yeah, just shit on the guy who tries to support you."

I cover my face with my hands. I don't know where to go from here. "I'm not shitting on you! Maverick, this is a time-sensitive opportunity. It's once in a lifetime! I'm sorry it conflicts with the show, but I'm not going to leave you up shit creek. I already have plans to replace myself—"

He laughs bitterly. "Replace yourself? Okay. Yeah. Because I want to work with some high schooler off the street."

My arms drop to my sides. "You're being ridiculous. This is going to be a good chance for you to get your feet wet in working with other professionals, finding employees—"

"I already have one, and it's you," he barks. The rawness edging his voice stuns me to silence. He throws the last of his clothes into his suitcase and then turns toward the shoes. "I don't need practice finding help. It was gonna be you and me. Lettie and Mav. That's what we fucking said."

The emotion overwhelms me, pushing more tears out. "But I never said that," I croak. "I never wanted to *be your employee*. I wanted to *help you out*. Once. For this."

"And look how well you're helping me out. Leaving before the hardest challenge." He scoffs, tossing his shoes into the suitcase. Everything in there is jumbled, which is an accurate representation of what's happening in this room right now. "You think I want to work with a stranger? I need someone who knows this shit. Someone who's not gonna fuck up and cost me the competition." He's spitting his words, every syllable lined with intensity. I've never seen him speak like this, not even close. He's twisted and seething, a brute force of anger. He throws his last shoe in so hard that it causes another shoe to fly out. "I spent my whole life savings on this! And now you're gonna walk away?"

"I'm going to help you," I insist through tears. There's so much more I want to add, including the fact that I reached out to Kru and I'm waiting for his response, but my throat won't unclench long enough for me to speak. Finally he turns to me, his chest heaving. He holds his arms out, palms up.

"So is it worth it? Tell me."

My body shakes with a contained sob. "What?"

"Starting this bullshit with me just to fucking ruin it all." He steps forward, his gaze angry enough to send me stepping backwards again. "Did you have fun? Was this just a rebound for you?"

"Maverick, I'm not—this isn't the end. Our relationship was never in question—"

"Not the end?" He laughs bitterly and heads for the bathroom. When he comes back out, his arms are full of his toiletries which he dumps ingloriously on a heap on top of his clothes and everything else. "Of course it's the fucking end."

"Just because I leave for this tour doesn't mean we can't still be together," I insist. I can barely see anymore, from the blur of tears. I wipe my forearm across my eyes. There's a smear of mascara on my arm, but I don't care. "I'll be coming back to Bayshore. It's not permanent. It's—"

"What is the point of being *together* if we're not *together*?" Condescension drips from his voice, like this is more obvious and basic than $1 + 1 = 2$.

"Oh. So for us to be an item, we have to physically be in each other's presence for the relationship to be valid?" I sniff hard, shaking my head. "That's not how relationships work. Not like you'd know that."

"You know what I do know? I expected more of you, *Scarlett.*"

"More of me how? I've given you literally all I have. And I want to continue doing that. Which is why we should work at this, long distance, until I'm back in Bayshore."

"Long distance." He scoffs. "Everyone knows that shit doesn't work. Would you trust me? Could I trust *you*?"

Now I know he's just spouting off. I'm the as loyal as they come, and his suggestion is so offensive I can't even form a response.

"Let's make it easy," he says. "You leave me now, you leave me forever."

I crumble under the weight of his ultimatum. I crouch in the doorway, covering my face with my hands while I run his words through my head. This is the most dramatic reenactment of what Flor and I go through on a weekly basis. But I don't want to be bullied into bending over. I'm so tired of it. And even though I never expected Maverick to be capable of it, here we are.

I don't want to give in. I want to stand up for myself and the life I've always wanted but have been too scared to go after.

"The choice is yours," he reminds me. "It's yours. And you fucking made it."

He finishes zipping his suitcase and jerks at the handle so that it tumbles to the ground. He storms toward me, but I don't move. Instead, I come to my feet, straightening my back. I'm not done fighting for us.

"I made a choice to follow my dream. Not to break up. You're making that choice."

He scoffs and brushes past me. I watch him leave. When he pulls open the door, I call out, "You're seriously leaving?" My voice is pinched. Unnaturally high.

"Why would I stay?" he challenges. "You were so worried about me hurting you, and you never even stopped to consider that you might be the one to rip *my* heart out." He scoffs, something dark twisting his features. "Whatever. I'm leaving. Plenty of adventures to be had without you. Plenty of new girls to get to know."

He shoulders past the door as grief starts dripping down and around me, coating me, filling all the cracks in my armor that the argument exposed. My throat tightens, and I sink to crouching yet again, watching as the door closes slowly on its own. And then, *click.*

He's gone.

I wait an eternity, which is maybe something like a half hour, alternating between sniffling and sobbing as I wait for Maverick to come back and reveal that he's calmed down now, he's had a chance to think things over, everything is actually fine.

But he doesn't come back.

There are no reassurances.

And the only question in my mind is whether following my greatest dream is worth losing my greatest love.

CHAPTER TWENTY-FIVE

MAVERICK

I'm twenty-five miles outside of Omaha, heading north to Minneapolis, when shit really starts to sink in.

I've been white-knuckle driving my max speed of sixty-five, glowering at the taillights of everyone who passes me. I can't get away from Scarlett any faster, and right now, I need every last sorry mile of space between us.

I would have hired a spaceship to get out of Omaha, if it has been an option, and spent every last cent of the competition pay-out to do so.

My entire body is tight, corded, brimming with discontent. I want to fight, vomit, and cry. I need to never look or speak to Scarlett again until I'm on my deathbed just as much as I need to melt into her arms and kiss her face until I'm dead.

And if this is what love feels like?

Fuck love, and fuck Scarlett too.

I sniff hard, fighting back the wave of anger and disappointment. Heartbreak is a classified medical condition, I can say that much so far. A doctor would fucking admit me to a hospital if they took my blood pressure right now. This broken heart might actually end up killing me. Good thing my dumb food truck only goes 65 miles per hour or else I'd be going 120 right now.

All I can say is, good thing I didn't name the business *Lettie & Mav.*

What a fucking ridiculous waste of time.

My thoughts cycle like this for hours. By the time darkness covers everything just after nine o'clock, I'm somewhere in the middle of the cornfields of Iowa once again.

Except this time, without Scarlett.

I pull over, and the truck shudders to a stop. I climb through the empty spot that she would normally occupy, yank open the door, and tumble out on the side of the road and right into the soft earth bordering a corn field.

Fuck cornfields, too.

And fuck Iowa, for good measure.

I look up into the sky and shout, "Fuuuuuck!"

I kick the front tire of the truck once, then again. I slam my first against the hood of the truck, leaving a trail of dents along the front. God, it feels good. It feels right. I make my way around the entire truck, kicking the tires, slamming the heel of my palm into the metal sides, leaving a meandering stream of dents along the way. I don't fucking care. I need this release, because this is the only thing that makes sense right now.

I'm only here because of her. Now I'm destined to lose because of her.

I think about the words as I kick the last tire. My ankle twists at a weird angle and I bark out a gruff stream of curse words before pounding my fist right into the cartoonish fork on the passenger side. My knuckles are bleeding. It's still not enough. I clamber back into the food truck, yank the door shut, and collapse into the passenger seat.

And then it hits me.

I fucking left her.

Alone.

In Omaha.

My chest is heaving, and I double over, fisting the front of my hair. Did I need any proof that I'm not fit for relationships? If I did, here's some. I'm aware of how crazy I'm being. How wild and weird and volatile. But the hurt screams louder than the logic. The parts of me that she wounded burrows deeper than the parts of me that can still see straight.

My phone beeps with a text. Every inch of my body lights up with hope that it is Scarlett. Though I'm not sure what she'd be willing to say to me at this point other than *fuck off for life.*

But it's Hartley.

HARTLEY: Did you leave? We can't find your truck or car.

MAV: Yep. En route to WI.

HARTLEY: You were supposed to wait for Keith!

Fuck. Fuck fuck fuck. I swipe to call Hartley, and he answers after it's barely rung.

"Why did you leave already? You were scheduled for a morning departure," he says, sounding production crew-level annoyed.

"Scarlett and I had a fight. I left."

"Okay. And where is your team member?"

"Uh, the hotel?" As soon as the words leave my mouth, I realize how awful it sounds. Because it *is* awful. Now that I've punched the shit out of my food truck in a cornfield in Iowa, some clarity is creeping in. It's amazing how much can be accomplished in cornfields in Iowa.

"You left her in Omaha?"

"Yeah." I pause, fisting the front of my hair. "We fought and broke up. She's not doing the show anymore. She's done."

Hartley heaves a sigh, and then he curses softly. "And you guys couldn't have done this for the cameras, huh?"

Of course that would be the first thing he thinks about. I'm over here about to have a fucking stroke because I lost my head by falling in love, and Hartley just wants the dramatic footage. "No fucking chance in hell."

"Fine. Listen, just snag the nearest motel and send me the address. Keith will meet you either tonight or tomorrow morning. Okay? We need all the footage possible leading up to the last challenge."

"Got it." We hang up, and I stare out at the inky Iowan night. Silence settles around me, profound and consuming.

And I sit in it. Drowning. After a little bit, the air in the truck goes stale, so I yank open the door again. I kick back in the passenger seat, propping my feet on the dashboard. As my head falls back against the seat, I'm bathed in the cool, fresh air of a rural night. And through the open door, I can see the spectacular constellations of stars dotting the sky. It's so stunning that I hold my breath, fearful of disturbing the expansive perfection of what I'm witnessing. I'm pinned to my seat. Riveted by the galaxy.

I stay like this for what feels like an hour, until the last dredges of my anger fade away and I'm left simply feeling spent. Exhausted. Utterly ready to ice my knuckles and pass out somewhere.

I haul the door closed and then start up the truck. The deep rumble makes me look to my right, the way I've done a billion times since this journey began three weeks ago.

Instead of Scarlett, I find empty space.

But not the dazzling kind. Nothing like the galactic swirl of light years of physical space to calm a soul.

No, this is the kind that threatens to unravel me. The space that I'd thought I'd avoid with contenting myself with just the hookups and the flings.

This is the space that's left when you lose the galaxy itself.

CHAPTER TWENTY-SIX

SCARLETT

I cry so much that I nearly puke. But I'm waiting. Somewhere, in the back of my mind, I think he's coming back. This is just him being upset, and he'll come back and we'll hug and kiss and fuck and be fine.

And then I go down to the hotel garage to verify the truth.

He fucking left.

Food truck and sedan, both gone. Along with our decades-long friendship, our recent romantic relationship, and every *I love you* and orgasm I ever dared to share with him.

I guess I'm not surprised. Somewhere between Chicago and Omaha, I opened myself up to a whirlwind romance with the biggest playboy I ever met. And even though I've known him my whole damn life, maybe I was wrong to think that he'd be open to a long-distance relationship. Or a relationship at all.

I should have known that we'd have a blissfully perfect honeymoon period. I just never imagined it would come crashing down like a meteorite aiming for the dinosaurs.

I cry until I'm too hungry to cry, and then I cry a little more. I order room service again, this time something I know Maverick hates—ravioli—because it feels like I should, now that he's spurned me.

Fuck you, Mav. I'll eat ravioli and *love every bite of it.*

I even take a picture of it when it arrives, just so I have it in my back pocket if I ever need to show him.

But the ravioli isn't that good, and I'm alone when I should be with Maverick, and all I can think is *Where is he?* and *Will we ever be friends again?*

Somehow, I make it through the night without crying more. In the bright and vibrant morning, my eyes are puffy, and I feel exhausted already. But I'm alive and not crying, so these are good signs. In fact, as I move to my yoga mat and start forcing myself to move through my sequence, a few other sensations bubble to the surface.

First and foremost, let's welcome crippling guilt to the Scarlett Emotional Rollercoaster Show. This familiar and beloved sensation always appears when I've disappointed someone, and now I realize it also likes to appear when I prioritize my happiness over someone else's.

And below that tectonic layer of guilt burbles something else. It's the hot magma of my hidden volcano, and it's urging me to email Momentum and tell them *I'M IN, MOTHERFUCKERS.*

The magma is so insistent, so impatient, that I stop my practice halfway through in order to send the email. And I don't stop my practice for anything except phone calls from Flor or that one time I had a weird gut after eating Taco Bell. My fingers are flying so fast as I write my response email to them that I type *Thamks, Scarlert* without noticing and hit Send. I grimace, opening up a second reply, and quickly explain that I was so excited I forgot how to type, even though it might appear that someone hijacked my email account because I misspelled my own name.

There. That's done.

It isn't ten minutes after I return to my mat, feeling both wild and relieved after accepting the troupe position, that another thought comes burbling down my magma veins.

I still need to help Maverick win the challenge. Even though he thinks I've ditched him—and I have, in a sense—it's not because I don't love him or want him to win. I feel both of those things more than I could ever explain to him. I thought I'd proven this to him by dedicating every ounce of my time to his endeavor.

My sister hardly speaks to me anymore. My job might not even want me back now that I've been traveling the Midwest for so long (let's be real, they thought we'd get eliminated quickly).

Haven't I earned choosing myself for once?

Maybe he'll see that someday. Maybe he won't. Once I'm sweaty and slightly less tense an hour later, my phone vibrates with a new message. Kru has responded.

KRU: Girl, Lobster on it! I'll reach out to my boy and hook up these lobster hands for him. Don't you worry. He and I are gonna take down Davie.

He sends about fifteen punk rock hand emojis, and all I can do is shriek with excitement.

The thought of Kru and Maverick taking on Davie and his Butter Boys is almost more perfect than I could have imagined. And now, I have a way to check on Maverick without actually talking to him. Because even though I love that man more than movies or poems or limericks can express, I refuse to reach out to him.

He's the one who broke up with me, after all. He's the one who bolted, who shouted, who cast all the first fucking stones.

He's the one who walked away, even when I will spend the rest of my life wanting him to walk back into my life.

The hotel reservation ends today, since the production crew is formally heading northeast. I don't see Hartley or Bennett or anyone once I turn in my room key. I linger in the lobby for a moment, checking my phone, acting like I know what I'm doing here. Like I'm not suddenly adrift and bobbing in the vast sea of the future. I gnaw on my lip, and it occurs to me that I need to tell my sister I won't be coming back for roughly sixteen more weeks.

But this time, I'm not going to be sorry about it.

SCARLETT: I was offered my dream job in California and I've taken it. I love you and Fifi and Louie. I'm not sure when I'll be back in Bayshore but I sincerely hope you can figure out the childcare situation. Please don't blame me for following my dream. I deserve this.

I'm the last trickle of the reality show to leave the hotel, and once I step out onto the sidewalk into the bright Omaha morning, it takes me a minute to remember that I have no idea what I'm doing.

I'm alone in Omaha, four hours fresh off accepting an aerial silks contract in California. I've got a couple grand in my bank account, I'm heartbroken, and I need to head west.

A sob hiccups in my chest, but it doesn't come out that way. Instead, it blossoms into a wild laugh. With tears in my eyes, I roll my luggage to the sidewalk and smile up at the sun.

Here it goes. The wild adventure.

I'm on my own, and I can't fucking wait to see how I get there.

CHAPTER TWENTY-SEVEN

MAVERICK

I can't stay mad forever. It's too fucking exhausting.

Instead, I segue pretty quickly into the moping stage. Once Keith and I meet up in the morning at my Podunk motel in northern Iowa, I resume my glum journey. Except now I have my very own cameraman to capture my descent into heartsickness. How thrilling.

It's only after mile fifty on the road together that he finally asks, "So where did Scarlett go?"

I smirk. "I don't fucking care."

He laughs a little. "Okay. I don't believe that."

"You don't have to. She left. That's all that matters." I can feel the dark cloud settling in again. "She abandoned me right before the last challenge."

Keith takes that intentional sort of silence, where I can tell that he's trying to just be nice or respectful or whatever. I look over at him after a minute, white-knuckling the steering wheel.

"What would you have thought if you and your wife were doing something like this and she just ditched before the end?"

"I guess that depends." Keith shifts in his seat, examining something on his big camera. "Mostly on what she left for."

I grit my teeth against the sickening lurch in my chest. "She's trying to be a performer. Aerial silks. She got picked for a high-profile troupe to become their next understudy." I sigh. "Don't get me wrong—I want her to do it. Just not *now*."

Keith nods sagely. "Of course. No time to launch a new career like at the climax of a reality TV show competition."

I laugh bitterly. "Exactly. She jumped ship. Not even a second thought."

"Well, that's how the entertainment and creative industry works," Keith goes on, squinting out the passenger side window. "Everything is urgent. Time sensitive. *Do or die.* I know this competition had a fast turnaround too. What did they give you? One week?"

I nod. "Yeah. That made for an edge-of-our-seat few weeks, that's for sure."

"Yeah, and she dropped everything to come with you," Keith says. "At least, I'm assuming she did." He looks over at me, sending me a knowing smile. "Maybe you owed her one."

I frown, and a mile disappears beneath us, silence filling the truck save the occasional rattle of the dangling tongs in the back.

"I do owe her," I finally say, when the sentiment has long disappeared behind us. And I hate to admit it. Not that I owe her, because that's more than obvious. But I hate admitting that I might have been wrong, even though he has no idea about our blow-up and break-up and all the things that came in between.

"I'm sure she'll make it up to you, and you'll make it up to her," Keith says. He reaches over the middle console to clap my shoulder.

"It's what happens when you're with your soul mate. That shit just sorta works itself out."

Soul mate. The words are jarring somehow, and I look over at him, spooked.

"Why do you say that?" I ask him.

"What?"

"Soul mate. I never—we never talked about—"

He laughs. "Oh, boy. No, we never talked about it, but it's obvious. You two are meant for each other. I've seen hundreds, if not thousands, of couples in my years, don't forget. And I've been filming you guys for three weeks—in both good times and bad. I'm pretty sure I'd know better than anyone."

Keith's words feel strange, both foreboding and the sweetest relief. Still, I just want to forget about everything. The final challenge is a week away, and I've got a lot of things to work on and figure out. The truck needs some minor repairs and upgrades once we get to Minneapolis—including some brand-new dent removal—and I've got to figure out why my grill burner is acting weird. There's a to-do list a mile long, actually, and that's not including finding a new right-hand. Processing this drama with Scarlett feels like it should be last on the list, because I can't spare any additional energy until I win this shit.

But now that Keith is making me think about it like this, it's hard to focus on what comes next. All I can think about is how bad things got. How ruined. How unrecognizable.

When we get to Minneapolis that afternoon, I'm limp as a dish rag from all the mental cycling and re-hashing. My plan is to console myself with beer and television until I can cobble together my former enthusiasm for life, if not a general ambivalence. As soon as we check into the ten-story hotel in downtown Minneapolis, my phone buzzes with a text. It's Kru, who's in my phone as UNK LOB.

UNK LOB: Little birdie tells me you need a right-hand man. I've got my application ready for your review, brother.

I reread the text a few times before it sinks in.

Kru.

Kru wants to be my right hand.

And I bet Scarlett was the little birdie.

My fingers are flying as I respond. In the dark night of this ocean I've been drowning myself in, his text is a beam of light from the surface. The helicopter search light reminding me that all is not lost. Everything will be okay. They just need to pull me out of the water.

MAV: Are you fucking serious? You're already hired. I thought you had to head home.

UNK LOB: I do, but whatever, I can spare a few days for my reality brother. You're 6 hours away, dude. Besides, you'll list me in the credits when you win, right?

MAV: You fucking know it.

UNK LOB: Lobster out...for now.

Time passes strangely in Minneapolis. Each hour feels like an eternity, yet the days melt away as quickly as sand disappears from a clenched palm. It takes me about three days and paying $500 to a propane technician to realize what feels the strangest about Minneapolis.

I'm on my fucking own.

I've never done this before. Been in a strange city without a guide, anchor, or lover. All my trips in the past—Chicago, Denver, Cincinnati, Key West—had been in the company of school buddies or my fling of the moment. Hell, on my trip to Key West, I went with a girl from Bayshore but ended up sleeping with a girl from Florida the entire trip, only to make up with the Bayshore girl at the end and fly back with her, everything hunky-dory. I was twenty-one and an idiot, but damn, it was fun at the time.

But now? I'm facing this new place with nobody. Well, nobody but Keith, but he hardly counts. He's got a wife and kids—he's practically an alien. In fact, he reminds me of my brothers. Now that they're all committed and *happy*.

And now that I've got a Scarlett-shaped hole in my heart, I'm thinking back on the rest of the trip when she was at my side. Reflecting on how committed and happy *I* was.

Just as much of an alien as the rest of them.

Being on my own isn't all bad, though. I've gotten an insane amount of work done on the truck, seen an impressive amount of Minneapolis, and met some new friends I never counted on. But nearly every hour, I look at my phone with something I want to text Scarlett then set it back down, unsure what to say or how to break the ice.

I miss her like crazy. My bones ache with wanting to check in on her, but I don't have the words for this type of shit. I still don't even understand what's happening inside me, much less between us. My go-to is to have an insane amount of sex, but I don't want it. I don't want anyone other than Scarlett, and she's the one person I can't have, and who invented this romantic love bullshit?

When the day of the big challenge arrives, I'm in the zone. I've never been so focused and *ready*. Kru backs me at every turn. And holy shit—it *is* kinda nice to work with someone who knows the food truck business from the same end that I do now. Nothing against Scarlett, but I'm seeing the ways in which an industry veteran like Kru could take my business to soaring heights.

The challenge focuses on bison meat. I come up with a ridiculous gourmet burger: bison meat mixed with cherries, topped with brie cheese, grilled onion, served on a toasted brioche bun. The cherry infusion is a nod to Scarlett, my personal dedication to her, whether or not she'll ever know.

Kru and I work like fiends. He's joking and laughing with everyone at the window, taking money and sending these burgers out the window like mad. We serve three hundred people in four hours for the final event. By the time we close the window, we both are groaning, collapsing to the floor, utterly spent.

"Dude," Kru starts after we've been staring at the ceiling for what feels like an hour. He's been sitting on the toasted top of a discarded brioche bun, but I don't have the energy to tell him. "Honestly, no matter what happens. You should be proud of today. Win or not, we just cranked that shit out."

I crack a grin. "Thanks, buddy."

"You're a winner in my lobster heart," he tells me.

"That means a lot to me." I reach for him, trying to touch his shoulder, but I can't reach. My arm drops like dead weight to the floor.

And it does mean a lot to me.

I just can't get around the throbbing absence of Scarlett. She is so boisterous and noisy in her absence that most days, it is all I can think about. I'm about to add that the only thing missing right now is Scarlett, but I stop.

I can't say the words.

Because she's not missing. She's exactly where she's dreamt of being. And that place is not at my side.

Not gonna lie, the heartbreak stains everything. It follows me as we struggle to clean up the truck. It lingers in the air as Kru and I go out for celebratory drinks that night.

It even follows me all the way to the final elimination ceremony. Davie's smug face alone is enough to send fresh waves of heartbreak through me. Not because I give a damn about *him*, but because he and I have one major thing in common, which is that we both wanted Scarlett.

And now she's nowhere to be seen.

Bennett and Hartley have perfected their poker faces as they mill around the conference room of the Minneapolis hotel, which has been temporarily re-outfitted to serve as our reality TV show decision room. The high-profile judges are seated, being touched up by the makeup crew before filming starts. I'm so nervous that I'm barely aware of anything except the painful wrench in my gut as time creeps toward the defining hour. Once filming is underway and the judges begin their well-practiced spiels, Kru practically needs to help keep me upright.

And then once the judges begin doling out their thoughts in cryptic, dramatic segments, all I can think about is that Scarlett is missing this. This fucking moment. And for how mad I am that she left, I still can't imagine myself with anyone else. Ever.

"Are we ready for the results?" One of the judges asks, as though I haven't been internally pissing myself with anxiety for an entire day waiting for this moment.

Kru squeezes my shoulder.

The main judge looks toward Davie then. "Butter Me Up. You have placed..." She looks down at her sheets then, allowing for the approximate half hour of dramatic silence to fill the room. Then she looks back up at Davie. "Second."

My eyes go wide as the news stutters through me. Kru is immediately whooping and pumping his fists in the air. The judges smile our way. Kru wraps me in a hug, pelting my back with encouraging slaps.

"You fucking did it, brother!" Kru says. "You fucking did it!"

Davie is stewing, arms crossed, his jaw moving back and forth like he's ready to fight me, or the judges, or maybe the entirety of the production crew.

It's when Davie's eyes finally meet mine across the room that his frothing, raw anger hits me. I remember all the snide insults he's delivered over the past few weeks, and the biggest smile of my life stretches across my face.

"*You* fucking did it too," I tell Kru, my brain finally starting to work again. I thought I couldn't do it without Scarlett, but maybe she was right that I didn't need her to pull this off.

I pull him into another hug, and while we're whooping and grinning, I deliver the most satisfying middle finger of my life to Davie.

The high lasts long enough that I make it back to Bayshore. Once I cross the city limits, I park my now-seasoned food truck back in storage and immediately head to the bank to deposit my enormous check for fifty grand.

I'm not sure where to go from there, though. I'd originally planned on giving half to Scarlett, but now I don't know what to do since she bolted. One day turns into two, and then three, under the pretense of "settling back into life in Bayshore". Except the more I try to rev myself up to call my boss to let him know that I'm home and ready to go back to the garage, the more I want to get back into the kitchen and face down another hungry line of people.

And the worst part? Each second spent in Bayshore without Scarlett to turn to, talk to, much less kiss for hours sends my heart breaking into tinier and tinier pieces.

After four days, I'm at a standstill. I should be refreshed, rejuvenated, invigorated. Instead, I'm moping and feeling worse than ever. Even with fifty grand in the bank and the biggest win of my life behind me.

It gets so bad that I try to eat a quesadilla for lunch one day and then physically can't. I might never be able to eat one again, in fact. I head to my mom's house one day while I know dad is at work. She's there, her brunette hair tied back in a low bun, plates clinking as she clears the dining room table. I step into the kitchen and I find Grayson and Dom there too.

Everyone's eyes light up.

"Maverick! What are you doing here?" A big grin overtakes her face as she sets the plates at the kitchen counter and then immediately pulls me into a big hug. "I feel like I haven't seen you in a year!"

"Brother! How's it feel to be the first Daly reality TV star?" Grayson asks as he comes over. He pulls me into a hug after mom, followed by Dom.

"Can you tell us what happened?" Dom asks.

Some of the old excitement returns to me, trickling through my veins. "Yeah. But you gotta keep it a secret." I smile for the first time since Minneapolis. "I fucking won."

The three of them cheer. Mom dances around the kitchen a little bit, pumping dirty forks in the air.

"Ohh, honey, this is amazing!" Mom gushes, pulling me into another hug.

"Just in time for the wedding, too," Dom says. He's getting married to London soon, and I'd been planning to take Scarlett, until we broke up. Even though I'm not entirely sure anymore that's what we are. In fact, I'm pretty sure I'm more devoted to her than ever, even though we have more miles between us than ever. "You can sign autographs for the family."

"But they can't know yet," Grayson reminds Dom. "It's secret until the show airs."

"Can I tell Connor and Weston?" Mom asks, clapping her hands together. "What about your father?"

"Let's just keep it quiet for now," I tell them.

"Okay, but we can tell the wives, right?" Grayson asks.

"Wife-to-be," Dom corrects.

Mom sends them a sidelong smirk. They've reconciled, but the ongoing competitive brotherhood will never go away between them.

I sigh. "I mean, do you have to?"

"I'm just asking," Grayson says, holding up his palms in defense. "Once you get married, the barriers dissolve and it gets a lot harder to keep secrets." Looking at Dom, he adds, "You'll find out soon enough."

All this talk about wives and dissolving barriers and ongoing love sends a special type of despair spiraling through me. I run a hand through my hair, feeling the need to either leave immediately, or spill my guts about Scarlett. "Yeah," I force out. "That's fine. Go ahead and tell them."

"Honey," Mom says suddenly, touching my arm. "What about Scarlett? Why isn't she here with you?"

The pit that has lived in my stomach for the past week and a half swells to double its size. "That's...kind of a story."

"What happened?" Mom asks.

I want to add that we don't need to go into it, that it doesn't matter, that everything is fine, but I can't. Because none of that is true. What happened with Scarlett is practically the only thing that matters—this much is clear as I try to resume normal life.

"Maverick," Mom prompts, squeezing my arm. Her blue eyes are soft, familiar. Reminding me that if I'm going to share this with anyone, it should be them. It should be now.

My throat tightens and I look over at the dining room table. "Can we all sit down and talk about it?"

My family sits down without question, and before long, I'm spilling all the details. The challenges. Our tumble down the long chute of love. Her opportunity, followed by her exit.

And the more I talk, the clearer some things become. And by the time I'm almost done with my story, I find three sets of understanding eyes watching me, all reflecting the same knowledge that is vibrating through me.

"I thought she'd betrayed me, but really she'd been supporting me." I drag my index finger across an invisible pattern over the wood grain of the dining room table. "And now that I lost her, nothing really feels complete. The win, the business, the future. None of it matters if she's not in my life."

My mom tuts softly, shaking her head. "Maverick, honey. I think you know what you need to do."

I do, but it's hard for me to talk right now with how tight my throat is, so I say nothing.

"I think he needs to start by going to Grammy Ethel's grave," Dom begins, looking deeply pleased, "and thanking her for the inheritance. And the rest will fall into place." He gives me a knowing wink.

I'm gearing up to be annoyed with him, but a laugh slips out instead.

Dammit, he's right.

"Start there," Grayson says, "but I would also start looking for rings."

Mom gasps, covering her mouth with her hands. "Do you think...?"

I roll my eyes. I come here to confess a deep and painful heartbreak, and they immediately pivot to when the wedding is.

"Not like you have to ask her right away," Grayson adds, "but you'll thank me later. Trust me on this. Because one thing is for certain, brother," he says, leveling me with a severe look. "When you know? You fucking know."

He's right. I fucking know.

I've known for a long time, too.

CHAPTER TWENTY-EIGHT

SCARLETT

One month into my tour with Momentum, there's only one way to describe my life:

Blissfully fucking mega-amazing holy-shit great, shadowed by a sad cloud.

That's way more than one word, actually. But there's no way to encapsulate how good this troupe is or how amazing the tour is. How many slushees one can actually consume while visiting all these big city festivals, or how many times I will remind myself that I lost my best friend despite desperately trying to avoid that very thing.

We're in Austin, Texas, for an arts and music festival in early September. Our tour moves from big city to big city, sometimes with multiple events in the same place. We provide artistic support and visual adornments to music gatherings, private events, art conclaves, and more. Every day is a brand-new adventure with Momentum. A new chance to practice my passion.

Thank God I have the distractions of this dream opportunity and the constantly revolving door of new places. Otherwise, I might have crumbled from the ongoing grief of losing Maverick. I can only assume I lost him, because we still aren't speaking five weeks after I left Omaha.

And for some reason, the nail in our mutual coffin came via another wedding. His older brother Dominic got married last month to London, which I noticed while scrolling through social media not too long ago. It seemed like the most potent symbol that Maverick and I aren't just on a hiatus, we're done with a capital Forever. I didn't have the heart to look through all the pictures. I should have been there on Maverick's arm, and I was too afraid to find proof that Maverick took someone else as his plus-one.

Luckily, I have Kru as my secret spy to get the occasional update while I tour. The final challenge was tough, but Maverick's cherry burger was a runaway hit at the final competition. Kru wrote at length about how much his legs hurt after their marathon serving session and reiterated no fewer than ten times how much of a badass Mav is in the kitchen.

And despite the sadness, I'm proud as fuck. This is the Maverick that I've seen inside him the whole time. The Mav who just needed someone to fan the flames of his passion.

Apparently Kru and Maverick are brainstorming a food truck concept that will be launching in Cleveland this fall, because Mav officially quit the garage. I try to get as many details as possible without seeming like a stalker, but I miss Maverick so much that my heart weeps as much as my eyes. Their new project started with 3,000 followers, which is insane because the show hasn't even aired yet, but also not surprising. Maverick was born for this, and he's rocking it.

I just wish I could make him understand how much I still love and support him, even though I left.

Maverick reached out to me about a week ago. This is what he sent.

MAV: Lettie.

MAV: I can't do this over text.

SCARLETT: Do what???

He never wrote back. So that's been a fun little cryptic stew to simmer in for a week.

Every time I go to his name in my contacts list, I stop. Because there's so much to say, and even the 5G network wouldn't be able to handle the amount of emotion I have brewing about our failed friendship.

But more than that? My aerial colleagues, who I think I can call my new best friends now, are helping me learn about boundaries. As in, I didn't have any. And I need to enforce them. And waiting for Maverick to reach out and make this right is just part of learning how to build up those boundaries where previously existed barren ditches.

At least Flor has started letting the kids do a video chat with me once a week. I'm taking that small win and adding it to my "Great Things About Life" list.

I can only hope that someday Maverick and I can meet in the middle again.

The troupe has been in the throes of setting up our performance area in Republic Square in downtown Austin. We're tucked between live food demonstrations—a wok chef is sending tantalizing aromas of garlic and beef our way—and endless stalls of handcrafted art. Further west are the food trucks, and dotted throughout the festival are little music stages, five total.

The urban green space is thrumming with life, smells, and movement. And soon, I'm about to be flying through the air in the middle of it all. I'm grinning despite the way my heart hangs in shatters.

And it's not because I want to convince anyone of anything. I'm not trying to put on a happy face. I'm just simply learning to enjoy life despite having disappointed someone.

I'm learning that life goes on. And I have to go with it.

By eleven a.m., our stage area is complete. Patrons are milling everywhere. I'm opening the set today, followed by a hula hoop performer named Candy, who is just as sweet as her name suggests. Others of our ilk are wandering the festival—heavily made-up fairies on stilts, clowns doing cartwheels, and more.

There is truly never a dull moment with Momentum. For how fun and awesome our shows are, the reactions of the crowd members are just as inspiring. Yet even after four cities and dozens of shows, no reaction will ever top the look that Maverick had on his face after I finished my sequence at AIR in Chicago.

It's a look that haunts me, especially as more and more time churns away beneath us with no contact. A look that was equal parts love, tenderness, and awe.

No stranger off the street could ever behold me like Maverick did. I'm thinking of this as I go into the changing area. Candy is there, and she helps me zip my jet-black leotard. Skintight black shorts go on next, and then Maggie from makeup comes to make me look wild. My hair is pulled into a high, slick ponytail, and once the mascara and dramatic eyeliner go on, I've got five minutes until music.

I hop around, staring up at the puffy clouds in the sky. The hum of humanity helps ground me—the scent of the wok-fired garlic and the random bursts of laughter from somewhere, everywhere. When my musical cue starts, I walk out onto our big, square stage. On this side of the protective fence that keeps spectators away from the performance area, black mats line the ground, just in case I should fall.

There aren't many people here, but they'll come. They always do, once they see a woman climbing into the sky on fabric strips. I grab the two black silks, some of my pre-show jitters dissolving as soon as I make my first fist. I don't spend long looking at who's watching. I never do, because if I do, I'll just freak myself out more. I launch forward, swinging like a pendulum as I hoist and hike myself up along the silks. The bass lounge-style electronic music is an additional balm to my nerves, the practiced moves flowing out of m e.

By the time I hit the top, my legs are wrapped three times and I'm in the splits. People are flocking now, pointing, shrieking while they drag over a bestie to watch. I take a deep breath, enjoying the view of the Austin skyline for just a moment longer than I otherwise would. God, this is fucking awesome. My heart swells, and I bring my legs together so that one leg falls free. I wrap and bend and fold through my sequence, until one of my newer—and harder—moves comes. I'm focused on what I'm doing, trying to remember where the slip-up happened during the last practice session.

Once I'm appropriately wrapped, I hoist myself up, crossing my ankles. I'm dangling upside down, arms hanging below my head, the brunt of my weight held by the silks crisscrossing my thighs. I dip my head back to find the upside-down crowd.

Magnetic ice-blue eyes are the first thing I see. Someone in the front row. Mussy, long hair swept off to the side only accentuates the gaze that pins me to my spot, even when I'm dangling upside down in the air. Chills shiver through my body, and I immediately look away, hauling myself back up to my seated perch on the silks.

That can't be Maverick. There's no way that is Maverick.

I swallow the knot in my throat, trying not to be hopeful or optimistic or anything of the sort, because I need to focus on my sequence. What's most likely? Someone else in the world possesses the Daly icy blues, and this is just a shimmer from the universe appearing to remind me that I am still in love with a man who is most definitely probably in Ohio right now.

That's all.

I do a somersault into another pose, where I'm suspended in the pigeon pose, one knee raised and cocked to the side with my leg out behind me. I raise my arms, looking out over the crowd with a grin. Applause erupts along with some shouts. Including a gruff one, followed by, "Go, Lettie!"

A sob hitches in my chest, and I don't look down. I can't. Emotion turns into a clamp, and I expel it with the force of hauling myself into my next posture. Air whooshes out of me, and I feel cleansed. A few tears are pinched out in the process too. Blank slate. I fist and knot my way up the silk again. My routine is almost over, and I need to stay present for the grand finale. I'm distantly aware of Candy off to the side of the stage, clapping with excitement.

Up. Up. Up. I knot my fists into the silks and pike my body up, executing a half headstand, half-plank in the air. No wrapped silks to support me, just the power of my wrists. And then I lower my legs, threading my ankles around and around the fabric until my thighs are wrapped. I'm tied by my right thigh, upside down, and drop my arm toward the ground.

With my other hand, I seek the special knot and *tug*. The silks come undone and I plummet to the ground in a controlled drop. The crowd shrieks with excitement as I land in my final posture, both arms extended to the ground maybe ten feet below me.

Applause erupts, and the music fades to nothing. I extricate myself from the position and slowly slide down the silks, beaming out at the crowd.

And Maverick is there at the front of them all. Clapping and then pumping his fists in the air.

Tears start to stream down my face before I'm even aware of the emotional release. I send air kisses toward the crowd and quickly hurry back to the prep area. Candy wraps me in a hug before I can get a word out. It's not uncommon to experience an emotional release after a performance. We're tapping into parts of ourselves that have gone overlooked and, well, as a new performer, I'll just say there's plenty I've been overlooking.

I dress on wobbly legs as Candy heads out to wow the assembled crowd with her hula hoop act. Normally, I linger and watch from the sidelines, but Maverick is out there.

In Austin. Waiting for me.

I shuck the leotard and opt for a shimmery black crop top with black jean shorts. Once I've popped my black boots on, I check myself in the mirror, though I'm not sure what I'm checking for. All I see is a wild-eyed lady with puffy eyes that can only see one man.

I push out of the staging area and into the festival. Maverick is the first person I see. He's got his hands shoved into the pockets of his board shorts, his broad, sculpted back toward me. He's jiggling all over—knees bouncing, shoulders swaying—and while he can't see me yet, I take it in. I already know how nervous he must be.

Because all it takes for most best-friends-turned-lovers is one glance, but with Maverick, I already fucking knew before I saw his face. I can feel him from across the damn country, and his showing up only proves that. All my doubts and wonders melt away, replaced only with knowing. On my first step toward him he turns, and everything around us flashes bright and then disappears into an insignificant blur.

Maverick fills my vision. I walk or run or teleport toward him—not sure, don't care—and we don't say anything, not even *hi*, before we're hugging, hugging, hugging like millennia have passed instead of weeks.

His thick arms wrap around me in the way I imagine Heaven feels to a new soul. I press my forehead against his neck, drinking in the musk and leather scent that has been haunting me for the past month. His lips are buried in my hair, and finally when the pounding of my heart recedes enough to let me hear again, I realize he's murmuring, "I'm sorry, I'm sorry."

"Maverick." I don't have anything else to say. Just his name is enough while I'm wrapped in his embrace.

"I love you, Lettie. So much. Please forgive me." He squeezes me tighter, lifting me off the ground. "Please forgive me for leaving you. For sucking. For doubting you." He sets me down and takes a deep breath. I pull back and smooth my hands over his chest, the ridges of his shoulders, absorbing him with enough detail that I never forget this moment, or how hard my heart can pound without actually expiring, or how heavy and freeing it feels to be filled with this much love for one person.

"I was angry that you left me, but I made it worse and left you too," he says. "And honestly...you leaving was a good thing. You helped me realize I can handle my own shit."

"I knew you could do it without me," I whisper, my voice cracking.

"I didn't want to. But if I hadn't, I wouldn't have linked up with Kru like I did. He and I are business partners now."

"I know," I say, laughing through some tears that squeak out of my eyes. "He's been keeping me in the loop. And it's perfect. It makes so much sense, Mav. You two are going to go far."

"I wanted to go that far with you," he says. "But I didn't realize that you weren't meant to walk that road with me. And there's only one thing I want to see you doing anyway—flipping around on those silks and making everybody's jaw drop. I want you to be doing this. I want you to follow this."

I nod fervently, searching his face. "Thank you. Me too. But I'm sorry that I made you doubt me and how much I love you," I croak.

Maverick's eyes are shimmering, and he watches me for a long time, shaking his head. "I can't believe this." He laughs a little, tugging me closer at the waist. "Every part of me is shaking right now."

We watch each other in bewildered silence, alternating between laughter, warm smiles, gentle caresses. The throngs moving past us don't even register. The swirl of the festival can't touch us. He and I are the only people who exist in this corner of Republic Square.

"I don't know if I can survive another month without you, Lettie," he says, his voice thick with emotion. His gaze drops to my crop top.

Fear begins a cold and slow unwinding at the base of my spine. I clutch his forearms.

"So you just flew to Austin to say you're sorry?" I ask, my voice hoarse.

"There were a few other things I wanted to say, too," he says, a grin tugging at his lips.

"And then? What do we get—one good day together before we're broken up again?"

Something dark slashes across his face. "I know I didn't do shit right. But I never broke up with you in my head or my heart."

His words are a salve I've been waiting for without realizing. I crumple into his arms. "You know I haven't either."

"Loyal Lettie," he says, swaying back and forth. He presses his forehead to mine, humming with an exhale. "Can I kiss you now, babe?"

I respond by pressing my lips to his. The kiss turns urgent, because they always are. Deep and exploring and brimming with need. The kiss turns indecent, and fast. I stop when he seeks out the back of my knee, hoisting my leg, and I've fisted the front of his shirt.

"Okay, whoa there. Hang on." I laugh weakly, standing on my own two feet again. "We're in public."

He grunts softly, coaxing another kiss from me. Softer this time, more thorough. He shakes his head when he pulls away, drawing a deep breath.

"I don't think I can survive another month without those kisses, much less twelve weeks." He sears me with a heartfelt look, something so raw and emotional that I couldn't look away if I tried. "But I'll do it. I'll wait for you, Lettie. If you can forgive me. If you want to be with me still, I'm fucking yours, girl." He laughs a little, giving both my ass cheeks a little squeeze. "I'll wait another five years if I have to."

The tears are returning now, brimming up and over onto my cheeks. Maverick alternates between brushing them away with his thumb and kissing them away with his lips.

"I'd be waiting for you even if you didn't want me to," he goes on. "Because we're Lettie and Mav. We're fucking made for each other, babe. Have you noticed recently?"

Laughter rolls out of me, delirious, blissful, full. "Yes. Yes, I have noticed. And trust me—there's nobody else in the world that I'd rather wait for."

He grabs my chin between his thumb and forefinger and kisses me again. When we part, he says, "Remember in Chicago what I told you about seeing your first live performance?"

My eyes go wide. So wide my eyeballs might damn well pop out of my head. Because I *do* remember.

"Are you—"

He grins as he pulls something out of his pocket. A ring box. He presses it into my hand and covers it with both of his.

I blink rapidly, trying to corral my surprise and happiness before it overwhelms me and I'm taken away in the back of an ambulance. *This girl was way too fucking happy,* the paramedic will report grimly to the newspaper. *She had a heart attack from everything in her life being just too good.*

I take a calming breath and pop open the box. A matte black band greets me.

"It's not a wedding ring," he whispers, "but a promise ring. An *I promise to wait for you* ring."

I start to giggle and cry. "The playboy gave me a promise ring."

His grin goes ear to ear. "I promise you that I'm yours. Even when I'm salty, jealous, pissed, flying high, manic, bursting, stressed, codependent, or any other state you've seen me in over the past twenty years."

I slip the ring onto the fourth finger of my right hand. It's gorgeous in its simplicity. It reminds me of the truth vibrating inside me: that my happiness *is* greater when it's shared. Not just with anyone, but with Mav.

"Good thing you didn't get me diamonds," I sniff.

"Like I'd attempt such a thing for my goth princess," he jokes.

"I love you so much, Mav," I whisper, resting my chin against his chest. "I promise I'll be your goth princess until the day we die."

A grin curls his lips. He smooths his palm over my hair, emotion shining in his eyes.

"I never thought it would feel so good to hear those words coming from somebody," he says. "But then I realized I don't want to hear them from just anybody. I only want to hear them from you."

I squeeze my arms around him, relishing the warmth and sturdiness of him. Because Maverick is the foundation of my being. Whether or not I wanted it—whether or not I counted on it—he is my rock. Now that things are right with him and we're on the same page, everything has clicked into place.

It doesn't matter where we go. Food truck challenges or festivals might separate us, but one simple truth remains.

When I'm in his arms, I'm home.

EPILOGUE

MAVERICK

9 MONTHS LATER

"Ooh! Ooh! Wait. Can you zip me?" Scarlett has been darting around the kitchen of the Bayshore Theatre like a madwoman for the past half hour, trying to help me get things ready for the dinner service.

It's Weston and Nova's wedding, and in the new Daly family tradition, they're getting married at the Theatre. I totally thought they'd get married in a sarcophagus in Egypt, but hey, they still have families to keep happy, and Mom would have shit a brick if she needed to renew her passport just to see her second youngest get hitched.

And of course, being the inspirational creative types they are, Weston and Nova hired us. As in, I'm cooking the dinner, and Scarlett is providing the entertainment. We convinced the city to let us set up a silks rig in the middle of the ballroom, and I've been fantasizing about this performance for the past five weeks. I don't get to see every single performance of hers—even though I'd like to—and I'm not missing this one, so help me God.

Our schedules keep us busy, especially since the TV show aired over the winter. Kru and I are something of a cult icon now, at least that's what the hashtags #TeamForked and #LobterMav demonstrate. I've never gotten fan mail before, but holy shit, there are a lot of people in the US who seriously dislike that douche canoe Davie, and I can't help but savor every bit of it.

I help Scarlett zip her leotard, which she then covers up with the white button-up shirt she's wearing to help us serve dinner. No, she's not gonna rip off her server clothes and segue into the silks set like a Chippendales dancer, but it will make the costume change easier after dinner. Besides, it's mostly for show. I hired a team of servers to take the load off of me and Scarlett, so we could enjoy more of the wedding.

Scarlett's gonna knock it out of the park. My meal, no matter how good it comes out, won't even register on her scale of awesomeness.

And I'm okay with it, because I'll be front and center to watch her fly.

"Hey! Got your veggie pans here," Kru barks as he comes into the kitchen. He moved to Cleveland six months ago as we got our business, Fork & Claw, off the ground. It's our next-gen food truck based on both of our styles and experience. Working with him has been a breeze, and he's entered the Daly fold easily as the unofficial sixth brother. He's played cornhole at Gray's house too many times to count, and I'm pretty sure my brothers like him more than they like me, but whatever.

"Great. Set those by the bisque," I tell him as he heads for the far tables. Yes, Uncle Lobster has graced Weston's wedding with his famous bisque. The one hundred eager mouths out there don't know what they're about to experience.

Weston pokes his head into the kitchen, all smiles. "Hey. Need any help?"

"Dude, you are the *groom*," I remind him, ushering him out of the kitchen. "You just exchanged vows. Can you please go suffer through pictures and not worry about helping me?"

"I'd take a beer," Kru says.

Weston cocks a finger gun at him. "You got it."

Dom comes into the kitchen suddenly, looking at us with his new brand of crazy grin. Ever since he became a dad, he's been relentlessly happy and effervescent about it. I'm actually surprised he's not wearing the baby carrier right now, which is his newest uniform. "What's going on in here, guys?"

"Just reminding Weston he's the groom and not first shooting assistant," I say, slinging my dish towel over my shoulder. I come over to my brothers and clamp both of them on the shoulders.

Dom looks over at Weston, emotion shining in his eyes. I swear to God, there's so much unspoken sap here I could bottle it and sell it as syrup. Before he can unleash his sermon on how our inheritances from Grammy Ethel changed all of our lives, or whatever he plans to talk about in new-Dom form, Grayson pushes through the door, followed by Connor.

"We having a party in here?" Grayson demands, holding his arms out to his sides. Connor shoves at Dom, and then at Weston.

"You guys need help that bad?" Connor goads. "Couldn't hack it on your own and had to tap the groom, huh?" He winks, shoving me in the shoulder.

"Please, I'm doing my best to get the groom *out* of my kitchen," I inform my brothers. With the way we're all gathered now, I know we look like weird, grinning twins. It's never felt this good to be with my brothers, not even during the golden years of childhood. I guess that's what growing up and falling in love can do for a guy. And for a family. Not to mention a healthy dose of heartbreak.

"If you guys stay here one more second, you're putting on an apron and turning into my serving girls," Kru warns from across the kitchen.

"Or you'll be forced to follow my silks performance with a circus act of your own making," Scarlett adds, pointing at each of my brothers as she whooshes by to help load up some plates.

"I'm okay with the circus thing," Weston says.

"Of course you would be," Grayson replies, clapping him on the shoulder.

"All right," another voice barks. From behind my brothers, I can see Mr. Damon Daly himself. Dad holds up his beer, jerking his head toward the dance floor. "Didn't come to this wedding to watch all my sons have fun without me. Now what should I carry out?"

I can't help but smile. My dad's got a little bit less jerk in his aura these days, specifically since Connor and Kinsley's wedding. I think the man is finally *enjoying* life.

"You can take the bread," Scarlett pipes up, pressing a bread basket into his hands. "The Daly-Henderson wedding will be served by the Daly patriarch himself."

Dad seems pleased and wanders into the reception hall with his one basket. My brothers follow him, Weston promising to bring Kru a fresh beer.

I smirk and watch them reintegrate into the reception through the serving window. While I'm peering, I catch sight of Nova, looking absolutely beautiful in her off-the-shoulder cream gown, all her red hair pulled up into an artfully messy updo that allows ringlets to spill around her face and down her back. Weston walks up to her, wraps his arms around her, whispers something in her ear that makes her blush, and then he heads to the bar to get Kru's beer.

"Whatcha looking at?" Scarlett appears at my side.

"Just thinking about how cool my family is," I say with a sigh. I sling my arm over her shoulders. "That includes you."

"You got lucky that your brothers are awesome," she tells me. It's not as much of a dig toward her sister as it might sound, because I know what she really means, which is that once upon a time, my brothers were *not* awesome.

She was there for all of it. Just like I've been there for all of it with her sister. Once her tour ended in mid-December and she came back to Bayshore, they made some steps at making amends. But Scarlett doesn't babysit like she used to—refuses to, actually. She only wants quality time with her niece and nephew on her schedule, which happens at least once a week.

She has the time, since she's not serving at E. Lago anymore. She moonlights at Fork & Claw only when our main window girl calls off, because Scarlett has a different full-time job.

She's the lead instructor at Fly-By in Cleveland, the aerial silks gym she used to frequent once a month or less. Now that she's got a bona fide performance tour under her belt and a whole new training regimen to call her own, she's one of the most experienced silks performers in the entire state.

And she's only going to get better. Her summer tour with Momentum starts next month.

If we're lucky, Fork & Claw will be appearing at some of the same festivals. Which means someone can officially slap my ass and call me fucking blissed out and fulfilled.

"Hey! You guys done canoodling?" Kru barks. "The fucking bisque is ready!"

I laugh and press a kiss to Scarlett's forehead. There's so much left to do. Not just today, but in the coming months and years. I got my team, my family, my love assembled around me.

Which is all I need.

All our individual parts come together to make this machine of life work flawlessly. And thanks to Scarlett, who pushed me over the edge of possibility, I'm able to see things way more clearly.

Scarlett wasn't a tomato in the fruit salad.

She's the chocolate in my chili powder. The pears mixed into my blue cheese tart. She makes my savory life so sweet—the ultimate balance.

Because that's what we've been for years, without even realizing it. And now that we do realize it? Watch out, world. I kiss her one last time before she slips away, squeezing my wrist before she goes back to arranging the dishes. We're ready to launch this latest adventure: Weston and Nova's wedding dinner.

Just one adventure of so many more that we have yet to experience. She's the only girl who's been with me since the beginning. And the only girl who will be here until the end.

Here's to Lettie and Mav, and our adventures for endless decades to come.

THE END

OMG. Is this the end?? Well...not QUITE.
Check out the final feel-good novella in the Bayshore series,
MAKE ME SMILE (http://books2read.com/make-me-smile),

where we revisit Kinsley and Connor as they attempt to unite their families before their wedding day.

Need more Lettie & Mav? Check out this deleted scene (https://BookHip.com/TLCATDC) – available to newsletter subscribers only!

Are you ready for another set of brothers? Time to meet the Fairchilds in my angsty, dramatic and high steam series, THE BAD BOYS OF WALL STREET. Start the series for FREE with The Price of a Promise (http://books2read.com/price-o f-promise).

Looking for more small-town vibes? Add in quirky side characters, family secrets, and a whole lotta steam and you've got my WINTER HARBOR series written with Whitley Cox...start getting to know these handsome, frustrating, and terribly alpha men in book #1, THE BASTARD HEIR (http ://books2read.com/the-bastard-heir).

AUTHOR'S NOTE

The choppy waters of Lake Erie in the summertime are a special sort of haven, shrieking sea gulls and all. This series is set in a fictionalized mixture of my hometown and a neighboring town in northern Ohio. Writing this series has become a love song to my homeland.

Even though I grew up mostly critical of my little slice of the world (like most moody, dissatisfied teens—HA!), I now recognize it for what it is: a gorgeous spot in the Midwestern landscape, one that is capable of producing all the love and emotion and depth that a romance author could hope for.

I sincerely hope you enjoy this visit to Bayshore...and I hope you'll continue this journey with the brothers of the Daly family!

LET'S STAY CONNECTED!

Stay connected with me via my newsletter (http://bit.ly/EL-news letter), where I share teasers, sales, and other exciting news. (Plus, if you haven't heard, I have an MMA romance series available, and **you'll get the prequel novella FOR FREE** when you sign up to my newsletter).

Or join my reader group, EMBER'S BLOSSOMS, to hang out up-close and personal! Early looks at new covers, exclusive access to ARC sign-ups, and more.

FACEBOOK
INSTAGRAM
GOODREADS
BOOKBUB
http://www.emberleighromance.com/

And before you go...

Please consider leaving an honest review about this book! Even just a few words or a line mean so much to us authors.

ALSO BY EMBER LEIGH

THE BAD BOYS OF WALL STREET
The Price of Revenge
The Price of Passion
The Price of Infamy
The Price of Forever

WINTER HARBOR
(co-written with Whitley Cox)
The Bastard Heir
The Asshole Heir
The Rebel Heir
The Matchmaking Heirs

THE BAYSHORE SERIES
Make Me Lose
Make Me Fall
Make Me Yours
Make Me Choose

Make Me Hot
Make Me Smile

THE BREAKING SERIES
Breaking the Rules
Changing the Game
Breaking the Sinner
Breaking the Habit
Breaking the Fall